Leslie Charteris

Leslie Charteris was born in Singapore on 12 May 1907. In 1919 he moved to England with his mother and brother and attended Rossall School in Lancashire before moving on to Cambridge University. His studies there came to a halt when a publisher accepted his first novel. His third book, entitled *Meet – The Tiger!*, was written when he was twenty years old and published in 1928. It introduced the world to Simon Templar, a.k.a. the Saint.

He continued to write about the Saint up until 1983, when the last book, *Salvage for the Saint*, was published by Hodder & Stoughton. The books, which have been translated into over twenty languages, have sold over 40 million copies around the world. They've inspired fifteen feature films, three TV series, ten radio series and a comic strip that was written by Charteris and syndicated around the world for over a decade.

Leslie Charteris enjoyed travelling, but settled for long periods in Hollywood, Florida, and finally in Surrey, England. In 1992 he was awarded the Cartier Diamond Dagger in recognition of a lifetime of achievement. He died the following year.

LESLIE CHARTERIS

Featuring the Saint

Series Editor: Ian Dickerson

MULHOLLAND
BOOKS
HODDER

First published in Great Britain in 1931 by Hodder & Stoughton

This paperback edition first published in 2013 by Mulholland Books
An imprint of Hodder & Stoughton
An Hachette UK company

1

A CIP catalogue record for this title is available from the British Library

Paperback ISBN 978 1 444 76264 8
eBook ISBN 978 1 444 76265 5

Typeset by Hewer Text UK Ltd, Edinburgh
Printed and bound by Clays Ltd, St Ives plc

Hodder & Stoughton policy is to use papers that are natural, renewable
and recyclable products and made from wood grown in sustainable
forests. The logging and manufacturing processes are expected to
conform to the environmental regulations of the country of origin.

Hodder & Stoughton Ltd
338 Euston Road
London NW1 3BH

www.hodder.co.uk

To Barbara

CONTENTS

INTRODUCTION

I intended to write this introduction wearing my scholar's cloak, with an academically freighted deconstruction utilizing references to Conan Doyle, Sir Walter Scott, the chivalric code and inevitably, Freud. The erudition of my arguments and analyses would not only elucidate the psycho-ontological motivations behind Simon Templar, but make me look pretty damn smart as well.

Then I picked up one of my ancient copies of Saint stories, selected 'The Wonderful War', and read about a banana republic invaded by one man with a delicious vision for justice. I smiled a lot and laughed aloud almost as often. I re-read passages to be tickled yet again. I set the book aside when finished, but had back it in my hands within an hour.

In short, I read with the giddy joy of a thirteen-year-old. Which makes perfect sense, since I was thirteen when I met the Saint. A reader leaning heavily toward the mystery/suspense genre, I had early immersion in the Bobbsey Twins, Seckatary Hawkins, and the Hardy Boys. I had read them to tatters when my father appeared in my bedroom one evening. 'I think you'll like these stories,' he said, bearing *The First Saint Omnibus*. 'They concern a man named Simon Templar, the Saint. They're more sophisticated than you're used to, and certainly racier, but I suspect you'll enjoy that aspect.'

With those cryptic words he set the book in my palms and retreated, singing an odd song about the bells of Hell. Hoping my old man had not gone fully round the bend, I opened the book and, in my own way, have never closed it.

I have read all the Saint sagas, including the three gems in *Featuring the Saint*, at least a dozen times each. If there is anything I as a writer have taken from my father's prescient gift – and I've taken as much from Leslie Charteris as from John D. MacDonald, Robert Parker and James Lee Burke – it is that a good hero always has a moral code (though it might not be yours or mine), the innocent must be protected, and when the bad get a comeuppance, it should fit the crime.

Oh . . . and beautiful women never detract from a story.

'The Wonderful War' is an all-time favourite, boasting nearly all of the hallmarks of a Saint mini-epic: a comely lady, a masterful plan, a Saintly versification, racy quotes regarding the actress and the Bishop, and The Song. Per a good Saint yarn, the malefactors are suitably venal and unattractive and – perhaps most irritating to Simon Templar – rude. All that's missing is an appearance by Inspector Teal, though I suspect he might not be much at home in a South American bananocracy.

And what grand invention is the country of Pasala . . . Charteris's setting is a rip-roaringly comic and deviously accurate caricature of the era and locale. The world stops for siesta. The army is five hundred strong, with a general or colonel for every nine men. The navy consists of . . . well, you get the idea.

The Saint stories are not for analysis, I realize, at least not by me. Not for deconstruction or preconstruction or anything akin to psychobabble. They're simply masterworks of delight, asking only that you pick up the pages of a champion storyteller, hold your breath, and step within.

You don't analyse joy, you revel in it.

Jack Kerley

FOREWORD

Eighteen years went by between the first Sherlock Holmes book, *A Study in Scarlet* (1887), and the last, *The Return of Sherlock Holmes* (1905), and Sir Arthur Conan Doyle went on to live 25 years after that, during which he saw great changes in the world. Throughout that time, so far as I know, the popularity of his detective was undimmed, and the books were always in print in some edition or other, as they are to this very day. But Sir Arthur never seems to have thought of revising them to keep them in touch with the changing times, and apparently found nothing incongruous in leaving Baker Street to the gaslight and hansom cabs which had long since been replaced by electricity and motor cars, to say nothing of radio in the home and airplanes roaring overhead.

The stories in this volume were written almost an equivalent quarter-century ago, during which the changes in the world have been more drastic even than in Doyle's. The radio has been supplanted by television, a science-fiction fantasy now made commonplace with commercials; aircraft still ply overhead, but they are jets at least, threatening to become supersonic, if they are not already rocket-launched satellites; and the automobiles, paradoxically, are mechanically capable of travelling about as fast on a good road as the planes that Doyle saw, but crawl through London traffic today at a pace which would have made one of those old horse carriages seem airborne. And I must admit that I don't have Doyle's self-restraint, and that I have often been tempted to bring the oldest Saint stories up to date, and in a few cases have done something about this when they were reprinted.

But that is a labour which could be endless, as my slothful instincts finally realized in the nick of time, and ultimately pointless anyhow, if my Immortal Works outlive me by a few centuries, as I expect them to.

Therefore let this book go out as another period piece in the making. I only ask readers not to be beguiled by any accidental modernities into forgetting how venerable the stories actually are, and how embryonic was the technology of the world in which they were laid.

And also, if you would be critically tolerant, how young was the author, and how correspondingly youthful was his hero.

Leslie Charteris

The Logical Adventure

I

If there must be more stories of the Saint, I prefer to choose them from among his later exploits, from the days when he was working practically alone – although Patricia Holm was never far away, and Roger Conway was always within call at times of need. I often think that it best suited the Saint's peculiar temper to be alone: he was so superbly capable himself, and so arrogantly confident of his own capability, that it irked him to have to deputise the least item of any of his schemes to hands that might bungle it, and exasperated him beyond measure to have to explain and discuss and wrangle his inspirations with minds that leapt to comprehension and decision less swiftly and certainly than his own. These trials he suffered with characteristic good humour; yet there is no doubt that he suffered sometimes, as may be read in other tales that have already been told of him. It is true that the Saint once became something perilously like a gang; there came about him a band of reckless young men who followed him cheerfully into all his crimes, and these young men he led into gay and lawless audacities that made the name of the Saint famous – or infamous – over the whole world; but even those adventures were no more than episodes in the Saint's life. They were part of his development, but they were not the end. His ultimate destiny still lay ahead; he knew that it still lay ahead, but he did not then know what it was. 'The Last Hero' he was called once; but the story of his last heroism is not to be told yet, and the manner of it he never foresaw even in his dreams.

This story, then, is the first of a handful that I have unearthed from my records of those days of transition, when the Saint was waiting upon Fate. They were days when he seemed to be filling up time; and, as might have been expected of the man, he beguiled the time in his own incomparable fashion, with his own matchless zest; but it is inevitable that his own moods should be reflected in these tales which are exclusively his – that the twist of the tales should write what he himself felt about them at the time, that they were not really important, and yet that they were none the less fantastically delightful interludes. For Simon Templar was incapable of taking anything of life half-heartedly – even an interlude. And it may be that because of all these things, because he had that vivid sense of the pleasant unimportance of all these adventures, the spirit of laughing devil-may-care quixotry that some have called his greatest charm dances through these tales as it does through few others.

I am thinking particularly of the story that stands first upon my list – a slight story, but a story. Yet it began practically from nothing – as, indeed, did most of the Saint's best stories. It has been said that Simon Templar had more than any ten men's fair share of luck in the way of falling into ready-made adventures; but nothing could be farther from the truth. It was the Saint's own unerring, uncanny genius, his natural instinct for adventure, that made him question things that no ordinary man would have thought to question, and sent him off upon broad, clear roads where no ordinary man would have seen the vestige of a trail; and some volcanic quality within himself that started violent action out of situations that the ordinary man would have found still-born. And if there is any story about the Saint that illustrates this fact to perfection it is this story which opens – ordinarily enough – upon the American Bar of the Piccadilly Hotel, two Manhattans, and a copy of the *Evening Record*.

'Eight to one,' murmured the Saint complacently – 'and waltzed home with two lengths to spare. That's another forty quid for the old oak chest. Where shall we celebrate, old dear?'

Patricia Holm smiled.

'Won't you ever take an interest in something outside the racing reports?' she asked. 'I don't believe you even know whether we've got a Conservative or a Labour Government at the moment.'

'I haven't the faintest idea,' said the Saint cheerfully. 'Apart from the fact that a horse we've never seen has earned us the best dinner that London can provide, I refuse to believe that anything of the least importance has happened in England to-day. For instance' – he turned the pages of the newspaper – 'we are not at all interested to learn that "Evidence of a sensational character is expected to be given at the inquest upon Henry Stobbs, a mechanic, who was found dead in a garage in Balham yesterday." I don't believe the man had a sensational character at all. No man with a really sensational character would be found dead in a garage in Balham ... Nor are we thrilled to hear that "Missing from her home at South Norwood since January last, the body of Martha Danby, a domestic servant, was discovered in a disused quarry near Tavistock early this morning by a tramp in an advanced state of decomposition." Not that we don't feel sorry for the tramp – it must be rotten for the poor fellow to have to cruise about the world in an advanced state of decomposition – but my point is—'

'That'll do,' said Patricia.

'O.K.,' said the Saint affably. 'So long as you understand why I'm so – Hullo – what's this?'

He had been folding the paper into a convenient size for the nearest waste-basket when his eye was caught by a name that he knew; and he read the paragraphs surrounding it with a sudden interest. These paragraphs figured in that admirable feature 'Here and There' conducted by that indefatigable and ubiquitous gossip 'The Eavesdropper.'

'Well, well, well!' drawled the Saint, with a distinct saintliness of intonation; and Patricia looked at him expectantly.

'What is it?'

'Just a little social chatter,' said Simon. 'Our friend is warbling about the progress of civil aviation, and how few serious accidents there have been since light aeroplane clubs started springing up all over the country, and how everyone is taking to the air as if they'd been born with wings. Then he says: "There are, of course, a few exceptions, Mr Francis Lemuel, for instance, the well-known cabaret impresario, who was one of the founders of the Thames Valley Flying Club, and who was himself making rapid progress towards his 'A' licence, was so badly shaken by his recent crash that he has been compelled, on medical advice, to give up all idea of qualifying as a pilot." The rest is just the usual kind of blurb about Lemuel's brilliant impresarioning. But that is interesting – now, isn't it – to know that dear Francis was sighing for the wings of a Moth!'

'Why?'

The Saint smiled beatifically, and completed the operation of preparing the *Evening Record* for its last resting-place.

'There are many interests in my young life,' he murmured, 'of which you are still in ignorance, dear lass. And little Francis is one of them – and has been for some time. But I never knew that he was a bold bad bird-man – outside of business hours ... And now, old Pat, shall we dine here or push on to the Berkeley Arms?'

And that was all that was said about Francis Lemuel that night, and for ten days afterwards; for at that time, bowing before Patricia's pleading, Simon Templar was trying to lead a respectable life. And yet, knowing her man, she was a little surprised that he dropped the subject so quickly; and, knowing her man again, she heaved a little sigh of rueful resignation when he met her for lunch ten days later and showed quite plainly in his face that he was on the trail of more trouble. At those times there was a renewed effervescence about the Saint's always electric personality, and a refreshed recklessness about the laughter that was never far from the surface of his blue eyes, that were unmistakable danger-signs. The smooth sweep of his patent-leather hair seemed to become sleeker and slicker than ever, and the keen brown face seemed to take on an even swifter and more rakish chiselledness of line than it ordinarily wore. She knew these signs of old, and challenged him before he had finished selecting the hors d'œuvre.

'What's on the programme, Saint?'

Simon sipped his sherry elegantly.

'I've got a job.'

'What's that?'

'You know – work. Dramatis persona: Simon Templar, a horny-handed son of toil.'

'Idiot! I meant – what's the job?'

'Private Aviator Extraordinary to Mr Francis Lemuel,' answered the Saint, with dancing eyes. 'And you can't laugh that off!'

'Is that what you've been so mysterious about lately?'

'It is. I tell you, it wasn't dead easy. Mr Lemuel has an eccentric taste in aviators. I got a lot of fun out of convincing him that I was really a shabby character. Try to imagine the late lamented Solomon applying, incog., for the job of "Ask Auntie Abishag" on the staff of the *Lebanon Daily Leader*. . .' The Saint grinned reminiscently. 'But as an ex-R.A.F. orficer, cashiered for pinching three ailerons, four longerons, and a brace of gliding angles, I had what you might call a flying start.'

'And what are you supposed to do?'

'Propel him about the bright blue sky.'

'Where?'

The Saint bisected a sardine with precision and dexterity.

'That,' he answered, 'is the point. According to rumours, Francis is proposing to extend his cabaristic activities into the other capitals of Europe. But why by air? "The latest and most rapid means of transport," says you, intelligent like. Oh, every time. But the whole of civilised Europe is served by very comfortable public airways – very comfortable – and my researches into Mr Lemuel's character never made me think he was the sort of cove who'd sacrifice his arm-chair in a pukka flying Pullman and go batting through the blue in an open two-seater air-louse just to save an hour here and there. Mystery Number One. That's why I was so interested to read that Brother Francis had been trying to aviate solo – you remember?'

Patricia nodded.

'I wondered—'

'Never give tongue before you've got the blue-bottle by the blunt end,' said the Saint. 'That's my motto. But I always believe in taking two looks at anything that seems to have slipped the least bit off the main line, and that was a case in point. Particularly with a man like Francis Lemuel. I've always thought he was far too respectable to be above suspicion. Now we may start to learn things.'

She tried to find out how he had contrived to discover that Mr Lemuel had been searching for a disreputable aviator; she was equally curious to know how the Saint had contrived to present himself for the job; but Simon Templar still had his own little secrets. About some of the preliminary details of his adventures he was often absurdly reticent.

'I heard about it,' he said, 'and a bloke I met in a pub out at Aldgate landed me on the front door, so to speak ...

Mystery Number Two, of course, is why the aviator should have been disreputable . . .'

He talked energetically about this problem, and left her first questions otherwise unanswered. And with that she had to be content – until, abruptly, he switched off the subject altogether, and for the rest of that day refused to talk any more about what he was pleased to call 'affairs of state.'

Other things happened afterwards – very shortly afterwards. A few other people entered the story, a few other threads came into it, a few diverting decorations blossomed upon it; but the foundations of the story were already laid, and it is doubtful whether any of the subsequent events herein described would have evented at all if Simon Templar had not chanced to catch sight of that innocent paragraph in the *Evening Record*. For of such material were the Saint's adventures made.

And nothing can be more certain than that if the Saint had not been a man of such peculiar genius and eccentric interests he would not to this day carry an eight-inch scar on his right forearm as a memento of the adventure, and Mr Francis Lemuel would not have experienced such a sudden and cataclysmic elevation, and one Jacob Einsmann might still have been with us, and M. Boileau, the French Minister of Finance, would not have been put to considerable inconvenience – and (which is perhaps even more important) a girl whose name used to be Stella Dornford would not now be married to a bank clerk with very ordinary prospects, and living in a very ordinary apartment in Battersea, and perfectly happy in spite of that.

2

The Calumet Club is situate (as the estate agents so beautifully put it) in a spacious basement in Deacon Street, Soho. This statement should be taken at its face value. There are, in fact, no premises whatsoever in any way ostensibly appertaining to the said club on the street level, or on any of the floors above. Entrance to the club is by means of a narrow flight of stone steps leading down into a microscopic area; and through a door opening upon this area one may (if one is known to the management) obtain access to the club itself, via a room which only an estate agent would have the nerve to describe as a vestibule, and past a porter who has been other things in his time.

The Calumet Club has an extensive if curiously exclusive membership. Things are discussed there – fascinating things. Money, and other objects of vertu, changes hands there. And, sometimes, strange things are said to have happened there – very strange things. The Saint was distinctly interested in the Calumet Club. It was one of the irregular interests of his young life.

Nevertheless, the visit he paid to it on a certain evening began as a mere matter of routine, and was embarked upon without immediate malice premeditated.

For thus is the way paved for adventure, as far as human ingenuity can contrive it, with good sound non-skid tarmac. Upon learning, almost beyond dispute, that Mr Phineas Poppingcove is a saccharine smuggler, you do not, whatever your principles and prowess, immediately invade his abode, beat him vimfully about the head with some blunt instrument, and so depart with the work of discouragement satisfactorily accomplished. If you discover, after patient investigation, that the rooms in which Miss Désirée Sausage professes to teach the latest ballroom dances (h. & c.) are in reality the dens where foolish men are fleeced of their fathers' money at wangled games of halma, you do not, even if you are the Saint, instantly force your way into those rooms, shoot the croupier, denounce Miss Sausage, and take the stake-money home with you as a souvenir. Or, if you do, your promising career is liable to terminate abruptly and in a manner definitely glutinous. The Saint, it should be remembered, had been in that sort of game for some time; and he knew, better than anyone, the value of painstaking preparation. When everything that could possibly be known about the lie of the land and the personal habits of its denizens was known, and the line of subsequent retreat had been thoroughly surveyed, mapped, dressed, ventilated, and upholstered – then, oh, yes, then the blunt instrument, wielded with decisive celerity and no uncertain hand. But not before.

This visit to the Calumet Club was definitely 'before'; and the Saint was therefore prepared and even expecting to behave himself with all the decorum that the occasion demanded.

He passed to a corner table, ordered a drink, lighted a cigarette, and settled himself comfortably.

It was then barely eleven, and the club would not begin to do real business for about another half-hour. The nucleus of an orchestra was rhythmically, if a trifle unenthusiastically, insisting that it didn't care how much some lady unspecified made it blue. To the accompaniment of this declaration of an unselfish devotion of which the casual eye, judging the orchestra solely by appearances, would never have believed them capable, four self-appointed ladies, in two pairs, and two other self-appointed ladies paired with an equal number of temporary gentlemen, were travelling in small circles round a minute section of inferior parquet. At other tables round the floor a scattering of other clients, apparently male and female, were absorbing divers brands of alcohol in the lugubrious fashion in which alcohol is ordinarily absorbed in England during the hours in which the absorption is legal. In fact, the Calumet Club was just yawning and stretching itself preparatory to waking up for the night's festivities.

The Saint sighed, inhaled cigarette-smoke luxuriously, tasted the modest glass of beer which the waiter brought him, paid twice the usual retail price for it, added a fifty per cent bonus, and continued to inspect his fellow-members with a somewhat jaundiced eye.

One by one he dismissed them. Two men whom he had met there several times before saluted him, and he smiled back as if he loved them like brothers. An unattached damsel at an adjacent table smiled sweetly at him, and the Saint smiled back just as sweetly, for he had a reputation to keep up. And then, in another corner, his gaze came to rest upon a man he had seen before, and a girl he had never seen before, sitting together at a table beside the orchestra.

Simon's gaze rested upon them thoughtfully, as it had rested upon other people in that room; and it only rested upon them longer than it had rested upon anyone else that night, because at that moment, when his glance fell upon them, something stirred at the back of his brain and opened its inward intangible eye upon the bare facts of the case as conveyed by the optic nerves. The Saint could not have said what it was. At that moment there was nothing about that corner of the scenery to attract such an attention. They were talking quite ordinarily, to judge by their faces; and, if the face of the girl was remarkably pleasant to look upon, even that was not unprecedented in the Calumet Club and the entourage of Baldy Mossiter. And yet, in spite of these facts rather than because of them, Simon Templar's queer instinct for the raw material of his trade flicked up a ghostly eyelid in some dim recess of his mind, and forced him to look longer, without quite knowing why he looked. And it was only because of this that the Saint saw what he saw, when the almost imperceptible thing happened in the course of one of Mr Mossiter's frequent and expressive gestures.

'Have you got a cigarette?' murmured the unattached damsel at the adjacent table, hopefully; but the sweetness of the smile which illuminated the Saint's features as she spoke was not for her, and it is doubtful whether he even heard.

He lounged out of his chair and wandered across the room with the long, lazy stride that covered ground with such an inconspicuous speed; and the man and the girl looked up together as he loomed over their table.

'Hullo,' drawled the Saint.

He sat down in a vacant chair between them, without waiting to be invited, and beamed from one to the other in a most Saintly way.

'Beautiful weather we're having, aren't we, Baldy?'

'What the devil do you want, Templar?' snarled Mr Mossiter, with no cordiality. 'I'm busy.'

'I know, sweetheart,' said the Saint gently, 'I saw you getting busy. That's why I came over.'

He contemplated Mr Mossiter with innocent blue eyes, and yet there was something in the very innocence of that stare, besides its prolonged steadiness, that unaccountably prickled the short hairs on the back of Mossiter's bull neck. It did not happen at once. The stare had focused on its object for some time before that cold draught of perplexedly dawning comprehension began to lap Mossiter's spinal column. But the Saint read all that he wanted to read in the sudden darkening of the livid scar that ran down the side of Mossiter's face from his left temple to his chin; and the Saintly smile became dazzlingly seraphic.

'Exactly,' said the Saint.

His gaze shifted over to the girl. Her hand was still round her glass – she had been raising it when the Saint reached the table, and had put it down again untasted.

Still smiling, Simon took the girl's glass in one hand and Mossiter's in the other, and changed them over. Then he looked again at Mossiter.

'Drink up,' he said, and suddenly there was cold steel in his voice.

'What d'you mean?'

'Drink,' said the Saint. 'Open your mouth, and induce the liquid to trickle down the gullet. You must have done it before. But whether you'll enjoy it so much on this occasion remains to be seen.'

'What the hell are you suggesting?'

'Nothing. That's just your guilty conscience. Drink it up, Beautiful.'

Mossiter seemed to crouch in his chair.

'Will you leave this table?' he grated.

'No,' said the Saint.

'Then you will have to leave the club altogether . . . Waiter!'

The Saint took out his cigarette-case and tapped a cigarette meditatively upon it. Then he looked up. He addressed the girl.

'If you had finished that drink,' he said, 'the consequences would have been very unpleasant indeed. I think I can assure you of that, though I'm not absolutely certain what our friend put in it. It is quite sufficient that I saw him drop something into your glass while he was talking just now.' He leaned back in his chair, with his back half-turned to Mr Mossiter, and watched the waiter returning across the floor with the porter who had been other things in his time, and added, in the same quiet tone: 'On account of the failure of this bright scheme, there will shortly be a slight disturbance of which I shall be the centre. If you think I'm raving mad, you can go to hell. If you've got the sense to see that I'm telling the truth, you'll stand by to make your bolt when I give the word, and meet me outside in a couple of minutes.'

Thus the Saint completed his remarks, quite unhurriedly, quite calmly and conversationally; and then the waiter and the porter were behind his chair.

'Throw this man out,' said Mossiter curtly. 'He's making a nuisance of himself.'

It was the porter who had been other things in his time who laid the first rough hand upon the Saint; and Simon grinned gently. The next moment Simon was on his feet, and the porter was not.

That remark needs little explanation. It would not be profitable to elaborate a description of the pile-driving properties of the left hook that connected with the porter's jaw as Simon rose from his chair; and, in fact, the porter himself knew little about it at the time. He left the ground momentarily, and then he made contact with a lot more ground a little farther on, and then he slept.

The elderly waiter, also, knew little about that particular incident. The best and brightest years of his life were past and over, and it is probable that he was growing a little slow on the uptake in his late middle age. It is, at least, certain that he had not fully digested the significance of the spectacle to which he had just been treated, nor come to any decision about his own attitude to the situation, when he felt himself seized firmly by the collar and the seat of his pants. He seemed to rise astonishingly into the air, and, suspended horizontally in space at the full upward stretch of the Saint's arms, was for an instant in a position to contemplate the beauties of the low ceiling at close range. And the Saint chuckled.

'How Time flies,' murmured the Saint, and heaved the man bodily into the middle of the orchestra – where, it may be recorded, he damaged beyond repair, in his descent, a tenor saxophone, a guitar, and a device for imitating the moans of a stricken hyena.

Simon straightened his tie, and looked about him. Action had been so rapid, during those few seconds, that the rest of the club's population and personnel had not yet completely awoken to understanding and reprisal. And the most important thing of all was that the sudden sleep of the porter who had been other things in his time had not only demoralised the two other officials who were standing in the middle distance, but had also left the way to the exit temporarily clear.

Simon touched the girl's shoulder.

'I should push along now, old dear,' he remarked, as if there was all the time in the world and nothing on earth to get excited about. 'Stop a taxi outside, if you see one. I'll be right along.'

She looked at him with a queer expression; and then she left her chair and crossed the floor quickly. To this day she is not quite sure why she obeyed; but it is enough that she did, and the Saint felt a certain relief as he watched her go.

Then he turned, and saw the gun in Mossiter's hand. He laughed – it was so absurd, so utterly fantastic, even in that place. In London, that sort of thing only happens in sensational fiction. But there it was; and the Saint knew that Baldy Mossiter must have been badly upset to make such a crude break. And he laughed; and his left hand fell on Mossiter's hand in a grip of steel, but with a movement so easy and natural that Mossiter missed the meaning of it until it was too late. The gun was pointed harmlessly down into the table, and all Mossiter's strength could not move it.

'You had better know me,' said Simon quietly. 'I'm called the Saint.'

Baldy Mossiter heard him, staring, and went white.

'And you must not try to drug little girls,' said the Saint.

A lot of things of no permanent importance have been mentioned in this chapter; but the permanently important point of it is that Baldy Mossiter's beautiful front teeth are now designed to his measure by a gentleman in a white coat with a collection of antediluvian magazines in his waiting-room.

3

A few moments later, the Saint strolled up into the street. A taxi was drawn up by the kerb, and the Saint briefly spoke an address to the driver and stepped in.

The girl was sitting in the far corner. Simon gave her a smile, and cheerfully inspected a set of grazed knuckles. It stands to the credit of his happy disposition that he really felt at peace with the world, although the evening's amusement represented a distinct set-back to certain schemes that had been maturing in his fertile brain. As a rough-house it had had its virtues; but the truth was that the Saint had marked down the Calumet Club for something more drastic and profitable than a mere rough-house, and that idea, if it was ever to be materialised now, would have to be tackled all over again, from the very beginning and a totally different angle. A couple of months of shrewd and patient reconnaissance work had gone west that night along with Baldy Mossiter's dental apparatus, but Simon Templar was incapable of weeping over potential poultry annihilated in the egg.

'Have a cigarette,' he suggested, producing his case, 'and tell me your name.'

'Stella Dornford.' She accepted a light, and he affected not to notice the unsteadiness of her hand. 'Did you – have much trouble?'

The Saint grinned over his match.

'Well – hardly! I seemed to get a bit popular all at once – that was all. Nobody seemed to want me to go. There was a short argument – nothing to speak of.'

He blew out the match and slewed round, looking through the window at the back. There was another taxi close behind, which is not extraordinary in a London street; and, hanging out of the window of the taxi behind, was a man – or the head and shoulders of one – which, to the Saint's suspicious mind, was quite extraordinary enough. But he was not particularly bothered about it at the moment, for he had directed his own driver to the Criterion, and nothing would happen there.

'Where are we going?' asked the girl.

'Towards coffee,' said the Saint. 'Or, if you prefer it, something with more kick. Praise be to the blessed laws of England, we can drink for another half-hour yet, if we hire a sandwich to put on the table. And you can tell me the story of your life.'

In the better light of the restaurant, and at leisure which he had not had before, he was confirmed in the impression which he had formed at the Calumet. She was undeniably pretty, in a rather childish way, with a neat fair head and china-blue eyes. A certain grace of carriage saved her from mere fluffiness.

'You haven't told me your name,' she remarked, when he had ordered refreshment.

'I thought you heard Mossiter address me. Templar – Simon Templar.'

'You seem to be rather a remarkable man.'

The Saint smiled. He had been told that before, but he had no objection to hearing it again. He really had very simple tastes, in some ways.

'It's rather lucky for you that I am,' he answered. 'And now, tell me, what were you doing at the Calumet with Baldy?'

He had some difficulty in extracting her story – in fact, it required all his ingenuity to avoid making the extraction look too much like a cross-examination, for it was evident that she had not yet made up her mind about him.

He learned, after a time, that she was twenty-one years old, that she was the only daughter of a retired bank manager,

that she had run away from the dull suburban circle of her
family to try to find fortune on the wrong side of the foot-
lights. He might have guessed that much, but he liked to
know. It took some much more astute questioning to elicit a
fact in which he was really much more interested.

'. . . He's a junior clerk in the branch that used to be
Daddy's. He came to the house once or twice, and we saw
each other occasionally afterwards. It was all rather sweet and
silly. We used to go to the pictures together, and once we met
at a dance.'

'Of course, you couldn't possibly have married him,' said
the Saint cunningly, and waited thoughtfully on her reply.

'It would have meant that I'd never have got away from all
the mildewed things that I most wanted to run away from. I
wanted to see Life . . . But he really was a nice boy.'

She had got a job in a revue chorus, and another girl in the
same show had taken her to the Calumet one night. There
she had met Mossiter, and others. She was without friends in
London, and sheer loneliness made her crave for any society
rather than none. There had been difficulties, she admitted.
One man, a guest of Mossiter's – a German – had been
particularly unpleasant. Yes, he was reputed to be very
rich . . .

'Don't you see,' said the Saint, 'that Mossiter could only
have wanted to drug you for one of two reasons?'

'One of two?'

'When does this German go back to Germany?'

'I think he said he was going back tomorrow – that's Friday,
isn't it?'

Simon shrugged.

'Such is life,' he murmured; and she frowned.

'I'm not a child, Mr Templar.'

'No girl ever is, in her own estimation,' said the Saint
rudely. 'That's why my friends and I have been put to so

much trouble and expense in the past – and are likely to go on being bothered in the same way.'

He had expected her to be troublesome – it was a premonition he had had about her from the first – and, as was his way, he had deliberately preferred to precipitate the explosion rather than fumble along through smouldering and smoke. But he was not quite prepared for the reaction that he actually provoked, which was that she simply rose and left the table.

'I'm perfectly capable of taking care of myself, thank you,' was her parting speech.

He beckoned a waiter, and watched her go with a little smile of rueful resignation. It was not the first time that something of that sort had happened to him – cases of that type were always liable to be trying, and fulfilled their liability more often than not.

'And so she swep' out,' murmured Simon wryly, as he pocketed his change; and then he remembered the men who had followed them from the Calumet. 'Men' – it was unlikely to be 'man.' The Calumet bunch were not of that class.

There were, as a matter of fact, two of them, and their instructions had been definite. They were merely to obtain addresses. It was therefore doubly unfortunate for the one who was concerned to follow Stella Dornford that, when he grasped part of the situation, he should have elected to attempt a coup on his own.

Stella Dornford tenanted a minute apartment in a block close to the upper end of Wardour Street. The block was in the form of a hollow square, with a courtyard in the centre, communicating with the street by a short passage, and the entrances to all the main staircases opened on to this courtyard. Standing in this courtyard, facing the doorway by which the girl had entered, the sleuth glanced up curiously at the windows. A moment later he saw one of the windows light up.

It was then that he decided upon his folly. The window which had lighted up was a French window, and it gave on to a narrow balcony – and, most tempting of all, it stood ajar, for the night was warm. And the building had been designed in the style that imitates large blocks of stone, with substantial interstices between the blocks. To reach that balcony would be as easy as climbing up a ladder.

He glanced about him. The courtyard was deserted and the light was poor. Once off the ground, he was unlikely to be noticed even if some other tenant passed beneath him. In the full blaze of his unconscious foolishness the man buttoned his coat and began to climb.

Standing in the shadows of the passage communicating with the street, Simon Templar watched him go. And, as he watched, with a newborn smile of sheer poetic devilment hovering on his lips, the Saint loaded up his newest toy – a small but powerful air-pistol.

He had acquired it quite recently, out of pure mischief. It wasn't by any means a lethal weapon, and was never intended for the purpose, but its pellets were capable of making a very painful impression upon the recipient. It had occurred to Simon that, adroitly employed from his window, it might serve as a powerful discouragement to the miscellaneous collection of professional and amateur sleuths whom from time to time he found unduly interested in his movements. But this occasion he had not anticipated, and his pleasure was therefore all the keener.

As the man on the wall reached the level of the second floor and paused for breath, Simon took careful aim.

The bullet smacked into the man's hand with a force that momentarily numbed his fingers. With a sharp gasp of pain and fear, he became aware that his hold was broken, and he had not enough strength in his uninjured hand to support himself with that alone. He gasped again, scrabbling wildly at the stone – and then his foot slipped . . .

The Saint pocketed his toy, and stepped quickly back into the street – so quickly that the man who was waiting just outside the passage had no time to appreciate his danger before it was upon him. He felt his coat lapels gripped by a sinewy hand, and looked into the Saint's face.

'Don't follow me about,' said the Saint, in a tone of mild and reasonable remonstrance; and then his fist shot up and impacted crisply upon the man's jaw.

Simon turned and went back down the passage, and crossed the courtyard swiftly; and the first window was flung up as he slipped into the shadow of the doorway opposite.

He went quickly up the dark stone stairs, found a bell, and pressed it. The door was opened almost immediately, but the girl was equally quick to shut it when she saw who her visitor was.

The Saint, however, was even quicker – with the toe of his shoe in the opening.

'There's something outside you ought to see,' he said, and pushed quickly through the door while she hesitated.

Then she recovered herself.

'What do you mean by bursting in like this?' she demanded furiously.

'I told you – there's a special entertainment been put on for your benefit. Come and cheer.'

He opened the nearest door, and went through the tiny sitting-room as if he owned the place. She followed him.

'If you don't get out at once I shall shout for help. There are people all round, and a porter in the basement, and the walls aren't very thick – so you needn't think no one will hear.'

'I hadn't bothered to think,' said the Saint calmly. 'Besides, they're all busy with the other attraction. Step this way, madam.'

He passed through the open window and emerged on to the balcony. In a moment he found her beside him.

'Mr Templar—'

Simon simply pointed downwards. She looked, and saw the little knot of people gathering about the sprawled figure that lay moaning at the foot of the wall.

'So perish all the ungodly,' murmured the Saint.

The girl turned a white face.

'How did it happen?'

'He, and a pal of his, followed us from the Calumet. I meant to tell you, but you packed up in such a hurry and such a naughty temper. I followed. He was on his way up to this verandah when I hypnotised him into the belief that he was a performing seal and I was a piece of ripe herring, whereupon he dived after me.'

He turned back into the sitting-room, and closed the window after her.

'I don't think you need join the congregation below,' he remarked. 'The specimen will be taken for a promising cat burglar who's come down in the world, and he will probably get six months and free medical attention. But you might remember this incident – it will help you to take care of yourself.'

She looked him in the eyes for several seconds.

Then:

'I apologise,' she said quietly.

'So do I,' answered the Saint. 'That remark was unnecessarily sarcastic, and my only defence is that you thoroughly deserved it.'

He smiled; and then he reached for his cigarette-case.

'Gasper? . . . Splendid . . . By the way, I suppose you don't happen to have such a thing as a kipper about the place, do you? I was going to suggest that we indulged at the Cri, but you didn't give me time. And this is the hour when I usually kip . . .'

4

A few days later, Mr Francis Lemuel made his first long flight with his new pilot. They went first to Paris, and then to Berlin, in a week of perfect weather; and of the Saint's share in their wanderings abroad, on that occasion, there is nothing of interest to record. He drank French and German beers with a solid yearning for good English bitter, and was almost moved to assassinate a chatty and otherwise amiable Bavarian who ventured to say that in his opinion English beer was zu stark. Mr Lemuel went about his own business, and the Saint only saw him at sporadic meal-times in their hotels.

Lemuel was a man of middle age, with a Lombard Street complexion and an affectation of bluff geniality of which he was equally proud.

Except when they were actually in transit, he made few calls upon his new employee's time.

'Get about and enjoy yourself, Old Man' – everyone was Old Man to Mr Lemuel. 'You can see things here that you'll never see in England.'

The Saint got about; and, in answer to Lemuel's casual inquiries, magnified his minor escapades into stories of which he was heartily ashamed. He made detailed notes of the true parts of some of his stories, to be reserved for future attention; but the Saint was a strong believer in concentrating on one thing at a time, and he was not proposing to ball up the main idea by taking chances on side-issues – at the moment.

He only met one of Lemuel's business acquaintances, and this was a man named Jacob Einsmann, who dined with them one night. Einsmann, it appeared, had a controlling interest in two prosperous night-clubs, and he was anxious for Lemuel to arrange lavish cabaret attractions. He was a short, florid-looking man, with an underhung nose and a superfluity of diamond rings.

'I must have it der English or American girls, yes,' he insisted. 'Der continental – pah! I can any number for noddings get, aind't it, no? But yours—'

He kissed excessively manicured fingers.

'You're right, Old Man,' boomed Lemuel sympathetically. 'English or American girls are the greatest troupers in the world. I won't say they don't get temperamental sometimes, but they've got a sense of discipline as well, and they don't mind hard work. The trouble is to get them abroad. There are so many people in England who jump to the worst conclusions if you try to send an English girl abroad.'

He ranted against a certain traffic at some length; and the Saint heard out the tirade, and shrugged.

'I suppose you know more about it than I do, sir,' he submitted humbly, 'but I always feel the danger's exaggerated. There must be plenty of honest agents.'

'There are, Old Man,' rumbled Lemuel. 'But we get saddled with the crimes of those who aren't.'

Shortly afterwards, the conversation reverted to purely business topics; and the Saint, receiving a hint too broad to be ignored, excused himself.

Lemuel and the Saint left for England the next morning, and at the hour when he took off from Waalhaven Aerodrome on the last stage of the journey (they had descended upon Rotterdam for a meal) Simon was very little nearer to solving the problem of Francis Lemuel than he had been when he left England.

The inspiration came to him as they sighted the cliffs of Kent.

A few minutes later he literally ran into the means to his end.

It had been afternoon when they left the Tempelhof, for Mr Lemuel was no early riser; and even then the weather had been breaking. As they travelled westwards it had grown steadily worse. More than once the Saint had had to take the machine very low to avoid clouds; and, although they had not actually encountered rain, the atmosphere had been anything but serene ever since they crossed the Dutch frontier. There had been one very bumpy half-hour during which Mr Lemuel had been actively unhappy . . .

Now, as they came over English ground, they met the first of the storm.

'I don't like the look of it, Templar,' Mr Lemuel opined huskily, through the telephones. 'Isn't there an aerodrome near here that we could land at, Old Man?'

'I don't know of one,' lied the Saint. 'And it's getting dark quickly – I daren't risk losing my bearings. We'll have to push on to Croydon.'

'Croydon!'

Simon heard the word repeated faintly, and grinned. For in a flash he had grasped a flimsy clue, and had seen his way clear; and the repetition had confirmed him in a fantastic hope.

'Why Croydon?'

'It's the nearest aerodrome that's fitted up for night landings. I don't suppose we shall have much trouble with the Customs,' added the Saint thoughtfully.

There was a silence; and the Saint flew on, as low as he dared, searching the darkening country beneath him. And, within himself, he was blessing the peculiar advantages of his favourite hobby.

Times without number, when he had nothing else to do, the Saint had taken his car and set out to explore the unfrequented byways of England, seeking out forgotten villages and unspoilt country inns, which he collected as less robust and simple-minded men collect postage-stamps. It was his boast that he knew every other inch of the British Isles blindfolded, and he may not have been very far wrong. There was one village, near the Kent–Surrey border, which had suggested itself to him immediately as the ideal place for his purpose.

'I say, Old Man,' spoke Lemuel again, miserably.

'Hullo?'

'I'm feeling like death. I can't go on much longer. Can't you land in a field around here while there's still a bit of light?'

'I was wondering what excuse you'd make, dear heart,' said the Saint; but he said it to himself. Aloud, he answered cheerfully: 'It certainly is a bit bumpy, sir. I'll have a shot at it, if you like.'

As a matter of fact, he had just sighted his objective, and he throttled off the engine with a gentle smile of satisfaction.

It wasn't the easiest landing in the world to make, especially in that weather; but the Saint put the machine on the deck without a mistake, turned, and taxied back to a sheltered corner of the field he had chosen. Then he climbed out of the cockpit and stretched himself.

'I can peg her out for the night,' he remarked, as Lemuel joined him on the ground, 'and there shouldn't be any harm done if it doesn't blow much harder than this.'

'A little more of that flying would have killed me,' said Lemuel; and he was really looking rather pale. 'Where are we?'

Simon told him.

'It's right off the map, and I'm afraid you won't get a train back to town to-night; but I know a very decent little pub we can stay at,' he said.

'I'll phone for my chauffeur to come down,' said Lemuel. 'I suppose there's a telephone in this place somewhere?'

'I doubt it,' said Simon; but he knew that there was.

Again, however, luck was with him. It was quite dark by the time the aeroplane had been pegged out with ropes obtained from a neighbouring farm, and a steady rain was falling, so that no one was about to watch the Saint climbing nimbly up a telegraph-pole just beyond the end of the village street . . .

Lemuel, who had departed to knock up the post office, rejoined him later in the bar of the 'Blue Dragon' with a tale of woe.

'A telegraph-pole must have been blown down,' he said. 'Anyway, it was impossible to get through.'

Simon, who had merely cut the wires without doing any damage to the pole, nevertheless saw no reason to correct the official theory.

Inquiries about possible conveyance to the nearest main-line town proved equally fruitless, as the Saint had known they would be. He had selected his village with care. It possessed nothing suitable for Mr Lemuel, and no traffic was likely to pass through that night, for it was right off the beaten track.

'Looks as if we'll have to make the best of it, Old Man,' said Lemuel, and Simon concurred.

After supper Lemuel's spirits rose, and they spent a convivial evening in the bar.

It was a very convivial evening. Mr Lemuel, under the soothing influence of many brandies, forgot his day's misadventures, and embarked enthusiastically upon the process of making a night of it. For, he explained, his conversation with

Jacob Einsmann was going to lead to a lot of easy money. But he could not be persuaded to divulge anything of interest, though the Saint led the conversation cunningly. Simon smiled, and continued to drink him level – even taking it upon himself to force the pace towards closing time. Simon had had some opportunity to measure up Francis Lemuel's minor weaknesses, and an adroit employment of some of this knowledge was part of the Saint's plan. And the Saint was ordinarily a most temperate man.

'You're a goo' feller, Ole Man,' Mr Lemuel was proclaiming, towards eleven o'clock. 'You stick to me, Ole Man, an' don' worrabout wha' people tell you. You stick to me. I gorra lotta money. Show you trick one day. You stick to me. Give you a berra job soon, Ole Man. Pallomine . . .'

When at length Mr Lemuel announced that he was going to bed, the Saint's affable 'Sleep well, sir!' would have struck a captious critic as unnecessary; for nothing could have been more certain than that Mr Lemuel would that night sleep the sleep of the only just.

The Saint himself stayed on in the bar for another hour, for the landlord was in talkative mood and was not unique in finding Simon Templar very pleasant company. So it came to pass that, a few minutes after the Saint had said good night, his sudden return with a face of dismay was easily accounted for.

'I've got the wrong bag,' he explained. 'The other two were put in Mr Lemuel's room, weren't they?'

'Is one of them yours?' asked the publican sympathetically.

Simon nodded.

'I've been landed with the samples,' he said. 'And I'll bet Mr Lemuel's locked his door. He never forgets to do that, however drunk he is. And we'd have to knock the place down to wake him up now – and I'd lose my job if we did.'

'I've got a master key, sir,' said the landlord helpfully. 'You could slip in with that, and change the bags, and he wouldn't know anything about it.'

Simon stared.

'You're a blinkin' marvel, George,' he murmured. 'You are, really.'

With the host's assistance he entered Mr Lemuel's room, and emerged with the key of the door in his pocket and one of Lemuel's bags in his hand. Mr Lemuel snored rhythmically through it all.

'Thanks, George,' said the Saint, returning the master key. 'Breakfast at ten, and in bed, I think . . .'

Then he took the bag into his own room, and opened it without much difficulty.

Its weight, when he had lifted it out of the aeroplane, had told him not to expect it to contain clothes; but the most superficially interesting thing about it was that Mr Lemuel had not possessed it when he left England, and it was simply as a result of intensive pondering over that fact that the Saint had arrived at the scheme that he was then carrying out. And, in view of his hypothesis, and Mr Lemuel's reaction to the magic word 'Croydon', it cannot be said that the Saint was wildly surprised when he found what the bag actually held. But he was very, very interested, nevertheless.

There were rows and rows of neatly-packed square tins, plain and unlabelled. Fishing one out, the Saint gently detached the strip of adhesive tape which sealed it, and prised off the lid. He came to a white, crystalline powder . . . but that had been in his mind when he opened the tin. Almost perfunctorily, he took a tiny pinch of the powder between his finger and thumb, and laid it on his tongue; and the Saintly smile tightened a little.

Then he sat back on his heels, lighted a cigarette, and regarded his catch thoughtfully.

'You're a clever boy, Francis,' he murmured.

He meditated for some time, humming under his breath, apparently quite unmoved. But actually his brain was seething.

It would have been quite easy to dispose of the contents of the bag. It would have been quite easy to dispose of Mr Lemuel. For a while the Saint toyed with the second idea. A strong solution of the contents of one of the tins, for instance, administered with the hypodermic syringe which Simon had in his valise – Then he shook his head.

'Try to remember, Old Man,' he apostrophised himself, 'that you are a business organisation. And you're not at all sure that Uncle Francis has left you anything in his will.'

The scheme which he ultimately decided upon was simplicity itself – so far as it went. It depended solely upon the state of the village baker's stock.

Simon left the 'Blue Dragon' stealthily, and returned an hour later considerably laden.

He was busy for some hours after that, but he replaced Lemuel's grip looking as if it had not been touched, opening the door with Lemuel's own key.

It is quite easy to lock a door from the outside and leave the key in the lock on the inside – if you know the trick. You tie a string to the end of a pencil, slip the pencil through the hole in the key, and pass the string underneath the door. A pull on the string turns the key; and the pencil drops out, and can be pulled away under the door.

And after that the Saint slithered into his pyjamas and rolled into bed as the first greyness of dawn lightened the sky outside his bedroom window, and slept like a child.

In the morning they flew on to Hanworth, where Lemuel's car waited to take them back to London.

The Saint was dropped at Piccadilly Circus and he walked without hesitation into the Piccadilly Hotel. Settling himself at a table within, he drew a sheet of the hotel's note-paper towards him, and devoted himself with loving care to the production of a Work of Art. This consisted of the picture of a little man, drawn with a round blank head and straight-lined body and limbs, as a child draws, but wearing above his cerebellum, at a somewhat rakish angle, a halo such as few children's drawings portray. Then he took an envelope, which he addressed to Francis Lemuel and omitted to embellish with a stamp. He posted his completed achievement within the hotel.

At half-past one he burst in upon Patricia Holm, declaring himself ravenous for lunch.

'With beer,' he said. 'Huge foaming mugs of it. Brewed at Burton, and as stark as they make it.'

'And what's Francis Lemuel's secret?' she asked.

He shrugged.

'Don't spoil the homecoming,' he said. 'I hate to tell you, but I haven't come within miles of it in a whole blinkin' week.'

He did not think it necessary to tell her that he had deliberately signed and sealed his own death-warrant, for of late she had become rather funny that way.

5

There are a number of features about this story which will always endear it – in a small way – to the Saint's memory. He likes its logical development, and the neat way in which the divers factors dove-tail into one another with an almost audible click; he likes the crisp precision of the earlier episodes, and purrs happily as he recalls the flawless detail of his own technique in those episodes; but particularly is he lost in speechless admiration when he considers the overpowering brilliance of the exercise in inductive psychology which dictated his manner of pepping up the concluding stages of the adventure.

Thus he reviewed the child of his genius:

'The snow retails at about sixty pounds an ounce, in the unauthorised trade; and I must have poured about seventy thousand pounds' worth down the sink. Oh, yes, it was a good idea – to fetch over several years' supply at one go, almost without risk. And then, of course, according to schedule, I should have been quietly fired, and no one but Uncle Francis would have been any the wiser. Instead of which, Uncle's distributing organisation, whatever that may be, will shortly be howling in full cry down Jermyn Street to ask Uncle what he means by ladling them out a lot of tins of ordinary white flour. Coming on top of the letter which will be shot in by the late post tonight, this question will cause a distinct stir. And, in the still small hours, Uncle Francis will sit down to ponder the ancient problem – What should "A" do?'

This was long afterwards, when the story of Francis Lemuel was ancient history. And the Saint would gesture with his cigarette, and beam thoughtfully upon the assembled congregation, and presently proceed with his exposition:

'Now, what should "A" do, dear old strepsicocco? . . . Should he woofle forth into the wide world, and steam into Scotland Yard, bursting with information? . . . Definitely not. He has no information that he can conveniently lay. His egg, so to speak, had addled in the oviduct . . . Then should he curse me and cut his losses and leave it at that? . . . Just as definitely not. I have had no little publicity in my time; and he knows my habits. He knows that I haven't finished with him yet. He knows that, unless he gets his counter-attack in quickly, he's booked to travel down the drain in no uncertain manner . . . Then should he call in a few tough guys and offer a large reward for my death-certificate? . . . I think not. Francis isn't that type . . . He has a wholesome respect for the present length of his neck; and he doesn't fancy the idea of having it artificially extended in a whitewashed shed by a gentleman in a dark suit one cold and frosty morning. He knows that that sort of thing is frequently happening – sometimes to quite clever murderers . . . So what does he do?'

And what Francis Lemuel did was, of course, exactly what the Saint had expected. He telephoned in the evening, three days later, and Simon went round to Jermyn Street after dinner – with a gun in his pocket in case of accidents. That was a simple precaution; he was not really expecting trouble, and he was right.

The instructions which he actually received, however, were slightly different from the ones he had anticipated. He found Lemuel writing telegrams; and the impresario came straight to the point.

'Einsmann – you remember the fellow who came to dinner? – seems to have got himself into a mess. He's opening a new night club to-morrow, and his prize cabaret attraction has let him down at the last minute. He hasn't been able to arrange a good enough substitute on the spot, and he cabled me for help. I've been able to find a first-class girl, but the trouble is to get her to Berlin in time for a rehearsal with his orchestra.'

'You want me to fly her over?' asked the Saint, and Lemuel nodded.

'That's the only way, Old Man. I can't let Einsmann down when he's just on the point of signing a big contract with me. You have a car, haven't you?'

'Yes, sir.'

'I'll give you this girl's address' – Lemuel took a slip of paper, and wrote. 'She's expecting you to pick her up at nine o'clock to-morrow morning. You must go straight to Hanworth . . .'

Simon folded the paper and stowed it carefully away in his pocketbook, while Lemuel gave further instructions.

Lemuel was showing signs of the strain. There was a puffiness about his eyes, and his plump cheeks seemed to sag flabbily. But he played his part with a grim restraint.

Leaving Jermyn Street, the Saint found himself heading mechanically for the Piccadilly Hotel. There he composed, after some careful calculations with the aid of a calendar, a brief note:

Unless the sum of £20,000 (Twenty Thousand Pounds) is paid into the account of J. B. L. Smith at the City and Continental Bank, Lombard Street, by 12 noon on Saturday, I shall forward to the Public Prosecutor sufficient evidence to assure you of five years' penal servitude.

The note was signed with one of the Saint's most artistic self-portraits, and it was addressed to Francis Lemuel.

This was on Thursday night.

As he strolled leisurely home the Saint communed with himself again.

'Uncle Francis wanted a disreputable aviator so that if anything went wrong the aviator could be made the scapegoat. But when he deduced that I was the Saint, that idea went west. What should I have done if I'd been Uncle Francis? ... I should have arranged for Mr Templar to fall out of an aeroplane at a height of about four thousand feet. A nasty accident – he stalled at the top of a loop, and his safety belt wasn't fastened ... And Uncle knows enough about the game to be able to bring the kite down ... And that's what I thought it was going to be, with a few drops of slumber mixture in my beer before we went up next time ... But this is nearly as good. I do my last job of work for Uncle, and doubtless there is an entertainment arranged for my especial benefit in Berlin to-morrow night – or a man hired to file my elevator wires ready for the return journey on Saturday. Yes – perhaps this is even cleverer than my own idea. The commission to take this girl to Berlin is intended to disarm my suspicions. I am meant to think that I'm not suspected. I'm supposed to think that I'm absolutely on velvet, and therefore get careless ... Oh, it should be a great little week-end!'

The only trouble he expected the next morning would not be directly of Lemuel's making – and in that, again, his deduction was faultless.

Stella Dornford was surprised to see him.

'What do you want?' she asked.

'I want you to fly with me,' said the Saint dramatically, and she was taken aback.

'Are you Lemuel's man?'

Simon nodded.

'Extraordinary how I get about, isn't it?' he murmured.

'Is this a joke?'

He shook his head.

'Anything but, as far as I'm concerned, old dear. Now, can you imagine anyone getting up at this hour of the morning to be funny?' He grinned at her puzzled doubts. 'Call it coincidence, sweetheart, and lead me to your luggage.'

At the foot of the stairs he paused, and looked thoughtfully round the courtyard.

'They seem to have scraped Cuthbert off the concrete,' he said; and then, abruptly: 'How did you get this job?'

'Lemuel was in front the other night,' she answered. 'He sent his card round in the interval—'

'Told you he was struck by your dancing, bought you out, signed you up—'

'How did you know?'

'I didn't. But it fits in so beautifully. And to make me the accessory – oh, it's just too splendiferous for words! I didn't know Francis had such a sense of humour.'

'What do you mean?'

'I'm right, am I? Listen. He said: "It's one of the worst shows I've ever seen, Old Man" – no, I suppose he'd vary that – "but your dancing, Old Woman, is the elephant's uvula." Or words to that effect. What?'

'He certainly said he liked my dancing—'

'Joke,' said the Saint sardonically.

She caught him up when he was loading her two suitcases into the back of his car.

'Mr Templar—'

'My name.'

'I don't understand your sense of humour.'

'Sorry about that.'

'I'd be obliged if you'd leave my dancing alone.'

'Darling,' said the Saint kindly, 'I'd like to maroon it on a desert island. After I'd met you for the first time I made a point of seeing your show; and I must say that I decided that you are beautiful and energetic and well-meaning, and your figure is a dream – but if your dancing is the elephant's uvula, then I think the R.S.P.C.A. ought to do something about it.'

Pale with fury, she entered the car, and there was silence until they were speeding down the Great West Road.

Then Simon added, as if there had been no break in his speech : 'If I were you, old dear, I'd be inclined to think very kindly of that nice boy in the bank.'

'I don't think I want your advice, Mr Templar,' she said coldly. 'Your job is to take me to Berlin – and I only wish I could get there in time without your help.'

All the instinctive antagonism that had come up between them like barbed wire at their first meeting was back again. After the accident to the amateur mountaineer there had been a truce; but the Saint had foreseen renewed hostilities from the moment he had read the name and address on the paper which Lemuel had given him, and he had been at no pains to avert the outbreak. Patricia Holm used to say that the Saint had less than no idea of the art of handling women. That is a statement which other historians may be left to judge; the Saint himself would have been the smiling first to subscribe to the charge, but there were times when Simon Templar's vanity went to strange extremes. If he thought he had any particular accomplishment, he would either boast about it or disclaim it altogether, so you always knew where you were with him. So far as the handling of women was concerned, his methods were usually of the this-is-your-label-and-if-you-don't-like-it-you-can-get-to-hell-out-of-here school – when they were not exactly the reverse – and in this case, at least, he knew precisely what he was doing. Otherwise, he might have had a more entertaining journey to Berlin than he did; but he had developed a soft spot in his heart for the unknown nice boy who used to take Stella

Dornford to the movies – and, bless him, probably used to hold her hand in the same. Now, Jacob Einsmann would never have thought of doing a thing like that . . .

There was another reason – a subsidiary reason – for the Saint's aloofness. He wanted to be free to figure out the exact difference that had been made to the situation by the discovery of the identity of his charge. A new factor had been introduced which was likely to alter a lot of things. And it was necessary to find out a little more about it – a very little more.

So they travelled between Hanworth and the Tempelhof in a frost-bitten silence which the Saint made no attempt to alleviate; and in the same spirit he took Stella Dornford by taxi to the address that Lemuel had given him.

This was a huge, gloomy house nearly two miles away from the centre of fashionable gaiety, and anything less like a night club Simon Templar had rarely seen.

He did not immediately open the door of the taxi. Instead, he surveyed the house interestedly through a window of the cab; and then he turned to the girl.

'I'm sure Jacob Einsmann isn't a very nice man,' he said. 'In fact, he and I are definitely going to have words. But I'm ready to leave you at a hotel before I go in.'

She tossed her head, and opened the door herself.

The Saint followed her up the steps of the house. She had rung the bell while he was paying off the taxi, and the door was unbarred as he reached her side.

'Herr Einsmann wishes to see you also, sir.'

The Saint nodded, and passed in. The butler – he, like the porter at the Calumet Club, of hallowed memory, looked as if he had been other things in his time – led them down a bare sombre hall, and opened a door.

The girl passed through it first, and Simon heard her exclamation before he saw Einsmann.

Then her hand gripped his arm.

'I don't like this,' she said.

Simon smiled. He had read the doubt in her eyes when she first saw the house, and had liked the dam'-fool obstinacy that had marched her into it against his advice and her better judgment. But, while he approved her spirit, he had deliberately taken advantage of it to make sure that she should have her lesson.

'So!' Jacob Einsmann rose from his chair, rubbing his hands gently together. His eyes were fixed upon the girl. 'You vould not listen to it vot I say in London, no, you vere so prrroud, but now you yourself to me hof come, aind't it?'

6

'Aye, laad, we've coom,' drawled the Saint. 'So you hof got it vot you vanted, yes, no, aind't it?'

Einsmann turned his head.

'Ach! I remember you—'

'And I you,' said the Saint comfortably. 'In fact, I spent a considerable time on the trip over composing a little song about you, in the form of a nursery rhyme for the instruction of small children, which, with your permission, I will now proceed to sing. It goes like this:

> 'Dear Jacob is an unwashed mamser,
> We like not his effluvium, sir;
> If we can tread on Jacob's graft,
> *Das wird ja wirklich fabelhaft.*'

For that effort in trilingual verse I have already awarded myself the Swaffer Biscuit.'

Einsman leered.

'For vonce, Herr Saint, you hof a misdake made.'

'Saint?'

The girl spoke, at Simon's shoulder, startled, half incredulous. He smiled round at her.

'That's right, old dear. I am that well-known institution. Is this the Boche you mentioned at the Cri – the bird who got fresh at the Calumet?'

She nodded.

'I didn't know—'

'You weren't meant to,' said Simon coolly. 'That was just part of the deception. But I guessed it as soon as Lemuel gave me your name.'

'You vos clever, Herr Saint,' Einsmann said suavely.

'I vos,' the Saint admitted modestly. 'It only wanted a little putting two and two together. There was that dinner the other day, for instance. Very well staged for my benefit, wasn't it? All that trout-spawn and frog-bladder about your cabarets, and Lemuel warbling about the difficulty of getting English girls abroad ... I made a good guess at the game then; and I'd have laid anyone ten thousand bucks to a slush nickel, on the spat, that it wouldn't be long before I was asked to ferry over a few fair maidens in Lemuel's machine. I had your graft taped right out a few days ago, and I don't see that the present variation puts me far wrong. The only real difference is that Francis is reckoning to have to find another aviator to carry through the rest of the contract – aind't it?'

His hand went lazily to his hip pocket; and then something jabbed him sharply in the ribs, and he looked down at a heavy automatic in the hand of the imitation butler, who had not left the room.

'You vill bring your gun out verree slowly,' said Einsmann, succulently. 'Verree slowly . . .'

Simon smiled – a slow and Saintly smile. And, as slow as the smile, his hand came into view.

'Do you mind?' he murmured.

He opened the cigarette-case, and selected a smoke with care. The butler lowered his gun.

'Let us talk German,' said the Saint suddenly, in that language. 'I have a few things to say which this girl need not hear.'

Einsmann's mouth twisted.

'I shall be interested,' he said ironically.

With an unlighted cigarette between his lips, and the cigarette-case still open in his hands, Simon looked across at the German. Stella Dornford was behind the Saint; the imitation butler stood a little to one side, his automatic in his hand.

'You are a man for whom there is no adequate punishment. You are a buyer and seller of souls, and your money is earned with more human misery than your insanitary mind can imagine. To attempt to visit some of this misery upon yourself would do little good. The only thing to do is to see that you cease to pollute the earth.'

His cold blue eyes seemed to bore into Einsmann's brain, so that the German, in spite of his armed bodyguard, felt a momentary qualm of fear.

'I only came here to make quite sure about you, Jacob Einsmann,' said the Saint. 'And now I am quite sure. You had better know that I am going to kill you.'

He took a step forward, and did not hear the door open behind him.

Einsmann's florid face had gone white, save for the bright patches of colour that burned in either cheek. Then he spoke, in a sudden torrent of hoarse words:

'So! You say you will kill me? But you are wrong. I am not the one who will die to-night, I know you, Herr Saint! Even if Lemuel had not told me, I should still have known enough. You remember Henri Chastel? He was my friend, and you killed him. Ach! You shall not have a quick death, my friend—'

With the Saintly smile still resting blandly on his lips, Simon had closed his cigarette-case with a snap while Einsmann talked, and was returning it to his hip pocket, . . . He performed the action so quietly and naturally that, coming after the false alarm he had caused when he took it out of the same pocket, this movement of his hand passed almost unnoticed. Nor did it instantly seem strange to the audience when the Saint's hand did not at once return to view. He brought the hand up swiftly behind his back; he had exchanged the cigarette-case for a gun, and he nosed the muzzle of the gun through the gap between his left arm and his body.

'You may give my love to Henri,' he remarked, and touched the trigger.

He saw Einsmann's face twist horribly, and the German clutched at his stomach before he crumpled where he stood; but Simon only saw these things out of the tail of his eye. He had whipped the gun from under his armpit a second after his first shot; there was no time to fetch it round behind his body into a more convenient firing position, and he loosed his second shot with his forearm lying along the small of his back and the gun aimed out to his left. But the butler's attention had been diverted at the moment when the Saint fired first, and the man's reaction was not quite quick enough. He took the Saint's bullet in the shoulder, and his own shot blew a hole in the carpet.

Then the door slammed shut and Simon turned right round.

The man who had seized Stella Dornford from behind a moment before the Saint's first shot was not armed, and he had not taken a second to perceive the better part of valour. Unhappily for his future, the instinct of self-preservation had been countered by another and equally powerful instinct, and he had tried to compromise with the two. Perhaps he thought that the armed butler could be relied upon.

The speculation is interesting but unprofitable, for the man's mental processes are now beyond the reach of practical investigation. All we know is that at that precise instant of time he was heading down the hall with an unconscious burden.

And the Saint had wrenched at the handle of the door and found it locked upon the outside. Simon jerked up his gun again, and the report mingled with a splintering crash.

He jerked the door open, and looked up and down the dark hall. At the far end, towards the back of the house, another door was closing – he saw the narrowing strip of brighter light in the gloom. The strip vanished as he raced towards it, and he heard a key turn as he groped for the handle. Again he raised his automatic, and then, instead of the detonation he was expecting, heard only the click of a dud cartridge. He snatched at the sliding jacket, and something jammed. He had no time to find out what it was; he dropped the gun into his pocket, made certain of the position of the keyhole, and stepped back a pace. Then he raised his foot and smashed his heel into the lock with all his strength and weight behind it.

The door sprang open eighteen inches – and crashed into a table that was being brought up to reinforce it. The Saint leapt at the gap, made it, wedged his back against the jamb, and set both hands to the door. With one titanic heave he flung the door wide and sent the table spinning back to the centre of the room.

The girl lay on the floor by the doorway. On the other side of the room, beyond the up-turned table, the man who had brought her had opened a drawer in a desk, and he turned with an automatic in his hand.

'*Schweinhund!*' he snarled; and the Saint laughed.

The Saint laughed, took two quick steps, and launched himself headlong into space in a terrific dive. It took him clear over the table, full length, and muddled his objective's aim. The man sighted frantically, and fired; and the Saint felt something like a hot iron sear his right arm from wrist to elbow; then Simon had gathered up the man's legs in that fantastic tackle, and they went to the floor together.

The Saint's left hand caught the gunman's right wrist and pinned it to the floor; then, his own right hand being numb, he brought up his knee . . .

He was on his feet again in a moment, gathering the automatic out of the man's limp hand as he rose.

The girl's eyes fluttered as he reached her, but the Saint reckoned that freight would be less trouble than first aid. He put his captured gun on a chair; and, as the girl started to try to rise, he yanked her to her feet and caught her over his left shoulder before she could fall again.

Quickly he tested his right hand again, and found that his fingers had recovered from the momentary shock. He picked up the gun in that hand.

A faint sound behind him made him turn swiftly, and he saw the gunman crawling towards him with a knife. He had not meant to fire, but the trigger must have been exceptionally sensitive, and the gunman rolled over slowly and lay quite still.

Then the Saint broke down the hall.

A gigantic negro loomed up out of the twilight. Careful of the trigger this time, the Saint snapped the muzzle of the gun into the man's chest, and the negro backed away with rolling eyes. Keeping him covered, Simon sidled to the door and set the girl gently on her feet. She was able to stand then; and she it was who, under his directions, unbarred the door and opened it.

'See if there's a taxi,' rapped the Saint, and heard her hurry down the steps.

A moment later she called him.

He gave her time to get into the taxi herself; and then, like lightning, he sprang through the door and slammed it behind him.

The chauffeur, turning to receive his instructions through the little window communicating between the inside and outside of the cab, heard the shout from the house, and looked round with a question forming on his lips. Then something cold and metallic touched the back of his neck, and one of his fares spoke crisply.

'*Gehen Sie schnell, mein Freund!*'

The driver obeyed.

The fact that, having been given no destination to drive to, he was quietly steering his passengers in the direction of the nearest police station, is of no great historical interest. For, when he reached the station he was without passengers; and the officials who heard his story were inclined to cast grave doubts upon that worthy citizen's sobriety, until confirmation of some of his statements arrived through another channel.

Stella Dornford and the Saint had quietly left him in a convenient traffic block; for Simon had much more to do in the next twenty-four hours, and he was in no mood to be delayed by embarrassing inquiries.

7

'And if that doesn't learn you, my girl,' said the Saint, a trifle grimly, 'nothing ever will.'

They were in a room in the hotel where the girl had parked her luggage before proceeding to the interview with Einsmann. The Saint, with a cigarette between his lips and a glass tankard of dark syrupy Kulmbach on the table beside him, was sitting on the bed, bandaging his arm with two white linen handkerchiefs torn into strips. Stella Dornford stood by shame-facedly.

'I'm sorry I was such a fool,' she said.

Simon looked up at her. She was very pale, but this was not the pallor of anger with which she had begun the day.

'Can I help you with that?' she asked.

'It's nothing,' he said cheerfully. 'I'm never hurt. It's a gift . . .'

He secured his effort with a safety-pin, and rolled down his sleeve. Then he gave her one of his quick, impulsive smiles.

'Anyway,' he said, 'you've seen some Life. And that was what you wanted, wasn't it?'

'You can't make me feel worse than I do already.'

He laughed, and stood up; and she looked round as his hands fell on her shoulders.

'Why worry, old dear?' he said. 'It's turned out all right – so what the hell? You don't even have to rack your brains to think of an unfutile way of saying "Thank you." I've loved it. The pleasure of shooting Jacob in the tum-tum was worth a dozen of these scratches. So let's leave it at that.' He ruffled her hair absently. 'And now we'll beat it back to England, shall we?'

He turned away, and picked up his coat.

'Are you leaving now?' she asked in surprise.

Simon nodded.

'I'm afraid we must. In the first place, this evening's mirth and horseplay is liable to start a certain hue and cry after me in this bouncing burg. I don't know that that alone would make me jump for the departure platform; but there's also a man I want to see in England – about a sort of dog. I'm sorry about the rush, but things always seem to happen to me in a hurry. Are you ready?'

They landed for a late meal at Amsterdam; and they had not long left Schiphol behind when the darkness and the monotonous roar of the engine soothed Stella Dornford into a deep sleep of sheer nervous weariness. She awoke when the engine was suddenly silenced, and found that they were gliding down into the pale half-light before dawn.

'I think there's enough light to make a landing here,' Simon answered her question through the telephones. 'I don't want to have to go on to Croydon.'

There was, at least, enough light for the Saint to make a perfect landing; and he taxied up to the deserted hangars and left the machine there for the mechanics to find in the morning. Then he went in search of his car.

In the car, again she slept; and it is therefore not surprising that she never thought of Francis Lemuel until after he had unloaded her into one of the friendliest sitting-rooms she had ever seen, and after he had prepared eggs and bacon and coffee for them both, and after they had smoked two cigarettes together. And then it was Simon who reminded her.

'I want you to help me with a telephone conversation,' he said, and proceeded to coach her carefully.

A few minutes later she had dialled a number and was waiting for the reply.

Then:

'Are you Piccadilly thrrree-eight thrrree-four?' she asked sweetly.

The answer came in a decorated affirmative.

'You're wanted from Berlin.'

She clicked the receiver hook; and then the Saint took over the instrument.

'Dot vos you, Lemuel, no? . . . You vould like to hear about it der business, aind't it? . . . Ja! I hof seddled it altogether der business. Der man vill not more trrouble gif, andt der samples I hof also received it, yes . . .'

A couple of lines of brisk dialogue, this time in German, between the Saint and an excellent impersonator of the Berlin exchange, cut short the conversation with the Saint hurriedly concluding: 'Ja! I to you der particulars to-morrow vill wrrrite . . .'

'It's detail that does it,' murmured Simon complacently, as he replaced the receiver.

Stella Dornford was regarding him with a certain awe.

'I'm beginning to understand some of the things I've read about you,' she said; and the Saint grinned, for no false modesty had ever been numbered among his failings.

Shortly afterwards he excused himself; and when he returned to the sitting-room, which was in a surprisingly short space of time, he had changed out of the characteristically conspicuous suit in which he had travelled, and was wearing a plain and unnoticeable blue serge. The Saint's phenomenal speed of dressing would have made the fortune of a professional quick-change artist; and he was as pleased with the girl's unspoken astonishment at his feat as he had been with her first compliment.

'Where are you going?' she demanded, when she had found her voice.

'To see you home, first,' he answered briskly. 'And then I have a little job of work to do.'

'But why have you changed?'

The Saint adjusted a cheap black tie.

'The job might turn into a funeral,' he said. 'I don't seriously think it will, but I like to be prepared.'

She was still mystified when he left her at the door of her apartment.

From there he drove down to Piccadilly, and left his car in St. James's Street, proceeding afterwards on foot. Here the reason for his change of costume began to appear. Anyone might have remarked the rare spectacle of a truly Saintly figure parading the West End of London at six o'clock in the morning arrayed in one of the most dazzling creations of Savile Row; but no one came forward to describe the soberly dressed and commonplace-looking young man who committed the simplest audacity of the season.

Nor could he ever afterwards have been identified by the sleepy-eyed porter who answered his ring at a certain bell in Jermyn Street; for, when the door was opened, Simon's face was masked from eyes to chin by a handkerchief folded three-cornerwise, and his hat-brim shaded his eyes. So much the porter saw before the Saint struck once, swiftly, mercifully, and regretfully, with a supple rubber truncheon . . .

The Saint closed the door behind him, and unbuttoned his double-breasted coat. There were a dozen turns of light rope wound round his waist belt-fashion, and with these he secured the janitor hand and foot, completing the work with a humane but efficient gag. Then he lifted the unconscious man and carried him to a little cubicle at the back of the hall, where he left him – after taking his keys.

He raced up the stairs to the door of Lemuel's apartment, which was on the second floor. It was the work of a moment only to find the right key. Then, if the door were bolted . . .

But apparently Lemuel relied on the security of his Yale and the watchfulness of the porter . . .

The Saint passed like a cat down the passage mat opened before him, listening at door after door. Presently he heard the sound of rhythmic breathing; and he entered Lemuel's bedroom without a sound, and stood over the bed like a ghost.

He was certain that Lemuel must have spent a restless night until the recent telephone call came through to calm his fears. There was a bottle, a siphon, a glass, and an ash-tray heaped with cigarette-ends, on a table by the bedside, to support this assumption; but now Lemuel must be sleeping the sleep of the dead.

Gently Simon drew the edge of the sheet over the sleeping man's face; and on to the sheet he dripped a colourless liquid from a flask which he took from his pocket. The atmosphere thickened with a sickly reek . . .

Five minutes later, in another room, the Saint was opening a burglar-proof safe with Lemuel's own key.

He found what he was expecting to find – what, in fact, he had arranged to find. It had required no great genius to deduce that Lemuel would have withdrawn all his mobile fortune from his bank the day before; if there had been no satisfactory report from Einsmann before morning, Lemuel would have been on his way out of England long before the expiration of the time limit which the Saint had given him.

Simon burned twenty-five thousand pounds' worth of negotiable securities in the open grate. There was already a heap of ashes in the fireplace when he began his own bonfire and he guessed that Lemuel had spent part of the previous evening disinfecting his private papers; it would be a waste of time to search the desk. With about forty thousand pounds in Bank of England notes cunningly distributed about his person, the Saint closed the safe, after some artistic work on the interior, and returned to Lemuel's bedroom, where he replaced the key as he had found it. Before he left, he turned the sheet back from Lemuel's face; the bedroom windows were already open, and by morning the smell of ether should have dispersed.

'By morning . . .' The Saint glanced at his watch as he went down the stairs, and realised that he had only just given himself enough time. But he stopped at the janitor's cubicle on his way out, and the helpless man glared at him defiantly.

'I'm sorry I had to hit you,' said the Saint. 'But perhaps this will help to console you for your troubles.'

He took ten one-pound notes from his wallet, and bid them on the porter's desk; then he hurried down the hall, and slipped off his masking handkerchief as he opened the door.

Half an hour later he was in bed.

Francis Lemuel had arranged to be called early, in case of accidents, and the reassuring telephone message had come too late for him to countermand the order. He roused at half-past eight, to find his valet shaking him by the shoulder, and sat up muzzily. His head was splitting. He took a gulp at the hot tea which his man had brought, and felt sick.

'Must have drunk more whisky than I thought,' he reflected hazily; and then he became aware that his valet was speaking.

'There's been a burglary here, sir. About six o'clock this morning the porter was knocked out—'

'Here – in this apartment?' Lemuel's voice was harsh and strained.

'No, sir. At least, I've looked round, sir, and nothing seems to have been touched.'

Lemuel drew a long breath. For an instant an icy dread had clutched at his heart Then he remembered – the Saint was dead, there was nothing more to fear . . .

He sipped his tea again, and chuckled throatily.

'Then someone's been unlucky,' he remarked callously, and was surprised when the valet shook his head.

'That's the extraordinary thing, sir. They've been making inquiries all round, and none of the other apartments seem to have been entered either.'

Lemuel recalled this conversation later in the morning. He had declined breakfast blasphemously, and had only just managed to get up and dress in time to restore his treasures to the keeping of his bank.

He saw the emptiness of his safe, and the little drawing which the Saint had chalked inside it by way of receipt, and went a dirty grey-white.

The strength seemed to go from his knees; and he groped his way blindly to a chair, shaking with a superstitious terror. It was some time before he brought himself to realise that ghosts do not stun porters and clean out burglar-proof safes.

The valet, coming at a run to answer the frantic pealing of the bell, was horrified at the haggard limpness of his master.

'Fetch the police,' croaked Lemuel, and the man went quickly.

Chief Inspector Teal himself had just arrived to give some instructions to the detective-sergeant who had taken over the investigations, and he it was who answered the summons.

'Sixty-five thousand pounds? That's a lot of money to keep in a little safe like this.'

Teal cast sleepy eyes over the object, and then went down on his knees to examine it more closely. His heavy eyelids merely flickered when he saw the chalk-marks inside.

'Opened it with your own key, too.'

Lemuel nodded dumbly.

'I suppose he warned you?' said Teal drowsily – he was a chronically drowsy man.

'I had two ridiculous letters—'

'Can I see them?'

'I – I destroyed them. I don't take any notice of threats like that.'

Teal raised his eyebrows one millimetre.

'The Saint's a pretty well-known character,' he said. 'I should hate to have to calculate how many square miles of newspaper he's had all to himself since he started in business. And the most celebrated thing about him is that he's never yet failed to carry out a threat. This is the first time I've heard of anyone taking no notice of his letters.'

Lemuel swallowed. Suddenly, in a flash of pure agony, he understood his position. The Saint had ruined him – taken from him practically every penny he possessed – and yet had left him one fragile thing that was perhaps more precious than ten times the treasure he had lost – his liberty. And Lemuel's numbed brain could see no way of bringing the Saint to justice without imperilling that last lonely asset.

'What was the Saint's grouse against you?' asked Teal, like a sleep-walking Nemesis, and knew that he was wasting his time.

All the world knew that the Saint never threatened without good reason. To attempt to get evidence from his victims was a thankless task; there was so little that they could say without incriminating themselves.

And Lemuel saw the point also, and clapped quivering hands to his forehead.

'I – I apologise,' he said huskily. 'I see you've guessed the truth. I heard about the burglary, and thought I might get some cheap publicity out of it. There was nothing in the safe. I drew the picture inside – copied it from an old newspaper cutting . . .'

Teal heard, and nodded wearily.

But to Francis Lemuel had come one last desperate resolve.

8

There were many men in London who hated the Saint, and none of them hated him without cause. Some he had robbed; some he had sent to prison; some he had hurt in their bodies, and some he had hurt in their pride; and some, who had not yet met him, hated him because they feared what he might do if he learned about them all the things that there were to learn – which was, perhaps, the most subtle and deadly hatred of all.

Simon Templar had no illusions about his general popularity. He knew perfectly well that there were a large number of people domiciled between East India Dock and Hammersmith Broadway who would have been delighted to see him meet an end so sticky that he would descend to the place where they thought he would go like a well-ballasted black-beetle sinking through a pot of hot glue, and who, but for the distressing discouragements which the laws of England provide for such natural impulses, would have devoted all their sadistic ingenuity to the task of thus settling a long outstanding account. In the old days Simon had cared nothing for this; in those days he was known only as the Saint, and none knew his real name, or what he looked like, or whence he came; but those days had long gone by. Simon Templar's name and address and telephone number were now common property in certain circles; it was only in sheer blind cussedness, which he had somehow got away with, that he had scorned to use an alias in his dealings with Francis

Lemuel and the Calumet Club. And there had already been a number of enterprising gentlemen who had endeavoured to turn this knowledge to account in the furthering of their life's ambition – without, it must be admitted, any signal success.

While there were not many men at large who in cold blood could have mustered up the courage to actually bump the Saint off (for British justice is notoriously swift to strike, and English criminals have a greater fear of the rope than those of any other nationality), there were many who would have delighted to do the Saint grievous bodily harm; and Simon Templar had no great wish to wake up in his bed one night and find someone pouring vitriol over his face, or performing any similar kindly office. Therefore he had made elaborate arrangements, in the converted mews where he had taken up his new headquarters, to ensure the peace and safety of his slumbers.

He woke up, a few nights after his raid upon Jermyn Street, to the whirring of the buzzer under his pillow. He was instantly alert, for the Saint slept and woke like a cat; but he lay still in bed for a few moments before he moved, watching the flickering of tiny coloured lights in the panel on the opposite wall.

Johnny Anworth knew all that there was to know about the ordinary kind of burglar alarm, and had adroitly circumvented the dummy ones which the Saint had taken care to fix to his doors and windows. But what Johnny did not understand was the kind that worked without wires. There were wireless alarms all over the Saint's home – alarms that relied upon an invisible ray projected across a doorway, a stairway, or a corridor, upon a photoelectric cell on the opposite side. All was well so long as the ray continued to fall thus; but when anything momentarily obscured it, the buzzer sounded under the Saint's pillow, and a tiny bulb blinked a coloured eye in the indicator panel on the Saint's bedroom wall to show the exact locality of the intruder.

Johnny Anworth had made absolutely no sound, and had heard none; and, when the Saint took him suddenly by the throat from behind, he would have screamed aloud if his larynx had not been paralysed by the steely grip of the fingers that compressed it. He felt himself being lifted into the air and heaved bodily through a doorway, and then the lights went on and he saw the Saint.

'Don't make a noise,' drawled Simon. 'I don't want you to wake the house.'

He had slipped on a startling dressing-gown, and not a hair of his head was out of place. In defence of Simon, it must be mentioned that he did not sleep in a hair-net. He had actually stopped to brush his hair before he went in search of the visitor.

The capture was a miserable and unsavoury-looking specimen of humanity, his sallow face made even sallower by the shock he had received. The Saint, after a short inspection, was able to identify it.

'Your name is Anworth, isn't it, Beautiful? And I recently had the pleasure of socking you on the jaw – one night when you followed me from the Calumet.'

'I never seed yer before, guv'nor – strite, I never. I'm dahn an' aht – starvin'—'

Simon reached out a long, silk-sheathed arm for the cigarette-box – he had heaved the specimen into the sitting-room.

'Tell me the old, old story,' he sighed.

'I 'adn't 'ardly a bite to eat since Friday,' Johnny whined on mechanically. 'This is the fust time I ever went wrong. I 'ad ter do it, guv'nor—'

He stopped, as the Saint turned. Incredulous audiences Johnny Anworth had had, indignant audiences, often, and even sympathetic audiences, sometimes – but he had never met such a bleak light in any outraged householder's eyes as he met then. If he had been better informed, he would have known that there were few things to which the Saint objected more than being interrupted in his beauty sleep. This Simon explained.

'Also, you didn't come here on your own. You were sent.' The cold blue eyes never left Johnny's face. 'By a man named Lemuel,' Simon added, in a sudden snap, and read the truth before the crook had opened his mouth to deny it.

'I never 'eard of 'im, guv'nor. I was near starvin'—'

'What were you told to do?'

'I never—'

On those words, Johnny's voice trailed away. For he had heard, quite distinctly, the stealthy footfall in the passage outside.

The Saint also had heard it. He had not expected a man like Johnny Anworth to be on a job like that alone.

'You're telling naughty stories, Precious . . .'

The Saint spoke gently and dreamily, stepping back towards the door with the silence of a hunting leopard; but there was neither gentleness nor dreaminess in the eyes that held the burglar half-hypnotised, and Johnny did not need to be told what would happen to him if he attempted to utter a warning.

'Naughty, naughty stories – you've brought me out of my beautiful bed to tell me those. I think I shall have to be very cross with you, Johnny—'

And then, like an incarnate whirlwind, the Saint whipped open the door and sprang out into the passage. Baldy Mossiter had a gun, but the Saint was too quick for him, and Baldy only just relaxed his trigger finger in time to avoid shooting himself in the stomach.

'Step right in and join the merry throng, Hairy Harold,' murmured Simon; and Mossiter obeyed, the Saint speeding him on his way.

That Johnny Anworth, having started forward with the idea of taking the Saint in the rear, should have been directly in the trajectory of his chief, was unfortunate for both parties. Simon smiled beatifically upon them, and allowed them to regain their feet under their own power.

'You wait, Templar!' Mossiter snarled; and the Saint nodded encouragingly.

'Were you starving, too?' he asked.

There was some bad language – so bad that the Saint, who was perhaps unduly sensitive about these things, found it best to bind and gag both his prisoners.

'When you decide to talk, you can wag your ears,' he said.

There was a gas fire in the sitting-room, and this the Saint lighted, although the night was already torrid enough. In front of the burners, with ponderous deliberation, he set an ornamental poker to heat.

The two men watched with bulging eyes.

Simon finished his cigarette; and then he solemnly tested the temperature of the poker, holding it near his cheek as a laundryman tests an iron.

'Do you sing your song, Baldy?' he inquired – so mildly that Mossiter, who had an imagination, understood quite clearly that his own limits of bluff were likely to be reached long before the Saint's.

The story came with some profane trimmings which need not be recorded.

'It was Lemuel. We were to cosh you, and take your girl away. Lemuel said he knew for certain you'd got a lot of money hidden away, and we were going to make you pay it all over – while we held the girl to keep you quiet. We were going shares in whatever we got – What are you doing?'

'Phoning for the police,' said the Saint calmly. 'You must not commit burglary – particularly with guns.'

The law arrived in ten minutes in the shape of a couple of men from Vine Street; but before they came the Saint had made some things painfully plain.

'I'd guessed what you told me, but I always like to be sure. And let me tell you, you pair of second-hand sewer-skunks, that that sort of game doesn't appeal to me. Personally, I expect the most strenuous efforts to be made to bump me off – I'd be disappointed if they weren't – but my girl friends are in baulk. Get that. And if at any time the idea should come back to you that that would be a good way of getting at me – forget it. Because I promise you that anyone who starts that stuff on me is going for a long ride, and he'll die in a way that'll make him wish he'd never been born. Think that over while you're carving rocks on the Moor!'

Then the police came and took them away. They said nothing then, and went down for three years without speaking.

But the Saint was a thoughtful man at breakfast the next morning.

In the old days, Patricia Holm had shared his immunity. Now that his was gone, her own went also. The knowledge of her existence, and what she might be assumed to mean to the Saint, was free to anyone who took the trouble to watch him. The plan of campaign that the facts suggested was obvious; the only wonder was that it had not been tried before. For one thing, of course, the number of the Saint's enemies whose minds would take that groove was limited, and the number who would be capable of actually travelling along the groove was more limited still – but the idea must not be allowed to grow. And Lemuel had lost much – he would have a long memory.

'I don't think he's a useful citizen,' concluded the Saint, out of the blue; and Patricia Holm looked up blankly from her newspaper.

'Who's that?'

'Uncle Francis.'

Then she heard of the nocturnal visitors.

'He doesn't know that all the money I took off him has gone to Queen Charlotte's Hospital – a most suitable charity – less only our regular ten per cent fee for collection,' said the Saint. 'And if I told him, I don't think he'd believe me. As long as he's at large, he'll be thinking of his lost fortune – and you. And, as I said, I don't think he's a useful citizen.'

'What can you do?' she asked.

Simon smiled at her. He really thought that she grew more beautiful every day.

'Sweetheart,' he said, 'you're the only good thing this rolling stone's collected out of all the world. And there's only one logical thing to do.'

But he left her to guess what that was; he had not worked out the details himself at that moment. He knew that Francis Lemuel owned a large country house standing in its own spacious grounds just outside Tenterden, and the next day he learned that Lemuel had established himself there – 'to recover from a severe nervous collapse,' the newspaper informed him – but it was not for another two days, when another item of news came his way, that the Saint had his inspiration for the manner in which Francis Lemuel should die.

9

I shall call on Wednesday at 3 p.m. You will be at home.

Francis Lemuel stared at the curt note, and the little sketch that served for signature, with blurring eyes. Minutes passed before he was able to reach shakily for the decanter – his breakfast was left untasted on the table.

An hour later, reckless of consequences, he was speaking on the telephone to Scotland Yard.

At the same time Simon Templar was speaking to Patricia Holm, what time he carefully marmaladed a thin slice of brown bread and a thick slice of butter.

'There are three indoor servants at Tenterden – a butler and a cook, man and wife, and the valet. The rest of the staff have been fired, and half the house is shut up – I guess Francis is finding it necessary to pull in his horns a bit. The butler and cook have a half-day off on Wednesday. The valet has his half-day on Thursday, but he has a girl at Rye. He has asked her to marry him, and she has promised to give her answer when she sees him next – which will, of course, be on Thursday. He has had a row with Lemuel, and is thinking of giving notice.'

'How do you know all this?' asked Patricia. 'Don't tell me you deduced it from the mud on the under-gardener's boots, because I shan't believe you.'

'I won't,' said the Saint generously. 'If you want to know, I saw all that last part in writing. The valet is an energetic correspondent. Sometimes he goes to bed and leaves a letter half finished, and he's a sound sleeper.'

'You've been inside Lemuel's house?'

'These last three nights. The burglar alarms are absolutely childish.'

'So that's why you've been sleeping all day, and looking so dissipated!'

Simon shook his head.

'Not "dissipated",' he said. ' "Intellectual" is the word you want.'

She looked at him thoughtfully.

'What's the game, lad?'

'Is your memory so short, old Pat? Why, what should the game be but wilful murder?'

Patricia came round the table and put her hands on his shoulders.

'Don't do it, Saint! It's not worth it.'

'It is.' He took her hands and kissed them, smiling a little. 'Darling, I have hunches, and my hunches are always right. I know that the world won't be safe for democracy as long as Francis continues to fester in it. Now listen, and don't argue. As soon as you're dressed, you will disguise yourself as an elderly charwoman about to visit a consumptive aunt at Rye. At Rye you will proceed to the post office and send a telegram which I've written out for you – here.' He took the form from his pocket, and pressed it into her hand. 'You will then move on to Tenterden.' He gave an exact description of a certain spot, and of an instrument which she would find there. 'If you observe a crowd and a certain amount of wreckage in the offing, don't get excited. They won't be near where you've got to go. Collect the gadget and et ceteras, and push them into the bag you'll have with you . . . Then, returning to the blinkin' Bahnhof, you will leap into the first train in which you see a carriage that you can have all to yourself, and in that you will remove your flimsy disguise, disembark as your own sweet self at the next stop, catch the first train back to

Town, and meet me for dinner at the Embassy at eight. Is that clear?'

She opened the telegraph form, and read it.

'But what's the idea?'

'To clear the air, darling.'

'But—'

'Uncle Francis? . . . I've worked that out rather brilliantly. The time has gone by, sweetheart, when I could bounce in and bump off objectionable characters as and when the spirit moved. Too much is known about me – and robbery may be a matter for the robbed, but murder is a matter for the Lore. But I think this execution ought to meet the case. Besides, it will annoy Teal – Teal's been a bit uppish lately.'

There was no doubt that his mind was made up; yet it was not without misgivings that Patricia departed on her mission. But she went; for she knew the moods in which the Saint was inflexible.

It was exactly three o'clock when the Saint, a trim and superbly immaculate and rather rakish figure, climbed out of his car at the end of Lemuel's drive, and sauntered up to the house.

'Dear old Francis!' The Saint was at his most debonair as he entered the celebrated impresario's library. 'And how's trade?'

'Sit down, Templar.'

The voice was so different from Lemuel's old sonorous joviality that the Saint knew that the story of 'a severe nervous collapse' was not a great exaggeration. Lemuel's hand was unsteady as he replaced his cigar between his teeth.

'And what do you want now?'

'Just a little chat, my cherub,' said the Saint.

He lighted a cigarette, and his eyes roved casually round the room. He remarked a tiny scrap of pink paper screwed up in an ash-tray, and a tall Chinese screen in one corner, and a slow smile of satisfaction expanded within him – deep within him. Lemuel saw nothing.

'It's a long time since we last opened our hearts to each other, honeybunch,' said the Saint, sinking back lazily into the cushions, 'and you must have so much to tell me. Have you been a good boy? No more cocaine, or little girls, or anything like that?'

'I don't know what you mean. If you've come here to try to blackmail me—'

'Dear, dear! Blackmail? What's that, Francis? – or shall I call you Frank?'

'You can call me what you like.'

Simon shook his head.

'I don't want to be actually rude,' he said. 'Let it go at Frank. I once knew another man, a very successful scavenger, named Frank, who slipped in a sewer, and sank. This was after a spree; ever afterwards he was teetotal – but, oh, how unpleasant he smelt. Any relation of yours?'

Lemuel came closer. His face looked pale and bloated; there was a beastly fury in his eyes.

'Now listen to me, Templar. You've already robbed me once—'

'When?'

'D'you have to bluff when there isn't an audience? D'you deny that you're the Saint?'

'On the contrary,' murmured Simon calmly. 'I'm proud of it. But when have I robbed you?'

For a moment Lemuel looked as if he would choke.

Then:

'What have you come for now?' he demanded.

Simon seemed to sink even deeper into his chair, and he watched the smoke curling up from his cigarette with abstracted eyes.

'Suppose,' he said lazily – 'just suppose we had all the congregation out in the limelight. Wouldn't that make it seem more matey?'

'What d'you mean?'

Lemuel's voice cracked on the question.

'Well,' said Simon, closing his eyes, with a truly sancti-monious smile hovering on his lips, 'I really do hate talking to people I can't see. And it must be frightfully uncomfort-able for Claud Eustace, hiding behind that screen over there.'

'I don't understand—'

'Do you understand, Claud?' drawled the Saint; and Chief Inspector Claud Eustace Teal answered wearily that he understood.

He emerged mountainously, and stood looking down at the Saint with a certain admiration in his bovine countenance.

'And how did you know I was there?'

Simon waved a languid hand towards the table. Teal, following the gesture, saw the ash-tray, and the discarded pink overcoat of the gum which he was even then chewing, and groaned.

'Wrigley,' sighed the Saint, succinctly.

Then Lemuel turned on the detective, snarling.

'What the hell did you want to come out for?'

'Chiefly because there wasn't much point in staying where I was, Mr Lemuel,' replied Teal tiredly.

Simon chuckled.

'It's as much your fault as his, Francis, old coyote,' he said. 'If you must try to pull that old gag on me, you want to go into strict training. A man in your condition can't hope to put it over . . . Oh, Francis! To think you thought I'd bite that bit of cheese – and land myself in good and proper, with Teal taking frantic notes behind the whatnot! You must take care not to go sitting in any damp grass, Francis – you might get brain fever.'

'Anyway,' said Teal, 'it was a good idea.'

'It was a rotten idea,' said the Saint disparagingly. 'And always has been. But I knew it was ten to one it would be tried – I knew it when I sent that note to Francis. I'm glad you came, Claud – I really did want you here.'

'Why?'

Lemuel cut in. His face was tense and drawn.

'Inspector, you know this man's character—'

'I do,' said Teal somnolently, 'That's the trouble.'

'He came here to try to blackmail me, and he'd have done it if he hadn't discovered you. Now he's going to try to get out of it on one of his bluffs—'

'No,' said the Saint; and he said it in such a way that there was a sudden silence.

And, in the stillness, with his eyes still closed, the Saint listened. His powers of hearing were abnormally acute: he heard the sound he was waiting for when neither of the other two could hear anything – and even to him it was like nothing more than the humming of a distant bee.

And then he opened his eyes. It was like the unmasking of two clear blue lights in the keen brown face; and the eyes were not jesting at all. He stood up.

'As you said – you know me, Teal,' he remarked. 'Now I'll tell you what you don't know about Francis Lemuel. The first thing is that he's at the head of the dope ring you've been trying to get at for years. I don't know how he used to bring the stuff into the country; but I do know that when I was his private pilot, a little while ago, he came back from Berlin one time with enough snow in his grip to build a ski-slope round the Equator—'

'It's a lie! By God, you'll answer for that, Templar—'

'Now I come to think of it,' murmured Teal, 'how do you know his real name?'

Simon laughed softly. The humming of the bee was not so distant now – the other two could have heard it easily, if they had listened.

'Don't haze the accused,' he said gently. 'He'll get all hot and bothered if you start to cross-examine him. Besides, the charge isn't finished. There's another matter, concerning a girl named Stella Dornford – and several others whose names I couldn't give you, for all I know—'

'Another lie!'

Teal turned heavy eyes on the man. 'You're a great clairvoyant,' he said, judicially.

'At this man's request,' said the Saint quietly, 'I flew Stella Dornford over to Berlin. She was supposed to be going to a cabaret engagement with a man called Jacob Einsmann. The place I took her to was not a cabaret – I needn't mention what it was. The Berlin police will corroborate that—'

Lemuel grated: 'They want you for the murder of Einsmann—'

'I doubt it,' said the Saint. 'I certainly shot him, but it shouldn't be hard to prove self-defence.' The bee was very much closer. And the Saint turned to Teal. 'I have one other thing to say,' he added, 'for your ears alone.'

'I have a right to hear it,' barked Lemuel shakily.

'Inspector—'

'Naturally you'll hear it, Mr Lemuel,' said Teal soothingly. 'But if Mr Templar insists on telling me alone, that's his affair. If you'll excuse us a moment . . .'

Lemuel watched them go, gripping the table for support. Presently, through the french windows, he saw them strolling across the lawn, side by side. The air was now full of the drone of the bee, but he did not notice it.

He stumbled mechanically towards the side-table where bottle and glasses were set out, but the bottle was nearly empty. Savagely he jabbed at the bell, and waited an impatient half-minute; but no one answered. Cursing, he staggered to the door and opened it. 'Fitch!' he bawled.

Still there was no answer. The house was as silent as a

tomb. Trembling with terror of he knew not what, Lemuel reeled down the hall and flung open the door of the servants' quarters. There was no one in sight.

On the table, he saw an orange envelope with a buff slip beside it. Impelled by an unaccountable premonition, he picked up the form and read.

Come at once. I want you.
Eileen.

Fitch was already on his way to Rye. The Saint was thorough.

As Lemuel crumpled the telegram with furious hands, the bee seemed to be roaring directly over his head.

10

Simon Templar gazed thoughtfully at the sky.

'Cloudy,' he remarked thoughtfully. 'The weather forecasts said it would be cloudy to-day, and for once they're right.'

Teal looked back over his shoulder.

'That aeroplane's flying pretty low,' he said.

'Owing to cloud,' said the Saint; and the detective glanced at him quickly.

'What's the big idea, Saint?' he demanded.

Simon smiled.

'I've been getting rather tired of answering that question lately,' he said.

They had reached a clump of trees at the edge of the wide lawn, a couple of hundred yards away from the house; and here the Saint stopped. Both the men turned.

The aeroplane was certainly low – it was flying under five hundred feet, and the racket of its engine was deafening.

'I know your habits,' said Teal sourly. 'If you weren't here with me, Saint, I'd be inclined to think you were up there – getting ready to do some illegal bombing practice.' He was watching the aeroplane with screwed-up eyes, while he took a fresh purchase on his gum; and then he added suddenly: 'Do any of the other guys in your gang fly?'

'There ain't no gang,' said the Saint, 'and you ought to know it. They broke up long ago.'

'I wouldn't put it above you to have recruited another,' said Teal.

Simon leaned against a tree. His hand, groping in a hollow in the trunk, found a tiny switch. He took the lever lightly between his finger and thumb. He laughed, softly and lazily, and Teal faced round.

'What's the big idea?' he demanded again. 'I don't know what it is, but you're playing some funny game. What did you fetch me out here to tell me?'

'Nothing much,' answered the Saint slowly, 'I just thought—'

But what he thought was not destined to be known. For all at once there came a titanic roar of sound, that was nothing like the roar of the aeroplane's engine – a shattering detonation that rocked the ground under their feet and hurled them bodily backwards with the hurricane force of its breath.

'Good God!'

Teal's voice came faintly through the buzzing in the Saint's ears.

Simon was scrambling rockily to his feet.

'Something seems to have bust, old water-melon—'

'F-ZXKA,' Teal was muttering. 'F-ZXKA; F-ZXKA—'

'Ease up, old dear!' Simon took the detective by the shoulder. 'It's all over. Nothing to rave about.'

'I'm not raving,' snarled Teal. 'But I've got the number of that machine—'

He was starting off across the lawn, and the Saint followed. But there was nothing that they or anyone else could do, for Francis Lemuel's house was nothing but a great mound of rubble under a mushroom canopy of smoke and settling dust, through which the first tongues of flame were starting to lick up towards the dark clouds. And the aeroplane was dwindling into the mists towards the north.

Teal surveyed the ruin; and then he looked round at the crowd that was pattering up the road.

'You're arrested, Saint,' he said curtly; and Simon shrugged.

They drove to Tenterden in the Saint's car, and from there Teal put a call through to headquarters.

'F-ZXKA,' he said. 'Warn all stations and aerodromes. Take the crew, whatever excuse they try to put up, and hold them till I come.'

'That's the stuff,' said the Saint approvingly; and Teal was so far moved as to bare his teeth.

'This is where you get what's coming to you,' he said.

It was not Teal's fault that the prophecy was not fulfilled.

Simon drove him back to London with a police guard in the back of the car; and Teal was met almost on the doorstep of Scotland Yard with the news that the aeroplane had landed at Croydon. The prisoners, said the message, had put up a most audacious bluff; they were being sent to headquarters in a police car.

'Good!' said Teal grimly; and went through to Cannon Row Police Station to charge the Saint with wilful murder.

'That's what you've got to prove,' said the Saint, when the charge was read over to him. 'No – I won't trouble my solicitor. I shall be out in an hour.'

'In eight weeks you'll be dead,' said the detective.

He had recovered some of his old pose of agonised boredom; and half an hour later he needed it all, for the police car arrived from Croydon as the newspaper vans started to pour out of E.C.4 with the printers' ink still damp on the first news of the outrage at Tenterden.

Two prisoners were hustled into Teal's office – a philosophical gentleman in flying overalls, and a very agitated gentleman with striped cashmere trousers and white spats showing under his leather coat.

'It is an atrrrrocity!' exploded the agitated gentleman. 'I vill complain myself to ze Prime Ministair! Imbecile! Your poliss, zey say I am arrrrest – zey insult me – zey mock zemselves of vat I say – zey trreat me like I vas a criminal – me! But you shall pay—'

'And who are you pretending to be?' asked Teal, lethargically unwrapping a fresh wafer of his favourite sweetmeat.

'Me? You do not know me ? You do not know Boileau—'

Teal did not.

'Take that fungus off his face,' he ordered, 'and let's see what he really looks like.'

Two constables had to pinion the arms of a raving maniac while a third gave the agitated gentleman's beard a sharp tug.

But the beard failed to part company with its foundations; and, on closer examination, it proved to be the genuine home-grown article.

Teal blinked as the agitated gentleman, released, danced in front of his desk, semaphoring with frantic arms.

'Nom d'un nom! You are not content viz insult me, you must attack me, you must pull me ze beard! Aaaaah!'

Words failed the man. He reeled against the desk, clawing at his temples.

Teal ran a finger round the inside of his collar, which seemed to have suddenly become tight.

Then the philosophical gentleman in overalls spoke.

''E 'as say true, m'sieu. 'E is M. Boileau, ze French Finance Minister, 'oo come ovair for confer—'

Teal signed to one of the constables.

'Better ring up the Embassy and see if someone can come over and identify him,' he said.

'Merde alors!' screamed the agitated gentleman. 'I vill not vait! I demand to be release!'

'I'm afraid you'll have to be identified, sir,' said Teal unhappily.

And identified M. Boileau was, in due course, by a semi-hysterical official from the Embassy; and Teal spent the most uncomfortable half-hour of his life trying to explain the mistake.

He was a limp wreck when the indignation meeting finally broke up; and the telephoned report of the explosives expert who had been sent down to Tenterden did not improve Teal's temper.

'It was a big aerial bomb – we've found some bits of the casing. We didn't find much of Lemuel . . .'

'Could it have been fired by a timing device?'

'There's no trace of anything like that, sir. Of course, if there had been, it might have been blown to bits.'

'Could it have been fired electrically?'

'I haven't found any wires yet, sir. My men are still digging round the wreckage. On the other hand, sir, if it comes to that, it might have been fired by radio, and if it was radio we shan't find anything at all.'

Teal had his inspiration some hours too late.

'You'd better search the grounds,' he said, and gave exact instructions.

'Certainly, sir. But what about the aeroplane that went over?'

'That,' said Teal heavily, 'contained the French Minister of Finance, on his way to a reparations conference.'

'Well, it couldn't have been him,' said the expert sagely, and Teal felt like murder.

A few days later the Saint called on Stella Dornford. He had not seen her since the morning when he dropped her on his way to Jermyn Street, and she had not communicated with him in any way.

'You must think me a little rotter,' she said. 'It seems such a feeble excuse to say I've been too busy to think of any thing—'

'I think it's the best excuse in the world,' said the Saint.

He pointed to the ring on her finger.

'When?'

'Ten days ago. I – I took your advice, you see . . .'

Simon laughed.

' "To those about to marry",' he quoted softly. 'Well, you must come round to a celebratory supper, and bring the Beloved. And Uncle Simon will tell you all about married life.'

'Why, are you married?'

He shook his head. For a moment the dancing blue eyes were quiet and wistful. And then the old mocking mirth came back to them.

'That's why I'll be able to tell you so much about it,' he said.

Presently the girl said: 'I've told Dick how much we owe you. I'll never forget it. I don't know how to thank you—'

The Saint smiled, and put his hands on her shoulders.

'Don't you?' he said.

The Wonderful War

INTRODUCTION BY LESLIE CHARTERIS*

At various points in the chronicle of the Saint's exploits there are vague references to his adventures in the far corners of the earth. This particular story, however, is the only one of its kind which is completely on record; and his followers have mentioned it often enough to convince me that it is one of their favourite recollections of his early days. The Saint himself derives so much obvious fun from it that I am bound to believe that it must still be one of his most enjoyable memories. I suppose that one of the so-called 'comic opera' South American republics has at one time or another been almost every man's imaginative playground; and it is only to be expected that Simon Templar would have used such a setting for one of his most riotous escapades.

Note from the March 1965 issue of The Saint Mystery Magazine:

Without even glancing at the copyright date, even Claud Eustace Teal would not have to read far to deduce that this story was written in the happy days before Castro, when Latin-American 'banana republics' were still rather comical and revolutions were uncomplicated by cosmic ideologies. And when, as a matter of history, one or two daredevil soldiers of fortune actually could (and did) topple governments and change the histories of foreign lands.

*From *The First Saint Omnibus* and *The Saint Mystery Magazine* (March 1965)

I

The Republic of Pasala lies near the northward base of the Yucatan peninsula in Central America. It has an area of about 10,000 square miles, or roughly the size of England from the Tweed to a line drawn from Liverpool to Hull. Population, about 18,000. Imports, erratic. Exports, equally erratic, and consisting (when the population can be stirred to the necessary labour) of maize, rice, sugar-cane, mahogany, and – oil.

'You can hurry up and warble all you know about this oil, Archie,' said Simon Templar briskly, half an hour after he landed at Santa Miranda. 'And you can leave out your adventures among the Señoritas. I want to get this settled – I've got a date back in England for the end of May, and that doesn't give me a lot of time here.'

Mr Archibald Sheridan stirred slothfully in his long chair and took a pull at a whisky-and-soda in which ice clinked seductively.

'You've had it all in my letters and cables,' he said. 'But I'll just run through it again to connect it up. It goes like this. Three years ago almost to the day, a Scots mining engineer named McAndrew went prospecting round the hills about fifty miles inland. Everyone said he was crazy – till he came back six months later with samples from his feeler borings. He said he'd struck one of the richest deposits that ever gushed – and it was only a hundred feet below the surface. He got a concession – chiefly because the authorities still couldn't believe his story – staked his claim, cabled for his daughter to come over and join him, and settled down to feel rich and wait for the plant he'd ordered to be shipped over from New Orleans.'

'Did the girl come?' asked Templar.

'She's right here,' answered Sheridan. 'But you told me to leave the women out of it. She doesn't really come into the story anyway. The man who does come in is a half-caste bum from God knows where, name of Shannet. Apparently Shannet had been sponging and beachcombing here for months before McAndrew arrived. Everyone was down on him, and so McAndrew, being one of these quixotic idiots, joined up with him. He even took him into partnership, just to defy public opinion; and, anyhow, he was wanting help, and Shannet had some sort of qualifications. The two of them went up into the interior to take a look at the claim. Shannet came back, but McAndrew didn't. Shannet said a snake got him.'

Simon Templar reached for another cigarette.

'Personally, I say that snake's name was Shannet,' remarked Archie Sheridan quietly. 'Lilla – McAndrew's daughter – said the same thing. Particularly when Shannet produced a written agreement signed by McAndrew and himself, in which it was arranged that if either partner should die, all rights in the claim should pass to the other partner. Lilla swore that McAndrew, who'd always thought first of her, would never have signed such a document, and she got a look at it and said the signature was forged. Shannet replied that McAndrew was getting over a bout of malaria when he signed it, and his hand was rather shaky. The girl carried it right to the court of what passes for justice here, fighting like a hero, but Shannet had too big a pull with the judge, and she lost her case. I arrived just after her appeal was turned down.'

'What about McAndrew's body?'

'Shannet said he buried it by the trail; but the jungle trails here are worse than any maze that was ever invented, and you can almost see the stuff grow. The grave could quite reasonably be lost in a week. Shannet said he couldn't find it again. I took a trip that way myself, but it wasn't any use. All I got out of it was a bullet through a perfectly good hat from some sniper in the background – Shannet for a fiver.'

'After which,' suggested Simon Templar thoughtfully, 'Shannet found he couldn't run the show alone, and sold out to our dear friend in London, Master Hugo Campard, shark, swindler, general blackguard, and promoter of unlimited dud companies—'

'Who perpetrated the first sound company of his career, Pasala Oil Products, on the strength of it,' Sheridan completed. 'Shares not for public issue, and sixty per cent of them held by himself.'

Simon Templar took his cigarette from his mouth and blew a long, thin streamer of smoke into the sunlight.

'So that's what I've come over to deal with, Archibald?' he murmured. 'Well, well, well! . . . Taken by and large, it looks like a diverting holiday. Carol a brief psalm about things political, son.'

'Just about twice as crooked as anything south of the United States border,' said Sheridan. 'The man who matters isn't the President. He's under the thumb of what they call the Minister for the Interior, who finds it much more convenient and much safer to stay in the background – they never assassinate Ministers for the Interior, apparently, but Presidents are fair game. And this man – Manuel Concepcion de Villega is his poetic label – is right under the wing of Shannet, and is likely to stay there as long as Shannet's money lasts.'

The Saint rose and lounged over to the verandah rail. At that hour (which was just after midday) the thermometer stood at a hundred and two in the shade, and the Saint had provided himself suitably with white ducks. The dazzling whiteness of them would have put snow to shame; and he wore them, as might have been expected of him, with the most cool and careless elegance in the world. He looked as if he would have found an inferno chilly. His dark hair was brushed smoothly back; his lean face was tanned to a healthy brown; altogether he must have been the most dashing and immaculate sight that Santa Miranda had set eyes on for many years.

Sheridan was in despair before that vision of unruffled perfection. His hair was tousled, his white ducks looked somewhat limp with the heat, and his pleasantly ugly face was moist.

'What about the rest of the white, or near-white, inhabitants?' inquired the Saint.

'A two-fisted, rip-roaring giant of a red-headed Irishman named Kelly,' was the reply. 'His wife – that's two. Lilla McAndrew, who's staying with them – I wouldn't let her put up at the filthy hotel in the town any longer – three. Four and five, a couple of traders, more or less permanently drunk and not worth considering. Six – Shannet. That's the lot.'

The Saint turned away and gazed down the hillside. From where he stood, on the verandah of Sheridan's bungalow, he could look down on to the roofs of Santa Miranda – the cluster of white buildings in the Moorish style which formed the centre, and the fringe of adobe huts on the outskirts. Left and right of him, on the hill above the town, were other bungalows. Beyond the town was the sea.

The Saint studied the view for a time in silence; then he turned round again.

'We seem to be on to the goods,' he remarked. 'Shannet, the small fish, but an undoubted murderer – and, through him, our real man, Campard. I had a hunch I shouldn't be wasting your time when I sent you out here as soon as I heard Campard was backing Pasala Oil Products. But I never guessed P.O.P. would be real till I got your first cable. Now we're on a truly classy piece of velvet. It all looks too easy.'

'Easy?' queried Sheridan sceptically. 'I'm glad you think it's easy. With Shannet's claim established, and the concession in writing at Campard's London office, and Lilla McAndrew's petition dismissed, and Shannet twiddling the Government, the Army, the police, and the rest of the bunch, down to the last office-boy, round and round his little finger with the money he gets from Campard – and the man calls it easy. Oh, take him away!'

The Saint's hands drove even deeper into his pockets. Tall and trim and athletic, he stood with his feet astride, swaying gently from his toes, with the Saintly smile flickering faintly round his mouth and a little dancing devil of mischief rousing in his blue eyes.

'I said easy,' he drawled.

Sheridan buried his face in his hands.

'Go and put your head in the ice-bucket,' he pleaded. 'Of course, it's the sun. You're not used to it – I forgot that.'

'How big is the Army?'

'There's a standing army of about five hundred, commanded by seventeen generals, twenty-five colonels, and about fifty minor officers. And if your head hurts, just lie down, close the eyes, and relax. It'll be quite all right in an hour or two.'

'Artillery?'

'Three pieces, carried by mules. If you'd like some aspirin—'

'Navy?'

'One converted tug, with 5-9 quick-firer and crew of seven, commanded by two admirals. I don't think you ought to talk now. I'll put up the hammock for you, if you like, and you can sleep for an hour before lunch.'

'Police force?'

'There are eleven constables in Santa Miranda, under three superintendents. And in future I shouldn't have any whisky before sundown.'

The Saint smiled.

'I'm probably more used to the sun than you are,' he said. 'This is merely common sense. What's the key to the situation? The Government. Right. We don't propose to waste any of our good money bribing them – and if we did, they'd double-cross us. Therefore they must be removed by force. And at once, because I can't stay long. Long live the Revolution!'

'Quite,' agreed Sheridan helplessly. 'And the Revolutionary Army? This State is the only one in South America that's never had a revolution – because nobody's ever had enough energy to start one.'

The Saint fished for his cigarette-case.

'We are the Revolutionary Army,' he said. 'I ask you to remember that we march on our stomachs. So we'll just have another drink, and then some lunch, and then we'll wander along and try to enlist the mad Irishman. If we three can't make rings round six hundred and fifteen comic-opera dagoes, I'm going to retire from the fighting game and take up knitting and fancy needlework!'

2

'My dear soul,' the Saint was still arguing persuasively at the close of the meal, 'it's so simple. The man who manages the Government of this two-by-four backyard is the man who holds the fate of Pasala Oil Products in his hands. At present Shannet is the bright boy who manages the Government, and the master of P.O.P. is accordingly walking around under the Shannet hat. We'll go one better. We won't merely manage the Government. We'll be the Government. And Pop is ours to play hell with as we like. Could anything be more straightforward? as the actress said when the bishop showed her his pass-book.'

'Go on,' encouraged Sheridan weakly. 'Don't bother about my feelings.'

'As the actress said to the bishop shortly afterwards,' murmured the Saint. 'Blessed old Archie, it's obvious that three months in this enervating climate and the society of Lilla McAndrew have brought your energy down to the level of that of the natives you spoke of so contemptuously just now. I grant you it's sudden, but it's the only way. Before I knew the whole story I thought it would be good enough if we held up the post office and sent Campard a spoof cable purporting to come from Shannet, telling him the Government had been kicked out, the concession revoked, and the only thing to do was to sell out his Pop holdings as quickly as possible. What time our old friend Roger, back in London, snaps up the shares, discreetly, as fast as they come on the market.'

'Why won't that work now?'

'You're forgetting the girl,' said Templar, 'This oil is really her property, so it isn't good enough just to make Campard unload at a loss and sell back to him at a premium when the rumour of revolution is exploded. The concession has really got to be revoked. Therefore I propose to eliminate the present Government, and make Kelly, your mad Irishman, the new Minister of the Interior. That is, unless you'd take the job.'

'No, thanks,' said Sheridan generously. 'It's not quite in my line. Pass me up.'

The Saint lighted a cigarette.

'In that case Kelly is elected unanimously,' he remarked with charming simplicity. 'So the only thing left to decide is how we start the trouble. I've been in South American revolutions before, but they've always been well under way by the time I arrived. The technique of starting the blamed things was rather missed out of my education. What does one do? Does one simply wade into the Presidential Palace, chant "Time, gentlemen, please!" in the ear of his Illustrious Excellency, and invite him to close the door as he goes out? Or what?'

'What, probably,' said Sheridan. 'That would be as safe as anything. I might get you reprieved on the grounds of insanity.'

The Saint sighed.

'You aren't helpful, Beautiful Archibald.'

'If you'd settle down to talk seriously—'

'I am serious.'

Sheridan stared. Then:

'Is that straight, Saint?' he demanded.

'From the horse's mouth,' the Saint assured him solemnly. 'Even as the crowd flieth before the pubs open. Sweet cherub, did you really think I was wasting precious time with pure pickled onions?'

Sheridan looked at him. There was another flippant rejoinder on the tip of Archie Sheridan's tongue, but somehow it was never uttered.

The Saint was smiling. It was a mocking smile, but that was for Sheridan's incredulity. It was not the sort of smile that accompanies a test of the elasticity of a leg. And in the Saint's eyes was a light that wasn't entirely humorous.

Archie Sheridan, with a cigarette in his mouth, fumbling for matches, realised that he had mistaken the shadow for the substance. The Saint wasn't making fun of revolutions. It was just that his sense of humour was too big to let him plan even a revolution without seeing the funny side of the show.

Sheridan got a match to his cigarette.

'Well?' prompted the Saint.

'I think you're pots, bats, and bees,' he said. 'But if you're set on that kind of suicide – lead on. Archibald will be at your elbow with the bombs. You didn't forget the bombs?'

The Saint grinned.

'I had to leave them behind,' he replied lightly. 'They wouldn't fit into my sponge-bag. Seriously, now, where and how do you think we should start the trouble?'

They were sitting opposite one another at Sheridan's bare mahogany dining-table, and at the Saint's back was the open door leading out on to the verandah and commanding an uninterrupted view of the approach to the bungalow.

'Start the thing here and now and anyhow you like,' said Sheridan, and he was looking past the Saint's shoulder towards the verandah steps.

Simon Templar settled back a little more lazily into his chair, and a very Saintly meekness was spreading over his face.

'Name?' he inquired laconically.

'Shannet himself.'

The Saint's eyes were half-closed.

'I will compose a little song about him immediately,' he said.

Then a shadow fell across the table, but the Saint did not move at once. He appeared to be lost in a day-dream.

'*Buenos dias*, Shannet,' said Archie Sheridan. 'Also, as soon as possible, *adios*. Hurry up and say what you've got to say before I kick you out.'

'I'll do any kicking out that's necessary, thanks,' said Shannet harshly. 'Sheridan, I've come to warn you off for the last time. The *Andalusia* berthed this morning, and she sails again on the evening tide. You've been nosing around here too long as it is. Is that plain enough?'

'Plainer than your ugly face,' drawled Sheridan. 'And by what right do you kick me out? Been elected President, have you?'

'You know me,' said Shannet. 'You know that what I say here goes. You'll sail on the *Andalusia* – either voluntary or because you're put on board in irons. That's all ... What's this?'

The Saint, perceiving himself to be the person thus referred to, awoke sufficiently to open his eyes and screw his head round so that he could view the visitor.

He saw a tall, broad-shouldered man of indeterminate age, clad in a soiled white suit of which the coat was unbuttoned to expose a grubby singlet. Shannet had certainly not shaved for two days; and he did not appear to have brushed his hair for a like period, for a damp, sandy lock drooped in a tangle over his right eye. In one corner of his mouth a limp and dilapidated cigarette dangled tiredly from his lower lip.

The Saint blinked.

'Gawd!' he said offensively. 'Can it be human?'

Shannet's fists swept back his coat and rested on his hips.

'What's your name, Cissy?' he demanded.

The Saint flicked some ash from his cigarette, and rose to his feet delicately.

'Benito Mussolini,' he answered mildly. 'And you must be one of the corporation scavengers. How's the trade in garbage?' His gentle eyes swept Shannet from crown to toe. 'Archie, there must have been some mistake. The real scavenger has gone sick, and one of his riper pieces of refuse is deputising for him. I'm sorry.'

'If you—'

'I said I was sorry,' the Saint continued, in the same smooth voice, 'because I'm usually very particular about the people I fight, and I hate soiling my hands on things like you.'

Shannet glowered.

'I don't know who you are,' he said, 'and I don't care. But if you're looking for a fight you can have it.'

'I am looking for a fight, dear one,' drawled the Saint. 'In fact, I'm looking for a lot of fights, and you're the first one that's offered. "Cissy" is a name I particularly object to being called, O misbegotten of a pig!'

The last words were spoken in colloquial Spanish, and the Saint made more of them than it is possible to report in printable English. Shannet went white, then red.

'You—'

His answering stream of profanity merged into a left swing to the Saint's jaw, which, if it had landed, would have ended the fight there and then. But it did not land.

Simon Templar swayed back, and the swing missed by a couple of inches. As Shannet stumbled, momentarily off his balance, the Saint reached round and took the jug of ice water off the table behind him. Without any appearance of effort or haste, he side-stepped and poured most of the contents of the jug down the back of Shannet's neck.

Shannet swung again. The Saint ducked, and sent the man flying with a smashing jab to the nose.

'Look out, Saint!' Sheridan warned suddenly.

'Naughty!' murmured the Saint, without heat.

Shannet was getting to his feet, and his right hand was drawing something from his hip pocket.

The Saint took two steps and a flying leap over Shannet's head, turning in the air as he did so. Shannet had only got to his knees when the Saint landed behind him and caught his opponent's throat and right wrist in hands that had the strength of steel cables in their fingers. Shannet's wrist was twisted behind his back with an irresistible wrench . . .

The gun clattered to the floor simultaneously with Shannet's yelp of agony, and the Saint picked up the gun and stepped away.

'A trophy! Archie!' he cried, and tossed the weapon over to Sheridan. 'Guns I have not quite been shot with – there must be a drawer full of them at home . . . Let's start, sweet Shannet!'

Shannet replied with a chair, but the Saint was ten feet away by the time it crashed into the opposite wall.

Then Shannet came in again with his fists. Any one of those whirling blows carried a kick that would have put a mule to sleep, but the Saint had forgotten more about ringcraft than many professionals ever learn. Shannet never came near touching him. Every rush Shannet made, somehow, expended itself on thin air, while he always seemed to be running his face slap into the Saint's stabbing left.

And at last the Saint, scorning even counter-attack, dropped his hands into his pockets, and simply eluded Shannet's homicidal onslaught by sheer brilliant footwork – ducking, swaying, swooping, as calm and unruffled as if he were merely demonstrating a few ballroom steps, and as light and graceful on his toes as a ballet dancer – until Shannet reeled limply back against the wall with the sweat streaming into his eyes, utterly done in.

The Saint's mocking smile had never left his lips, and not one hair of his head had shifted.

'Want a rest?' he asked kindly.

'If you'd come in and fight like a man,' gasped Shannet, his tortured chest heaving, 'I'd kill you!'

'Oh, don't be silly!' said the Saint in a bored voice, as though he had no further interest in the affair. 'Hurry up and get out – I'm going to be busy.'

He turned away, but Shannet lurched after him.

'Get out yourself!' snarled the man thickly. 'D'you hear? I'm going right down to fetch the police——'

The Saint sat down.

'Listen to me, Shannet,' he said quietly. 'The less you talk about police when I'm around, the better for you. I'm telling you now that I believe you murdered a man named McAndrew not so long ago, and jumped his claim on a forged partnership agreement. I'm only waiting till I've got the proof. And then – well, it's too much to hope that the authorities of this benighted republic will execute the man who pays half their salaries, and so in the name of Justice I shall take you myself and hang you from a high tree.'

For a moment of silence the air seemed to tingle with the same electric tension as heralds the breaking of a thunderstorm, while the Saint's ice-blue eyes quelled Shannet's re-awakening fury; and then, with a short laugh, the Saint relaxed.

'You're a pawn in the game,' he said, with a contrasting carelessness which only emphasised the bleak implacability of his last speech. 'We won't waste good melodrama on you. We reserve that for clients with really important discredit accounts. Instead, you shall hear the epitaph I've just composed for you. It commemorates a pestilent tumour named Shannet, who disfigured the face of this planet. He started some fun, but before it was done he was wishing he'd never began it. That otherwise immortal verse is greatly marred by a grammatical error, but I'm not expecting you to know any better . . . Archibald – the door!'

Archie Sheridan had no reason to love Shannet, and the kick with which he launched the man into the garden was not gentle, but he seemed to derive no pleasure from it.

He came back with a grave face, and resumed his chair facing the Saint.

'Well,' he said, 'you've done what you wanted. Now shall we sit down and make our wills, or shall we spend our last hours of life in drinking and song?'

'Of course, we may be shot,' admitted the Saint calmly. 'That's up to us. How soon can we expect the Army?'

'Not before five. They'll all be asleep now, and an earthquake wouldn't make the Pasala policeman break off his siesta. Much less the Army, who are inclined to give themselves airs. We might catch the *Andalusia*,' he added hopefully.

The Saint surveyed him seraphically.

'Sweetheart,' he said, 'that joke may now be considered over. We've started, and we've got to keep moving. As I don't see the fun of sitting here waiting for the other side to surround us, I guess we'll bounce right along and interview Kelly. And when you two have coached me thoroughly in the habits and topography of Santa Miranda, we'll just toddle along and capture the town.'

'Just toddle along and which?' repeated Sheridan dazedly.

The Saint spun a cigarette high into the air, and trapped it neatly between his lips as it fell.

'That is to say, I will capture the town,' he corrected himself, 'while you and Kelly create a disturbance somewhere to distract their attention. Wake up, sonny! Get your hat, and let's go!'

3

The Saint's breezy way of saying that he would 'just toddle along and capture the town' was a slight exaggeration. As a matter of fact, he spent nearly four days on the job.

There was some spade-work to be done, and certain preparations to be made, and the Saint devoted a considerable amount of care and sober thought to these details. Though his methods, to the uninformed observer, might always have seemed to savour of the reckless, tip-and-run, hit-first-and-ask-questions-afterwards school, the truth was that he rarely stepped out of any frying-pan without first taking the temperature of the fire beyond.

Even in such a foolhardy adventure as that in which he was then engaged, he knew exactly what he was doing, and legislated against failure as well as he might; for, even in the most outlandish parts of the world, the penalty of unsuccessful revolution is death, and the Saint had no overwhelming desire to turn his interesting biography into an obituary notice.

He explained his plan to Kelly, and found the Irishman an immediate convert to the cause.

'Shure, I've been thinkin' for years that it was time somebody threw out their crooked Government,' said that worthy, ruffling a hand like a ham through his tousled mop of flaming hair. 'I'm just wonderin' now why I niver did ut meself.'

'It's a desperate chance,' Simon Templar admitted. 'But I don't mind taking it if you're game.'

'Six years I've been here,' mused Kelly ecstatically, screwing up a huge fist, 'and I haven't seen a real fight. Exceptin' one or two disagreements with the natives, who run away afther the first round.'

The Saint smiled. He could not have hoped to find a more suitable ally.

'We might easily win out,' he said. 'It wouldn't work in England, but in a place like this—'

'The geography was made for us,' said Kelly.

On a scrap of paper he sketched a rough map to illustrate his point.

Pasala is more or less in the shape of a wedge, with the base facing north-east on the sea-coast. Near the centre of the base of the wedge is Santa Miranda. In the body of the wedge are the only other three towns worth mentioning – Las Flores, Rugio, and, near the apex, Esperanza. They are connected up by a cart-track of a road which includes them in a kind of circular route which starts and finishes at Santa Miranda, for the State of Pasala does not yet boast a railway. This is hardly necessary, for the distance between Santa Miranda and Esperanza, the two towns farthest apart, is only one hundred and forty miles.

It should also be mentioned that the wedge-shaped territory of Pasala cuts roughly into the Republic of Maduro, a much larger and more civilised country.

'Of course, we're simply banking on the psychology of revolutions and the apathy of the natives,' said the Saint, when they had finished discussing their plan of campaign, 'The population aren't interested – if they're shown a man in a nice new uniform, and told that he's the man in power, they believe it, and go home and pray that they won't be any worse off than they were before. If we take off a couple of taxes or something like that, as soon as we get in, the mob will be with us to a man. I'm sure the Exchequer can stand it – I don't imagine Manuel Concepcion de Villega has been running this show without making a substantial profit on turnover.'

'That'll fetch 'em,' Kelly averred. 'They're bled dhry with taxes at present.'

'Secondly, there's the Army. They're like any other army. They obey their officers because it's never occurred to them to do anything else. If they were faced with a revolution they'd fight it. So instead of that we'll present the revolution as an accomplished fact. If they're like any other South American army, they'll simply carry on under the new Government – with a bonus of a few pesos per man to clinch the bargain.'

They talked for a while longer; and then they went out and joined Archie Sheridan, who had not been present at the council, being otherwise occupied with Lilla McAndrew on the verandah.

The Saint had a little leisure to admire the girl. She was rather tall, fair-haired and blue-eyed, superbly graceful. Her sojourn in that sunny climate had coloured her skin a pale golden-brown that was infinitely more becoming than mere pink-and-white; but the peach-like bloom of her complexion had not had time to suffer.

It was plain that Archie Sheridan was fatally smitten with the inevitable affliction, and the Saint was mischievously delighted.

'You want to be careful of him, Miss McAndrew,' he advised gravely. 'I've known him since he was so high, and you wouldn't believe what a past he's collected in his brief career of sin. Let's see ... There was Gladys, the golden-haired beauty from the front row of the Gaiety chorus, Susan, Beryl – no, two Beryls – Ethel, the artist's model, Angela, Sadie from California, Joan – two Joans – no, three Joans—'

'Don't believe him, Lilla,' pleaded Archie. 'He's been raving all day. Why, just before lunch he said he was Benito Mussolini!'

The girl laughed.

'It's all right,' she told Simon. 'I don't take him seriously.'

'There's gratitude for you!' said Sheridan wildly. 'After all I've done for her! I even taught her to speak English. When she arrived here she had a Scots accent that would have made a bawbee run for its life. She reeked of haggis—'

'Archie!'

'Haggis,' persisted Sheridan. 'She carried one around in her pibroch till it starved to death.'

'What are pibroch?' asked the Saint curiously. 'Are they something you wear under a kilt?'

When the girl had recovered her composure:

'Is he really so impossible?' she exclaimed.

'I don't know you well enough to tell you the whole truth,' said the Saint solemnly. 'The only hope I can give you is that you're the first Lilla in his life. Wait a minute – sorry – wasn't Lilla the name of the barmaid—'

'Go away,' said Sheridan morosely. 'With sudden death staring you in the face, you ought to be spending your time in prayer and repentance. You'll be shot at dawn to-morrow, and I shall look over the prison walls and cheer on the firing squad.'

He watched Kelly and the Saint retire to the other end of the verandah, and then turned to the girl, with his pleasant face unusually serious.

'Lilla,' he said, 'I don't want to scare you, but it isn't all quite as funny as we make out. The Saint would still be laughing in the face of the firing squad I mentioned; but that doesn't make the possibility of the firing squad any less real.'

She looked at him with sober eyes.

'Then it's easily settled,' she said. 'I won't let you do it.'

Sheridan laughed.

'It isn't me you've got to deal with,' he replied, 'It's the Saint. Nothing you could say would stop him. He'd simply tell me to beat it with you on the *Andalusia* this evening if I was scared. And I'd rather face the said firing squad than have the Saint say that to me.'

She would have protested further, but something in the man's tone silenced her. She knew that he was making no idle statement. She had no experience whatever of such things, and yet she realised intuitively what she was up against, recognised the heroic thing when she met it – the blind, unswerving loyalty of a man to his friend, the unshakable obedience of a man to a loved leader. And she knew that any attempt she made to seduce her man from that reality would only lower herself in his eyes.

Perhaps there are few women who could have shown such an understanding, but Lilla McAndrew was – Lilla McAndrew.

She smiled suddenly.

'I've always wanted to see a revolution,' she said simply.

Moments passed before Sheridan could grasp the full wonder of her sympathy and acquiescence. And then his arms went round her, and her hands tousled his hair.

'Dear Archie!' she said, and found herself unaccountably breathless.

'I admit every girl the Saint mentioned,' said Sheridan defiantly. 'And a few more. But that doesn't alter the fact that I love you, and as soon as this comic revolution's over I'm going to marry you.'

'I'll believe that when you do it,' she teased him; but her heart was on her lips when he kissed her . . .

Some almost offensively discreet coughing from the Saint interrupted them ten minutes later.

'I tried to save you,' said the Saint, declining to avert his shamelessly quizzical gaze from the girl's efforts to straighten her hair inconspicuously. 'And I'm sorry to have to butt in on your downfall, but your boy friend and I have work to do. If you look down towards the town you'll see a file of men advancing up the main street in our direction, led by two men on horseback in the uniform of commissionaires. The entire police force of Santa Miranda, as far as I can make out from this distance, is on its way up here to arrest me for assaulting and battering one of their most prominent citizens, and to arrest Archie as an accessory before, after, and during the fact. They have just woken up from their afternoon snooze, and have been put on the job by the aforesaid citizen with commendable rapidity. Will you excuse us if we escape?'

They went to the edge of the verandah and looked down. Below them, about a mile away, Santa Miranda, as yet hardly astir from its siesta, lay bathed in the afternoon sunshine.

The town, indeterminately vignetted at the edges, had a definite core of nearly modern white buildings ranged down its principal streets. These numbered two, and were in the form of a T. The top of the T ran parallel with the waterfront; the upright, half-way down which was the Presidential Palace, ran inland for nearly a mile, tailing off in the mass of adobe huts which clustered round the core of the town.

From where they stood they could look down the length of the street which formed the upright of the T; and the situation was even as the Saint had diagnosed it . . .

'One minute for the fond farewell, Archie,' said the Saint briskly, and Sheridan nodded.

Simon Templar drew Kelly inside the bungalow.

'By the way,' he said, 'do you happen to have such a thing as a good-looking pot of paint?'

'I've got some enamel,' replied the mystified Kelly.

He produced a couple of tins, and the Saint selected one with every appearance of satisfaction.

'The very idea,' he said. 'It's just an idea of mine for dealing with this arrest business.'

Kelly was suspicious.

'I don't seem to have much to do,' he complained aggrievedly. 'It's hoggin' the best of the fightin' yez are. Now, if I had my way, I'd be sthartin' the throuble with these policemen right away, I would.'

'And wreck the whole show,' said the Saint. 'No, it's too soon for that. And if you call being fifty percent of an invading army "having nothing to do" I can't agree. You're one of the most important members of the cast. Besides, if your bus doesn't break down, you'll be back here just when the rough stuff is warming up. You get it both ways.'

He adjusted his hat to an appropriately rakish and revolutionary angle on his head, and went out to collect Archie Sheridan.

They shook hands with the still grumbling Kelly; but the Saint had the last word with Lilla McAndrew.

'I'm sorry I've got to take Archie,' he said. 'You see, he's the one man I can trust here who can tap out Morse fluently, and I sent him out from England for that very reason, though I didn't know it was going to pan out as it's panning out now. But I'll promise to get him back to you safe and sound. You needn't worry. Only the good die young. I wonder how you've managed to live so long, Lilla?'

He smiled; and when the Saint smiled in that particularly gay and enchanting manner, it was impossible to believe that any adventure he undertook could fail.

'Archie is marked "Fragile – With Care" for this journey,' said the Saint, and went swinging down the verandah steps.

He walked back arm-in-arm with Sheridan to the latter's bungalow at a leisurely pace enough, for it was his last chance to give Sheridan his final instructions for the opening of the campaign.

Archie was inclined to voice much the same grievance as Kelly had vented, but Templar dealt shortly with that insubordination.

'I'm starting off by having the most boresome time of any of you,' he said. 'If I could do your job, I promise you I'd be making you do mine. That being so, I reckon I deserve a corresponding majority ration of excitement at the end. Anyway, with any luck we'll all be together again by Thursday, and we'll see the new era in in a bunch. And if you're going to say you've thought of another scheme that'd be just as effective, my answer is that you ought to have spoken up before. It's too late to change our plans now.'

At the bungalow the Saint made certain preparations for the arrival of the police posse which to some extent depleted Archie Sheridan's travelling athletic outfit. That done, he sent Sheridan to his post, and himself settled down with a cigarette in an easy chair on the verandah to await the coming of the Law.

4

The *guindillas* came toiling up the last two hundred yards of slope in a disorderly straggle. The hill at that point became fairly steep, they were in poor condition, and, although the sun was getting low, the broiling heat of the afternoon had not yet abated; and these factors united to upset what might otherwise have been an impressive approach. The only members of the squad who did not seem the worse for wear were the two *comisarios*, who rode in the van on a pair of magnificent high-stepping horses, obvious descendants of the chargers of Cortes' invading Spaniards, the like of which may often be seen in that part of the Continent. The Saint had had an eye for those horses ever since he spied them a mile and a half away, which was why he was so placidly waiting for the deputation.

He watched them with a detached interest, smoking his cigarette. They were an unkempt and ferocious-looking lot (in Pasala, as in many other Latin countries, Saturday night is Gillette night for the general public), and every man of them was armed to somewhere near the teeth with a musket, a revolver, and a sabre. The Saint himself was comparatively weaponless, his entire armoury consisting of a beautifully-fashioned little knife, strapped to his left forearm under his sleeve, which he could throw with a deadly swiftness and an unerring aim. He did not approve of firearms, which he considered messy and noisy and barbarous inventions of the devil. Yet the opposition's display of force did not concern him.

His first impression, that the entire police force of Santa Miranda had been sent out to arrest him, proved to be a slight over-estimate. There were, as a matter of fact, only ten *guardias* behind the two mounted men in resplendent uniforms.

The band came to a bedraggled and slovenly halt a few yards from the verandah, and the *comisarios* dismounted and ascended the short flight of steps with an imposing clanking of scabbards and spurs. They were moustached and important.

The Saint rose.

'*Buenos tardes, Señores,*' he murmured courteously.

'*Señor,*' said the senior *comisario* sternly, unfolding a paper overloaded with official seals, 'I regret that I have to trouble a visitor illustrious, hut I am ordered to request your honour to allow your honour to be taken to the *prevencion,* in order that in the morning your honour may be brought before the tribunal to answer a charge of grievously assaulting the *Señor* Shannet.'

He replaced the document in his pocket, and bowed extravagantly.

The Saint, with a smile, surpassed the extravagance of the bow.

'*Señor polizante,*' he said, 'I regret that I cannot come.'

Now the word '*polizante*' while it is understood to mean 'policeman,' is not the term with which it is advisable to address even an irascible *guardia* – much less a full-blown *comisario*. It brought to an abrupt conclusion the elaborate ceremony in which the *comisario* had been indulging.

He turned, and barked an order; and the escort mounted the steps and ranged themselves along the verandah.

'Arrest him!'

'I cannot stay,' said the Saint sadly. 'And I refuse to be arrested. *Adios, amigos*!'

He faded away – through the open door of the dining-room. The Saint had the knack of making these startlingly abrupt exits without any show of haste, so that he was gone before his audience had realised that he was on his way.

Then the *guardias*, led by the two outraged *comisarios*, followed in a body.

The bungalow was small, with a large verandah in front and a smaller verandah at the back. The three habitable rooms of which it boasted ran through the width of the house, with doors opening on to each verandah. The dining-room was the middle room, and it had no windows.

As the *guardias* surged in in pursuit, rifles at the ready, with the *comisarios* waving their revolvers, the Saint reappeared in the doorway that opened on to the back of the verandah. At the same moment the doors to the front verandah were slammed and barred behind them by Archie Sheridan, who had been lying in wait in an adjoining room for that purpose.

The Saint's hands were held high above his head, and in each hand was a gleaming round black object.

'*Señores*,' he said persuasively, 'I am a peaceful revolutionary, and I cannot be pestered like this. In my hands you see two bombs. If you shoot me, they will fall and explode. If you do not immediately surrender I shall throw them – and, again, they will explode. Is it to be death or glory, boys?'

He spoke the last sentence in English; but he had already said enough in the vernacular to make the situation perfectly plain. The *guardias* paused, irresolute.

Their officers, retiring to a strategic position in the background from which they could direct operations, urged their men to advance and defy death in the performance of their duty; but the Saint shifted his right hand threateningly, and the *guardias* found the counter-argument more convincing. They threw down their arms; and the *comisarios*, finding themselves alone, followed suit as gracefully as they might.

The Saint ordered the arsenal to be thrown out of the door, and he stepped inside the room and stood aside to allow this to be done. Outside, the guns were collected by Archie Sheridan, and their bolts removed and hurled far away into the bushes of the garden. The cartridges he poured into a large bag, together with the contents of the bandoliers which the Saint ordered his prisoners to discard, for these were required for a certain purpose. Then the Saint returned to the doorway.

'*Hasta la vista!*' he murmured mockingly. 'Until we meet again!'

And he hurled the two gleaming round black objects he carried, and a wail of terror went up from the doomed men.

The Saint sprang back, slamming and barring the doors in the face of the panic-stricken stampede; and the two tennis-balls, which he had coated with Kelly's providential enamel for the purpose, rebounded off the heads of the cowering *comisarios*, leaving great splashes of paint on the gorgeous uniforms and the gorgeous moustachios of Santa Miranda's Big Two, and went bouncing insolently round the room.

The Saint vaulted over the verandah rail and ran round to the front of the bungalow. Sheridan, his bag of cartridges slung over his shoulder, was already mounted on one of the police horses, and holding the other by the bridle. From inside the dining-room could be heard the muffled shouting and cursing of the imprisoned men, and on the panels of the barred doors thundered the battering of their efforts to escape. The Saint sprang into the saddle.

'*Vamos!*' he cried, and smacked his hand down on the horse's quarters.

The pounding of departing hoofs came to the ears of the men in the locked room, and redoubled the fury of their onslaught on the doors. But the mahogany of which the doors were made was thick and well-seasoned, and it was ten minutes before they broke out. And then, on foot, and unarmed, there was nothing for them to do but to return to Santa Miranda and confess defeat.

The which they did, collaborating on the way down to invent a thrilling tale of a desperate and perilous battle, in which they had braved a hundred deaths, their heroism availing them naught in the face of Simon Templar's evil cunning. But first, to restore their shattered nerves, they partook freely of three bottles of Sheridan's whisky which they found. And it may be recorded that on this account the next day found them very ill; for, before he left, Archie Sheridan had liberally adulterated the whisky with Epsom salts, in anticipation of this very vandalism. But, since *guardia* and *comisario* alike were unfamiliar with the flavour of whisky, they noticed nothing amiss, and went unsuspecting to their hideous fate.

But when they returned to Santa Miranda they said nothing whatever about bombs, wisely deeming that the inclusion of that episode in their story could not but cover them with derision.

Meantime, Simon Templar and Archie Sheridan had galloped neck and neck to Kelly's bungalow, and there Kelly was waiting for them. He had a kit-bag already packed with certain articles that the Saint had required, and Simon took the bag and lashed it quickly to the pommel of his saddle.

Sheridan dismounted. The Saint shook hands with him, and took the bridle of the spare horse.

'All will be well,' said the Saint blithely. 'I feel it in my bones. So long, souls! See you all again soon. Do your stuff – and good luck!'

He clapped his heels to his horse, and was gone with a cheery wave of his hand.

They watched him till the trees hid him from view, and then they went back to the bungalow.

'A piece of wood, pliers, screws, screwdriver, and wire, Kelly, my bhoyl' ordered Sheridan briskly. 'I've got some work to do before I go to bed to-night. And while I'm doing it you can gather round and hear the biggest laugh yet in this revolution, or how the Battle of Santa Miranda was nearly won on the courts of Wimbledon.'

'I thought you weren't coming back,' said the girl accusingly.

'I didn't know whether I was or not,' answered the shameless Archie. 'It all depended on whether the Saint's plan of escape functioned or not. Anyway, a good-bye like you gave me was far too good to miss just because I might be coming back. And don't look so disappointed because I got away, I'll go down to the town and surrender, if that's what you want.'

Towards sundown a squadron of cavalry galloped up to the bungalow, and the officer in command declared his intention of making a search. Kelly protested.

'You have no right,' he said, restraining an almost irresistible desire to throw the man down the steps and thus precipitate the fighting that his fists were itching for.

'I have a warrant from the Minister of the Interior, *El Supremo é Ilustrisimo Señor* Manuel Concepcion de Villega,' said the officer, producing the document with a flourish.

'El Disgustando y Horriblisimo Señor!' muttered Kelly.

The officer shrugged, and indicated the men who waited below.

'I do not wish to use force, *Señor* Kelly,' he said significantly, and Kelly submitted to the inevitable.

'But,' he said, 'I do not know why you should suspect me to be hiding him.'

'You are known to be a friend of the *Señor* Sheridan,' was the brief reply, 'and the *Señor* Sheridan is a friend of this man. We are looking for both of them.'

Kelly followed the officer into the house.

'What did you say was the name of this man you are look-ing for?' he inquired.

'To the *Señor* Shannet, whom he attacked,' said the officer, 'he gave his name as Benito Mussolini.'

He was at a loss to understand Kelly's sudden earthquak-ing roar of laughter. At last he gave up the effort, and put it down to another manifestation of the well-known madness of all *ingleses*. But the fact remains that the joke largely compen-sated Kelly for the indignity of the search to which his house was subjected.

The officer and half a dozen of his men went through the bungalow with a small-toothed comb, and not a cubic inch of it, from floor to rafters, escaped their attention. But they did not find Archie Sheridan, who was sitting out on the roof, on the opposite side to that from which the soldiers had approached.

At last the search-party allowed themselves to be shep-herded out, for barely an hour's daylight was left to them, and they had already fruitlessly wasted much valuable time.

'But remember, *Señor* Kelly,' said the officer, as his horse was led up, 'that both Sheridan and Mussolini have been declared outlaws for resisting arrest and assaulting and threatening the lives of the *guardias civiles* sent to apprehend them. In the morning they will be proclaimed; and the *Señor* Shannet, who has heard of the insolence offered to the Law, has himself offered to double the reward for their capture, dead or alive.'

The troopers rode off on their quest, but in those latitudes the twilight is short. They scoured the countryside for an hour, until the fall of night put an end to the search, and five miles away they found the horses of the two *comisarios* graz-ing in a field, but of the man Mussolini there was no trace. The Saint had had a good start; and what he did not know about the art of taking cover in the open country wasn't worth knowing.

He was stretched out on a branch of a tall tree a mile away from where the horses were found when the troop of cavalry reined in only twelve feet beneath him.

'We can do no more now,' said the officer. 'In the morning we shall find him. Without horses he cannot travel far. Let us go home.'

The Saint laughed noiselessly in the darkness.

5

That night there came into Santa Miranda a *peón*.

He was dirty and disreputable to look upon. His clothes were dusty, patched in many places, and threadbare where they were not patched; and his hair was long, and matted into a permanent thatch, as is the slovenly custom of the labourers of that country.

Had he wished to do so, he might have passed unnoticed among many other similarly down-at-heel and poverty-stricken people; but this he did not seem to want. In fact, he went out of his way to draw attention to himself; and this he found easy enough, for his poverty-stricken appearance was belied by the depth of his pocket.

He made a fairly comprehensive round of the inferior cafés in the town, and in each he bought wine and *aguardiente* for all who cared to join him. Naturally, it was not long before he acquired a large following; and, since he seemed to account for two drinks to everybody else's one, there was no surprise when he became more and more drunk as the evening wore on.

It was not to be expected that such display of affluence on the part of one whose outward aspect argued against the probability that he would have more than a few *centavos* to his name could escape comment, and it was not long before the tongues that devoured the liquor which he bought were busy with rumour. It was whispered, as with authority, that he was a bandit from the Sierra Maduro, over the border

beyond Esperanza, who had crossed into Pasala to spend his
money and rest until the *rurales* of Maduro tired of seeking
him and he could return to his old hunting-grounds with
safety. Then it was remarked that on his little finger was a
signet ring bearing a heraldic device, and with equal authority it was said that he was the heir to a noble Mexican family
indulging his hobby of moving among the peónes as one of
themselves and distributing charity where he found it
merited. Against this, another school of thought affirmed
that he was a *peón* who had murdered his master and stolen
his ring and his money.

The *peón* heard these whisperings, and laughingly ignored
them. His manner lent more support, however, to either of
the two former theories than to the third. He was tall for a
peón, and a man of great strength, as was seen when he
bought a whole keg of wine and lifted it in his hands to fill his
goblet as if it had weighed nothing at all. His eyes were blue,
which argued that he was of noble descent, for the true *peón*
stock is so mixed with the native that the eyes of that sea-blue
colour are rare. And again, the bandit theory was made more
plausible by the man's boisterous and reckless manner, as
though he held life cheap and the intense enjoyment of the
day the only thing of moment, and would as soon be fighting
as drinking. He had, too, a repertoire of strange and barbarous songs which no one could understand.

'Drink up, *amigos*!' he roared from time to time, 'for this is
the beginning of great days for Pasala!'

But when they asked him what they might mean, he turned
away their questions with a jest, and called for more wine.

Few of his following had seen such a night for many years.

From house to house he went, singing his strange songs,
and bearing his keg of wine on his shoulder. One or two *guardias* would have barred his way, or, hearing the rumours
which were gossiped about him, would have stopped and

questioned him; but the *peón* poured them wine or flung them money, and they stood aside.

Towards midnight, still singing, the man led his procession up the Calle del Palacio. The crowd followed, not sure where they were going, and not caring, for they had drunk much.

Now, the Calle del Palacio forms the upright of the T which has been described, and half-way down it, as has been stated, is the palace from which it takes its name.

In the street opposite the palace gates the *peón* halted, set down his keg, and mounted unsteadily upon it. He stood there, swaying slightly, and his following gathered round him.

'*Viva! Viva!*' they shouted thickly.

The *peón* raised his hands for silence.

'Citizens!' he cried, 'I have told you that this is the beginning of great days for Pasala, and now I will tell you why. It is because at last we are going to suffer no more under this Manuel Concepcion de Villega. May worms devour him alive, for he is a thief and a tyrant and the son of a dog! His taxes bear you down, and you receive nothing in return. The President is his servant, that strutting nincompoop, and they are both in the pay of the traitor Shannet, who is planning to betray you to Maduro. Now I say that we will end this, to-night.'

'*Viva!*' responded a few doubtful voices.

'Let us finish this slavery,' cried the *peón* again. 'Let us storm this palace, which was built with money wrung from the poor, where your puppet of a President and this pig of a de Villega sleep in luxury for which you have been tortured! Let us tear them from their beds and slay them, and cast them back into the gutter from which they came!'

This time there were no '*Vivas!*' The awfulness of the stranger's blasphemy had sobered the mob as nothing else could have done. It was unprecedented – incredible. No one had ever dared to speak in such terms of the President and his Minister – or, if they had, it was reported by spies to the *comisarios*, and *guardias* came swiftly and took the blasphemers away to a place where their treason should not offend the ears of the faithful. Of course, the *peón* had spoken nothing but the truth. But to tear down the palace and kill the President! It was unheard of. It could not be done without much discussion.

The stranger, after his first speech, had seen the sentries at the palace gates creep stealthily away; and now, over the heads of the awestruck crowd, he saw a little knot of *guardias* coming down the street at the double. Whistles shrilled, and the mob huddled together in sudden terror.

'*Amigos*,' said the stranger urgently, in a lower voice, 'the hour of liberation will not be long coming. To-night you have heard me sing many strange songs, which are the songs of freedom. Now, when you hear those songs again, and you have thought upon the words I have said to-night, follow the man who sings such songs as I sang, for he will be sent to lead you to victory. But now go quickly, or you will be taken and punished.'

The mob needed no encouragement for that. Even while the *peón* spoke many of them had sneaked away into the dark side-streets. As he spoke his last sentence, it was as if a cord had been snapped which held them, and they fled incontinently.

The *peón* straightened up and shook his fists at their backs.

'Fools!' he screamed. 'Cowards! Curs! Is it thus that ye fight? Is it thus that ye overthrow tyrants?'

But his audience was gone, and from either side the *guardias* were closing in on him with drawn sabres.

'*Guarro!*' challenged one of them. 'What is this raving?'

'I speak for liberty!' bawled the *peón*, reeling drunkenly on his pedestal. 'I speak against the President, who does not know the name of his father, and against the Minister for the Interior, Manuel Concepcion de Villega, whom I call Señor

Jugo Procedente del Estercolero, the spawn of a dunghill – *guarros, perruelos, hijos de la puts adiva . . .'*

He let loose a stream of the vilest profanity and abuse in the language, so that even the hardened guardias were horrified.

They dragged him down and hustled him ungently to the police station, where they locked him up in a verminous cell for the night; but even then he cursed and raved against the President and the Minister for the Interior, mingling his maledictions with snatches of unintelligible songs, until the jailer threatened to beat him unless he held his tongue. Then he was silent, and presently went to sleep.

In the morning they brought him before the magistrate. He was sober, but still rebellious. They asked him his name.

'Don Fulano de Tal,' he replied, which is the Spanish equivalent of saying 'Mr So-and-So, Such-and-Such.'

'If you are impertinent,' said the magistrate, 'I shall order you to receive a hundred lashes.'

'My name is Sancho Quijote,' said the *peón* sullenly.

He was charged, and the sentries from the palace testified to the treason of his speeches. So also did the *guardias* who had broken up his meeting. They admitted, in extenuation of his offence, that he had been very drunk.

He was asked if he had anything to say.

'I have nothing to say,' he answered, 'except that, drunk or not, I shall spit upon the name of the President and the Minister for the Interior till the end of my days. As for you, *Señor jeuz*, you are no better than the *guindillas* who arrested me – you are all the miserable hirelings of the oppressors, paid to persecute those who dare speak for justice. But it will not be long before your pride is turned to humiliation.'

'He is mad,' whispered one *guardia* to another.

The *peón* was sentenced to seven years' imprisonment with hard labour, for there are no limits to the powers of summary jurisdiction in Pasala. He heard the verdict without emotion.

'It does not matter,' he said. 'I shall not stay in prison seven days. It will not be long before you know why.'

When he reached the prison he asked to be allowed to send a message by telegraph to Ondia, the capital of Maduro.

'I am of Maduro,' he confessed. 'I should have returned to Ondia to-morrow, and I must tell my wife that I am detained.'

He had money to pay for the telegram, but it was evening before permission was received for the message to be sent, for nothing is done hurriedly in Spanish America.

Twenty-four hours later there came from Ondia a telegram addressed to Manuel Concepcion de Villega, and it was signed with the name and titles of the President of Maduro. A free translation would have read:

I am informed that a citizen of Maduro, giving the name of Sancho Quijote, has been imprisoned in Santa Miranda. If he is not delivered to the frontier by Wednesday noon my armies will advance into Pasala.

Shannet was closeted with de Villega when the message arrived, and for the moment he was no better able to account for it than was the Minister.

'Who is this man Quijote?' he asked. 'It's a ridiculous name. There is a book called "*Don Quijote*," Quixote in English, and there is a man in it called Sancho Panza.'

'I know that,' said Don Manuel, and sent for the judge.

He heard the story of the *peón*'s crime and sentence and was not enlightened. But he had enough presence of mind to accuse the magistrate of inefficiency for not having suspected that the name Sancho Quijote was a false one.

'It is impossible,' said de Villega helplessly, when the magistrate had been dismissed. 'By Wednesday noon – that hardly gives us enough time to get him to the frontier even if we release him immediately. And who is this man? A labourer, a stranger, of whom nobody knows anything, who suddenly appears in Santa Miranda with more money than he could have ever come by honestly, and preaches a revolution to a mob that he has first made drunk. He deserves his punishment, and yet the President of Maduro, without any inquiry, demands his release. It means war . . .'

'He knew this would happen,' said Shannet. 'The judge told us – he boasted that he would not stay in prison seven days . . .'

They both saw the light at the same instant.

'An agent provocateur—'

'A trap!' snarled de Villega. 'And we have fallen into it. It is only an excuse that Maduro was seeking. They sent him here, with money, for no other purpose than to get himself arrested. And then this preposterous ultimatum, which they give us no time even to consider . . .'

'But why make such an intrigue?' demanded Shannet. 'This is a poor country. They are rich. They have nothing to gain.'

Don Manuel tugged nervously at his moustachios.

'And we cannot even buy them off,' he said. 'Unless we appeal to the Estados Unidos—'

Shannet sneered.

'And before their help can arrive the war is over,' he said. 'New Orleans is five days away. But they will charge a high price for burying the hatchet for us.'

Don Manuel suddenly sat still. His shifty little dark eyes came to rest on Shannet.

'I see it!' he exclaimed savagely. 'It is the oil! You, and your accursed oil! I see it all! It is because of the oil that this country is always embroiled in a dozen wars and fears of wars. So far Pasala has escaped, but now we are like the rest. My

Ministry will be overthrown. Who knows what Great Power has paid Maduro to attack us? Then the Great Power steps in and takes our oil from us. I shall be exiled. Just now it is England, through you, who has control of the oil. Perhaps it is now America who tries to capture it, or another English company. I am ruined!'

'For God's sake stop whining!' snapped Shannet. 'If you're ruined, so am I. We've got to see what can be done about it.'

De Villega shook his head.

'There is nothing to do. They are ten to one. We shall be beaten. But I have some money, and there is a steamer in two days. If we can hold off their armies so long I can escape.'

It was some time before the more brutally vigorous Shannet could bring the Minister to reason. Shannet had the courage of the wild beast that he was. At bay, faced with the wrecking of his tainted fortunes, he had no other idea but to fight back with the desperate ferocity of a cornered animal.

But even when Don Manuel's moaning had been temporarily quietened they were little better off. It was useless to appeal to the President, for he was no more than a tool in de Villega's hands. Likewise, the rest of the Council were nothing but figureheads, the mere instruments of de Villega's policy, and appointed by himself for no other reason than their willingness, for a consideration, to oppose nothing that he put forward.

'There is but one chance,' said Villega. 'A radio-gram must be sent to New Orleans. America will send a warship to keep the peace. Then we will try to make out to Maduro that the warship is here to fight for us, and their armies will retire. To the Estados Unidos, then, we will say that we had made peace before their warship arrived; we are sorry to have troubled them, but there is nothing to do.'

It seemed a flimsy suggestion to Shannet, but it was typical of de Villega's crafty and tortuous statesmanship. Shannet doubted if America, having once been asked to intervene, would be so easily put off, but he had no more practical scheme to suggest himself, and he let it go.

He could not support it with enthusiasm, for an American occupation would mean the coming of American justice, and Shannet had no wish for that while there were still tongues wagging with charges against himself. But he could see no way out. He was in a cleft stick.

'Why not let this *peón* go?' he asked.

'And will that help us?' demanded Don Manuel scornfully. 'If we sent him away now he would hardly have time to reach the border by noon to-morrow, and they would certainly say that they had not received him. Is it not plain that they are determined to fight? When they have taken such pains to trump up an excuse, will they be so quickly appeased?'

A purely selfish train of thought led to Shannet's next question.

'This man Sheridan and his friend – has nothing been heard of them yet? They have been at large two days.'

'At a time like this, can I be bothered with such trifles?' replied de Villega shortly. 'The squadron of Captain Tomare has been looking for them, but they are not found.'

This was not surprising, for the searchers had worked outwards from Santa Miranda. Had they been inspired to work inwards they might have found Simon Templar, unwashed and unshaven, breaking stones in their own prison yard, chained by his ankles in a line of other unwashed and unshaven desperadoes, his identity lost in his official designation of Convicto Sancho Quijote, No. 475.

It was the Saint's first experience of imprisonment with hard labour, and he would have been enjoying the novel adventure if it had not been for various forms of microscopic animal life with which the prison abounded.

6

There came one morning to the London offices of Pasala Oil Products Ltd. (Managing Director, Hugo Campard) a cable in code. He decoded it himself, for it was not a code in general use; and his pink face went paler as the transliteration proceeded.

By the time the complete translation had been written in between the lines Hugo Campard was a very frightened man. He read the message again and again, incredulous of the catastrophe it foreboded.

Maduro declared war Pasala on impossible ultimatum.
Believe deliberately instigated America or rival combine.
Pasala army hopelessly outnumbered. No chance. Villega
appealed America. Help on way but will mean overthrow of
Government. Concession probably endangered. Sell out before
news reaches London and breaks market.
  Shannet.

Campard's fat hands trembled as he clipped the end of a cigar.

He was a big, florid man with a bald head and a sandy moustache. Once upon a time he had been a pinched and out-at-elbows clerk in a stockbroker's office, until his ingenuity had found incidental ways of augmenting his income. For a few years he had scraped and saved; then, with five hundred pounds capital, and an intimate knowledge of the share market, he had gone after bigger game.

He had succeeded. He was clever, he knew the pitfalls to avoid, he was without pity or scruple, and luck had been with him. In fifteen years he had become a very rich man. Innumerable were the companies with which he had been associated, which had taken in much money and paid out none. He had been 'exposed' half a dozen times, and every reputable broker knew his stock for what it was; but the scrip of the Campard companies was always most artistically engraved and their prospectuses couched in the most attractive terms, so that there was never a lack of small investors ready to pour their money into his bank account.

It is said that there is a mug born every minute, and Campard had found this a sound working principle. Many others like him, steering narrowly clear of the law, have found no lack of victims, and Campard had perhaps found more suckers than most.

But even the most triumphant career meets a check sometimes, and Campard had made a slip which had brought him into the full publicity of a High Court action. He had wriggled out, by the skin of his teeth and some expensive perjury, but the resultant outcry had told him that it would be wise to lie low for a while. And lying low did not suit Campard's book. He lived extravagantly, and for all the wealth that he possessed on paper there were many liabilities. And then, when his back was actually to the wall, had come the miracle – in the shape of the chance to buy the Pasala concession, offered him by a man named Shannet, whom he had employed many years ago.

Pasala oil was good. In the few months that it had been worked, the quality and quantity of the output had been startling. Campard enlisted the help of a handful of his boon companions, and poured in all his resources. More plant was needed and more labour, more expert management. That was now to be supplied. The directors of Pasala Oil Products sat down to watch themselves become millionaires.

And then, in a clear sky, the cloud.

Hugo Campard, skimming through his newspaper on his way to the financial pages, had read of the early manifestations of the Saint, and had been mildly amused. In the days that followed he had read of other exploits of the Saint, and his amusement had changed gradually to grave anxiety . . . And one day there had come to Hugo Campard, through the post, a card . . .

Each morning thereafter the familiar envelope had been beside his plate at breakfast; each morning, when he reached the offices of Pasala Oil Products, he had found another reminder of the Saint on his desk. There had been no message. Just the picture. But the newspapers were full of stories, and Hugo Campard was afraid . . .

Then, two days ago, the Saint had spoken.

Campard could not have told why he opened the envelopes in which the Saint sent his mementoes. Perhaps it was because, each time, Campard hoped he would be given some indication of what the Saint meant to do. After days of suspense, that had painted the black hollows of sleeplessness under his eyes and brought him to a state of nerves that was sheer physical agony, he was told.

On that day, underneath the crude outline, was pencilled a line of small writing:

In a week's time you will be ruined.

He had already had police protection – after the Lemuel incident there had been no difficulty in obtaining that, as soon as he showed the police the first cards. All night there had been a constable outside his house in St. John's Wood. All day a constable stood in the corridor outside his office, a plain-clothes detective rode in his car with him everywhere he went. Short of some unforeseeable masterpiece of strategy, or a recourse to the machine-gun fighting of the Chicago gangsters, it was impossible that the Saint could reach him as he had reached Lemuel.

Now, at one stroke, the Saint brought all these preparations to naught, and broke invisibly through the cordon. Against such an attack the police could not help him.

'In a week's time you will be ruined.'

An easy boast to make. A tremendous task to carry out.

And yet, even while he had been racking his brains to find out how the Saint might carry out his threat, he had his answer.

For a long time he stared blindly at the cable-gram, until every letter of the message was burned into his brain as with a hot iron. When he roused himself it was to clutch at a straw.

He telephoned to the telegraph company, and verified that the message had actually been received from Santa Miranda via Barbados and Pernambuco. Even that left a loophole. He cabled to an agent in New York, directing him to obtain authentic information from Washington at any cost; and by the evening he received a reply confirming Shannet's statement. The U.S.S. *Michigan* was on its way to Santa Miranda in response to an appeal from the President.

There was no catch in it. Shannet's code message was not a bluff, not even from an agent of the Saint in Santa Miranda. It was a grimly sober utterance of fact.

But the gigantic thoroughness of it! The colossal impudence of the scheme! Campard felt as if all the strength and fight had ebbed out of him. He was aghast at the revelation of the resources of the Saint. Against a man who apparently thought nothing of engineering a war to gain his ends, he felt as puny and helpless as a babe.

His hand went out again to the telephone, but he checked the impulse. It was no use telling the police that. They could do nothing – and, far too soon as it was, the news would be published in the Press. And then, with the name of Campard behind them, P.O.P. shares would tumble down the market to barely the value of their weight in waste paper.

Before he left the office that night he sent a return cable in code to Santa Miranda:

Believe war organised by criminal known as Saint, who has threatened me. Obtain particulars of any strange Englishman in Pasala or Maduro. Give descriptions. Report developments.

What the Saint had started, Campard argued, the Saint could stop. Campard might have a chance yet, if he could bargain . . .

But the declaration of war was announced in the evening paper which he bought on his way home, and Hugo Campard knew then that it was too late.

He had no sleep that night, and by nine o'clock next morning he was at the office, and speaking on the telephone to his broker.

'I want you to sell twenty thousand P.O.P.s for me,' he said. 'Take the best price you can get.'

'I wish I could hope to get a price at all,' came the sardonic answer. 'The market's full of rumours and everyone's scared to touch the things. You're too late with your selling – the Bears were in before you.'

'What do you mean?' asked Campard in a strained voice.

'There was a good deal of quiet selling yesterday and the day before,' said the broker. 'Somebody must have had information. They're covering to-day, and they must have made thousands.'

During the morning other backers of the company came through on the telephone and were accusing or whining according to temperament, and Campard dealt with them all in the same formula.

'I can't help it,' he said. 'I'm hit twice as badly as any of you. It isn't my fault. The company was perfectly straight; you know that.'

The broker rang up after lunch to say that he had managed to get rid of six thousand shares at an average price of two shillings.

'Two shillings for two-pound shares?' Campard almost sobbed. 'You're mad!'

'See if you can do any better yourself, Mr Campard,' replied the broker coldly. 'The market won't take any more at present, but I might be able to get rid of another couple of thousand before we close at about a bob each – to people who want to keep them as curios. A firm of wall-paper manufacturers might make an offer for the rest—'

Campard slammed down the receiver and buried his face in his hands.

He was in the same position three hours later when his secretary knocked on the door and entered with a buff envelope.

'Another cable, Mr Campard.'

He extracted the flimsy and reached out a nerveless hand for the code book.

He decoded:

Maduro armies advancing into Pasala. Only chance now sell any price. Answer inquiry. Man arrived nearly four months ago –

With a sudden impatience, Campard tore the cablegram into a hundred pieces and dropped them into the waste-paper basket There was no time now to get in touch with the Saint. The damage was done.

A few minutes later came the anticipated message from the firm that he had induced to back him over Pasala Oil Products. Rich as he had become, he would never have been able to acquire his large holding in the company without assistance. How, with his reputation, he had got any firm to back him was a mystery. But he had been able to do it on the system known as 'margins' – which, in this instance, meant roughly that he could be called upon immediately to produce fifty per cent of the amount by which the shares had depreciated, in order to 'keep up his margin.'

The demand, courteously but peremptorily worded, was delivered by special messenger; and his only surprise was that it had not come sooner. He scribbled a cheque, which there was no money in the bank to meet, and sent it back by the same boy.

He sent for his car, and left the office shortly afterwards. The paper which he bought outside told of the panic of P.O.P.s, and he read the article with a kind of morbid interest.

There was a letter, delivered by the afternoon post, waiting at his house when he got back.

I sold P.O.P.s and covered to-day. The profits are nearly twelve thousand pounds.

The expenses of this campaign have been unusually heavy; but, even then, after deducting these and my ten per cent collecting fee, I hope to be able to forward nine thousand pounds to charity on your behalf.

Received the above-named sum – with thanks.

The Saint

Enclosed was a familiar card, and one Pasala Oil Products share certificate.

Hugo Campard dined well that night, and, alone, accounted for a bottle of champagne. After that he smoked a cigar with relish, and drank a liqueur brandy with enjoyment.

He had dressed. He felt the occasion deserved it. His mind was clear and untroubled, for in a flash he had seen the way out of the trap.

When his cigar was finished, he exchanged his coat for a dressing-gown, and passed into his study. He locked the door behind him, and for some time paced up and down the room in silence, but no one will ever know what he thought. At ten o'clock precisely the pacing stopped.

The constable on guard outside heard the shot; but Hugo Campard did not hear it.

7

The men serving sentences of hard labour in the prison of Santa Miranda are allowed an afternoon siesta of three hours. This is not due to the humanity and loving-kindness of the authorities, but to the fact that nothing will induce the warders to forgo the afternoon nap which is the custom of the country, and no one has yet discovered a way of making the prisoners work without a wide-awake warder to watch them and pounce on the shirkers.

The fetters are struck off the prisoners' ankles, and they are herded into their cells, a dozen in each, and there locked up to rest as well as they can in the stifling heat of a room ventilated only by one small barred window and thickly populated with flies. The warders retire to their quarters above the prison, and one jailer is left on guard, nodding in the passage outside the cells, with a rifle across his knees.

It was so on the third day of the Saint's incarceration, and this was the second hour of the siesta, but the Saint had not slept.

His cell-mates were sprawled on the bunks or on the floor, snoring heavily. They were hardened to the flies. Outside, the jailer dozed, his sombrero on the back of his head and his coat unbuttoned. Through the window of the cell a shaft of burning sunlight cut across the moist gloom and splashed a square of light on the opposite wall.

The Saint sat by the gates of the cell, watching that creeping square of light. Each afternoon he had watched it, learning its habits, so that now he could tell the time by it. When the edge of the square touched a certain scar in the stone it was four o'clock . . . That was the time he had decided upon . . .

He scrambled softly to his feet.

The jailer's head nodded lower and lower. Every afternoon, the Saint had noted, he set his chair at a certain point in the passage where a cool draught from a cross-corridor would fan him. Therefore, on that afternoon, the Saint had taken pains to get into the nearest cell to that point.

He tore a button off his clothes, and threw it. It hit the jailer on the cheek, and the man stirred and grunted. The Saint threw another button. The man shook his head, snorted, and roused, stretching his arms with a prodigious yawn.

'*Señor!*' hissed the Saint.

The man turned his head.

'Loathsome disease,' he growled, 'why dost thou disturb my meditations? Lie down and be silent, lest I come and beat thee.'

'I only wished to ask your honour if I might give your honour a present of fifty pesos,' said the Saint humbly.

He squatted down again by the bars of the gate and played with a piece of straw. Minutes passed . . .

He heard the jailer get to his feet, but did not look up. The man's footsteps grated on the floor, and stopped by the cell door. In the cell the other convicts snored peacefully.

'Eater of filth and decomposing fish,' said the jailer's voice gruffly, 'did I hear thy coarse lips speak to me of fifty pesos? How hast thou come by that money?'

'Gifts break rocks,' replied the *peón*, quoting the Spanish proverb. 'I had rather my gifts broke them than I were compelled to break any more of them. I have fifty pesos, and I want to escape.'

'It is impossible. I searched thee—'

'It was hidden. I will give it to your honour as a pledge. I know where to find much more money, if your honour would deign to release me and let me lead you to where it is hidden. Have you not heard how, when I was arrested, it was testified that in the town I spent, in one evening, enough to keep you for a year? That was nothing to me. I am rich.'

The jailer stroked his stubbly chin.

'Verminous mongrel,' he said, more amiably, 'show me this fifty pesos and I will believe thee.'

The Saint ran his fingers through his tangled hair, and there fell out a note. The jailer recognised it, and his avaricious eyes gleamed.

He reached a claw-like hand through the bars, but the Saint jerked the note out of his reach. The jailer's face darkened.

'Abominable insect,' he said, 'thou hast no right to that. Thou art a convict, and thy goods are forfeit to the State. As the servant of the State I will confiscate that paper, that thy low-born hands may defile it no longer.'

He reached for his keys, but the Saint held up a warning hand.

'If you try to do that, *amigo*,' he said, 'I shall cry out so loudly that the other warders will come down to see what has happened. Then I shall tell them, and they will make you divide the fifty pesos with them. And I shall refuse to tell you where I have hidden the rest of my money. Why not release me, and have it all for yourself?'

'But how shall I know that thou dost not lie?'

The Saint's hands went again to his hair, and a rain of fifty-peso notes fell to the floor. He picked them up and counted them before the jailer. There were thirty of them altogether.

'See, I have them here!' he said. 'Fifteen hundred pesos is a lot of money. Now open this door and I will give them to you.'

The jailer's eyes narrowed cunningly. Did this fool of a *peón* really believe that he would be given his liberty in exchange for such a paltry sum? Apparently.

Not that the sum was so paltry, being equal to about two hundred pounds in English money; but if any prisoner escaped, the jailer would be blamed for it, and probably imprisoned himself. Yet this simpleton seemed to imagine that he had only to hand over his bribe and the jailer would risk punishment to earn it.

Very well, let him have his childish belief. It would be easily settled. The door opened, the money paid over, a shot . . . And then there would be no one to bear witness against him. The prisoner was known to be violent. He attempted to escape, and was shot. It would be easy to invent a story to account for the opening of the cell door . . .

'*Señor peón*,' said the jailer, 'I see now that your honour should not be herded in with these cattle. I will set your honour free, and your honour will give me the money, and I shall remember your honour in my prayers.'

He tiptoed back to his chair and picked up his rifle. Then, with elaborate precautions against noise, he unlocked the cell door, and the *peón* came out into the passage.

The other prisoners still snored, and there was no sound but the droning of the flies to arouse them. The whole colloquy had been conducted in whispers, for it was imperative for the jailer as for the *peón* that there should be no premature alarm.

'Now give me the money,' said the jailer huskily.

The Saint held out the handful of notes, and one broke loose and fluttered to the floor. As the jailer bent to pick it up, the Saint reached over him and slid the man's knife gently out of his belt. As the man straightened up the Saint's arm whipped round his neck, strangling his cry of fear before it could pass his throat. And the man felt the point of the knife prick his chest.

'Put thy rifle down against the wall,' breathed the Saint in his ear. 'If it makes a sound thou wilt not speak again.'

No rifle could ever have been grounded more silently.

The Saint withdrew the knife and picked the man off his feet. In an instant, and without a sound, he had him on the floor, holding him with his legs in a ju-jitsu lock so that he could not move.

'Be very quiet,' urged the Saint, and let him feel the knife again.

The man lay like one dead. The Saint, his hands now free, twisted the man's arms behind his back and tied them with the sling of his rifle. Then he rolled the man over.

'When you searched me,' he said, 'I had a knife. Where is it?'

'I am wearing it.'

The Saint rolled up the man's sleeve and unstrapped the sheath from his forearm. With loving care he transferred it to his own arm, for he had had Anna for years, and she was the darling of his heart. That little throwing-knife, which he could wield so expertly, had accompanied him through countless adventures, and had saved his life many times. He loved it like a child, and the loss of it would have left him inconsolable.

With Anna back in her place, the Saint felt more like himself – though it is doubtful if anyone could have been found to agree with him, for he could never in his life have looked so dirty and disreputable as he was then. He, Simon Templar, the Saint, the man who was known for his invariable elegance and his almost supernatural power of remaining immaculate and faultlessly groomed even in the most hectic rough-house and the most uncivilised parts of the world, had neither washed nor shaved for nearly four days. There was no provision for these luxuries in the prison of Santa Miranda. And his clothes had been dreadful enough when Kelly had borrowed them off his under-gardener for the purpose; now, after having been lived in day and night on the stone pile and in the filthy cell which they had just left, their condition may be imagined . . .

His greatest wish at that moment was to get near some soap and water; and already the time of grace for such a diversion was getting short. The square of light on the cell wall told him that he had barely half an hour at his disposal before Santa Miranda would be rousing itself for the second instalment of its day's work; and the other warders would soon be lurching down, yawning and cursing, to drive the prisoners back to their toil. It was time for the Saint to be moving.

He unfastened the jailer's belt and used it to secure the man's legs; then he rolled him over and stuffed his handkerchief into his mouth for a gag. He straightened up, hands on hips; and the helpless man glared up at him with bulging eyes.

'But I had forgotten!' cried the Saint, under his breath, and stooped again to take his money from the jailer's pocket.

The man squirmed, and the Saint swept him a mocking bow.

'Remain with God, my little ape,' he murmured. 'There will now be nothing to disturb thy meditations.'

Then he was gone.

He ran lightly down the corridor, and out at the end into the blazing sunlight of the prison courtyard. This he crossed swiftly, slowing up and moving a little more cautiously as he neared the gates. Within the courtyard, beside the gates, was a little sentry-box where the gatekeeper might take shelter from the sun.

The Saint stole up the last few yards on tiptoe, and sidled one eye round the doorway of the box.

The gatekeeper sat inside on a packing-case, his back propped against the wall. His rifle was leaning against the wall in one corner. He was awake, but his eyes were intent on a pattern which he was tracing in the dust with the toe of his boot.

The bare prison walls were too high to scale, and the only way out was by way of the gates.

The Saint's shadow suddenly blocked the light from the sentry-box, and the gatekeeper half-rose to his feet with a shout rising to his lips. It was rather like shooting a sitting rabbit, but the issues involved were too great to allow of making a more sporting fight of it. As the warder's head came up, the Saint hit him on the point of the jaw scientifically and with vim, and the shout died stillborn.

The Saint huddled the man back against the wall, and tipped his sombrero over his eyes as if he was asleep – which, in fact, he was. Then he scrambled over the gates, and dropped cat-footed into the dust of the cart-track of a road outside.

The prison of Santa Miranda lies to the east of the town, near the sea, among the slums which closely beset the bright main streets; and the Saint set himself to pass quickly through the town by way of these dirty, narrow streets where his disreputable condition would be most unnoticed, avoiding the Calle del Palacio and the chance of encountering a *guardia* who might remember him.

Santa Miranda had not yet awoken. In the grass-grown lanes between the rude huts of the labourers a child in rags played here and there, but paid no attention to his passing. In the doorway of one hut an old and wizened Indian slept in the sun, like a lizard. The Saint saw no one else.

He threaded the maze quietly but with speed, steering a course parallel to the Calle del Palacio. And then, over the low roofs of the adobe hovels around him, he saw, quite close, a tall white tower caught by the slanting rays of the sun, and he changed his plans.

That is to say, he resolved on the spur of the moment to dispense with making plans. His original vague idea had been to make for Kelly's bungalow, get a shave, a bath, some clean clothes, and a cigarette, and sit down to deliberate the best way of capturing the town. So far, in spite of his boast, the solution of that problem had eluded him, though he had no doubts that he would be given inspiration at the appointed time.

Now, looking at that tower, which he knew to be an ornament of the Presidential Palace, only a stone's throw away, the required inspiration came; and he acted upon it at once, branching off to his left in the direction of the tower.

It was one of those gay and reckless, dare-devil and foolhardy, utterly preposterous and wholly delightful impulses which the Saint could never resist. The breath-taking impudence of it was, to his way of thinking, the chief reason for taking it seriously; the suicidal odds against success were a conclusive argument for having a fling at bringing off the lone hundred-to-one chance; the monumental nerve that was plainly needed for turning the entertaining idea into a solemn fact was a challenge to his adventurousness that it was simply unthinkable to ignore. The Saint took up the gauntlet without the faintest hesitation.

For this was the full effrontery of his decision.

'Eventually,' whispered the Saint, to his secret soul – 'why not now?'

And the Saintly smile in all its glory twitched his lips back from his white teeth . . .

His luck had been stupendous, and it augured well for the future. Decidedly it was his day. A clean getaway from the prison, with no alarm. And he reached the high wall surrounding the palace grounds unobserved. And only a dozen feet away from the walls grew a tall tree.

The Saint went up the tree like a monkey, to a big straight branch that stuck out horizontally fifteen feet from the ground. Measuring the distance, he jumped.

The leap took him on to the top of the wall. He steadied himself for a moment, and then jumped again, twelve feet down into the palace gardens.

He landed on his toes, as lightly as a panther, and went zigzagging over the lawn between the flower-beds like a Red Indian. The gardens were empty. There was no sound but the murmuring of bees in the sun and the soft rustle of the Saint's feet over the grass.

He ran across the deserted gardens and up some steps to a flagged terrace in the very shadow of the palace walls. Eight feet above the terrace hung a low balcony. The Saint took two steps and a jump, hung by his finger-tips for a second, and pulled himself quickly up and over the balustrade.

An open door faced him, and the room beyond was empty. The Saint walked in, and passed through to the corridor on the other side.

Here he was at a loss, for the geography of the palace was strange to him. He crept along, rather hesitantly, without a sound. In the space of a dozen yards there was another open door. Through it, as he passed, the Saint caught a glimpse of the room beyond, and what he saw brought him to a sudden standstill.

He tiptoed back to the doorway, and stood there at gaze.

It was a bathroom.

Only a year ago that bathroom had been fitted up at enormous cost for the delectation of the Saturday nights of His Excellency the President and the Minister of the Interior. A gang of workmen specially sent down by a New York firm of contractors had affixed those beautiful sky-blue tiles to the walls, and laid those lovely sea-green tiles on the floor, and installed that superlative pale green porcelain bath with its gleaming silver taps and showers and other gadgets. Paris had supplied the great crystal jar of bath salts which stood on the window-sill, and the new cakes of expensive soap in the dishes.

The Saint's glistening eyes swept the room.

It was not Saturday, but it seemed as if someone was making a departure from the usual habits of the palace household. On a rack above the wash-basin were laid out razor, shaving-soap, and brush. On a chair beside the bath were snowy towels. On another chair, in a corner, were clothes – a spotless silk shirt, a sash, wide-bottomed Mexican trousers braided with gold, shoes . . .

For a full minute the Saint stared, struck dumb with wonder at his astounding good fortune. Then, in fear and trembling, he stole into the room and turned on a tap.

The water ran hot.

He hesitated no longer. War, revolution, battle, murder, and sudden death meant nothing to him then. He closed the door, and turned the key.

Blessings, like misfortunes, never come singly. There was even a packet of Havana cigarettes and a box of matches tucked away behind the bath salts . . .

Ten minutes later, already shaved, the Saint was stretched full length in a steaming bath into which he had emptied the best part of the Presidential jar of bath salts, innocently playing submarines with the sponge and a cake of soap.

A cigarette was canted jauntily up between his lips, and he was without a care in the world.

8

Archie Sheridan mopped his moist forehead and smacked viciously at a mosquito which was gorging itself on his bare forearm.

'Thank the Lord you're back,' he said. 'This blistered place gives me the creeps. Have you fixed anything?'

Kelly settled ponderously on the spread groundsheet.

'I have arranged the invadin' army,' he said. 'Anything come through while I've been away?'

'Nothing that matters. One or two private messages, which I duly acknowledged. I wonder what they're thinking at the Ondia end of the line.'

'There'll be a breakdown gang along some time,' pronounced Kelly. 'It's now the second day of the wire bein' cut. Within the week, maybe, they'll wake up and send to repair it. What's the time?'

Sheridan consulted his watch.

'A quarter-past eleven,' he said.

They sat under a great tree, in a small clearing in the jungle near the borders of Maduro, some ten miles east of Esperanza. A mile away was the rough track which led from Esperanza across the frontier to Maduro, and which formed the only road-link between the two countries; and there Kelly's Ford, in which they had made most of the journey, waited hidden between the trees at a little distance from the road.

But for all the evidence there was to the contrary they might have been a thousand miles from civilisation. At the edge of the tiny clearing colossal trees laced together with vines and creepers hemmed them in as with a gigantic palisade; high over their heads the entangled branches of the trees shut out the sky, and allowed no light to pass but a ghostly, grey twilight, in which the glaring crimsons and oranges and purples of the tropical blooms which flowered here and there in the marshy soil stood out with a shrieking violence.

Now and again, in the stillness of the great forest, there would be a rustle of the passing of some unseen wild thing. Under some prowling beast's paw, perhaps, a rotten twig would snap with a report like a rifle-shot. Sometimes the delirious chattering of a troop of monkeys would babble out with a startling shrillness that would have sent a shudder up the spine of an impressionable man. And the intervals of silence were not true silence, but rather a dim and indefinable and monotonous murmur punctuated with the sogging sound of dripping water. The air was hot and steamy and heavy with sickly perfumes.

'You get used to it,' said Kelly with a comprehensive wave of the stem of his pipe.

'Thanks,' said Sheridan. 'I'm not keen to. I've been here two days too long already. I have nightmares in which I'm sitting in an enormous bath, but as soon as I've finished washing a shower of mud falls on me and I have to start all over again.'

Now this was on the morning of the day in the afternoon of which the Saint escaped from prison.

On Sheridan's head were a pair of radio headphones. On the ground-sheet beside him was a little instrument, a Morse transmitter, which he had ingeniously fashioned before they left Santa Miranda. Insulated wires trailed away from him into the woods.

The telegraph line, for most of its length, followed the roads, but at that point, for some inexplicable reason, it took a shortcut across country. They had decided to attack it at that point on grounds of prudence; for, although the road between Esperanza and the Maduro frontier was not much used, there was always the risk of someone passing and commenting on their presence when he reached his destination.

The afternoon before, they had cut the line and sent through to Esperanza, to be relayed to Santa Miranda, the ultimatum purporting to come from the President of Maduro. Since then, night and day, one of them had sat with the receivers upon his ears, waiting for a reply. The arrangement was complicated, for Kelly could not read Morse, while Sheridan's Spanish was very haphazard; but they managed somehow. Several times when Archie had been resting Kelly had roused him to take down a message; but the translation had had no bearing on the threat of war, except occasionally from a purely private and commercial aspect. There had been no official answer.

Sheridan looked at his watch again.

'Their time's up in half an hour,' he said. 'What do you say to sending a final demand? – the "D" being loud and explosive, as in "Income Tax".'

'Shure – if there's no chance of 'em surrenderin',' agreed Kelly. 'But we can't let anything stop the war.'

The message they sent was worded with this in view:

Understand you refuse to release Quijote. Our armies will accordingly advance into Pasala at noon.

While they waited for zero hour, Kelly completed the task of breaking camp, strapping their tent and equipment into a workmanlike bundle. He finished this job just before twelve, and returned to his prostrate position on the ground-sheet.

'I wonder what that blackguard Shannet is doin'?' he said. 'I only hope he hasn't missed the news by takin' a thrip to the concession. It'd be unlucky for us if he had.'

'I think he'll be there,' said Sheridan. 'He was in Santa Miranda when we left, and he's likely to stay there and supervise the hunt for the Saint.'

'He's a good man, that,' said Kelly. 'It's a pity he's not an Irishman.'

Sheridan fanned himself with a handkerchief.

'He's one of the finest men that ever stepped,' he said. 'If the Saint said he was going to make war on Hell, I'd pack a fire extinguisher and go with him.'

Kelly sucked his pipe, and spat thoughtfully at an ant.

'That's not what I call your duty,' he remarked. 'In fact, I'm not sure that yez should have been in this at all, with a girl like Lilla watchin' for yez to come back, and worryin' her pretty head. And with a crawlin' sarpint like Shannet about . . .'

'He's tried to bother her once or twice. But if I thought—'

'I've been thinkin' a lot out here,' said Kelly. 'I'm not sayin' what I've thought. But it means that as soon as we've done what we're here to do we're goin' to hurry back to Santa Miranda as fast as Tin Lizzie'll take us. There's my missus an' Lilla without a man to look afther them; an' the Saint—'

Sheridan suddenly held up a hand for silence. He wrote rapidly on his little pad, and Kelly leaned over to read.

'What's it mean?'

'The war's on!' yelled Kelly ecstatically, 'Don Manuel ain't the quitter I thought he was or maybe he didn't see how he could get out of it. But the war's on! Hooroosh! There's goin' to be fightin'! Archie, me bhoy, the war's on!'

He seized Sheridan in a bear-hug of an embrace, swung him off the ground, dropped him, and went prancing around the clearing uttering wild Celtic cries. It was some minutes before he could be sobered sufficiently to give a translation of the message.

It was short and to the point :

'The Armies of Pasala will resist aggression to the death.'

Manuel Concepcion de Villega, being a civilian official, had thought this a particularly valiant and noble sentiment. In fact, he was so pleased with it that he used it to conclude his address to the Army when, with the President, he reviewed it before it rode out of Santa Miranda to meet the invaders. Of course the speech should have been made by the President, but His Excellency had no views on the subject.

At lunch-time the news came through from Esperanza that the enemy were attacking the town.

Although there had been ample warning, few of the inhabitants had left. The bulk of the population preferred to stay, secure in the belief that wars were the exclusive concern of the professional soldiers and had nothing to do with the general public, except for the inconvenience they might cause.

There was a small garrison stationed in the town, and they had barricaded the streets and settled down to await the attack. It came at about one o'clock.

The 'invading armies' which Kelly had prepared had been designed by Archie Sheridan, who was something of a mechanical genius.

In the woods on the east, three hundred yards from the front line of improvised fortifications, had been established a line of ten braziers of glowing charcoal, about twenty yards apart. Above each brazier was suspended a string of cartridges knotted at intervals of a few inches into a length of cord. The cord passed over the branch of a tree into which nails had been driven as guides. All these cords were gathered together in two batches of five each at a point some distance away, in such a way that one man, using both hands, could slowly lower the strings of cartridges simultaneously into all ten braziers, and so give the impression that there was firing over a front of two hundred yards. If they had had fireworks they could have saved themselves much trouble; but they had no fireworks, and Archie Sheridan was justly proud of his ingenious substitute.

Sheridan worked the 'invading armies,' while Kelly lay down behind a tree some distance away, sheltered from any stray bullets, and loaded his rifle. To complete the illusion it was necessary that the firing should seem to have some direction.

Sheridan, with a low whistle, signalled that he was ready, and the battle began.

The cartridges, lowered one by one into the braziers and there exploded by the heat, provided a realistic rattle up and down the line; while Kelly, firing and reloading like one possessed, sent bullets smacking into the walls of the houses and kicking up spurts of dust around the barricades. He took care not to aim anywhere where anyone might be hit.

The defence replied vigorously, though no one will ever know what they thought they were shooting at, and there were some spirited exchanges. When another whistle from Sheridan announced that the strings of cartridges were exhausted, Kelly rejoined him, and they crawled down to the road and the waiting Ford, and drove boldly towards the town, Kelly waving a nearly white flag.

The car was stopped, but Kelly was well known.

'They let me through their lines,' he explained to the officer of the garrison. 'That is why the firing has ceased. I was in Ondia when war was declared, and I came back at once.'

He told them that he was on his way to Santa Miranda.

'Then travel quickly, and urge them not to delay sending help,' said the officer, 'for it is clear that we are attacked by a tremendous number. I have sent telegraphs, but you can do more by telling them what you have seen.'

'I will do that,' promised Kelly, and they let him drive on.

As soon as the car was clear of the town he stopped and assisted Sheridan to unearth himself from under the pile of luggage; for, being now an outlaw, Sheridan had had to hide when they passed through the towns on the journey up, and it was advisable for him to do the same for most of the return.

A little farther down the road they stopped again, and Sheridan climbed a tree and cut the telegraph wires, so that the news of the fizzling out of the attack should not reach Santa Miranda in time for the troops that had been sent out to be recalled. Instead of organizing the 'invasion' they might have tapped the wire there and sent on messages from the commander of the garrison describing the progress of the battle, and so saved themselves much labour and thought; but the short road between Esperanza and Las Floras (the next town) was too well frequented for that to be practicable in broad daylight.

The Minister of the Interior was informed that it was no longer possible to communicate with Esperanza, and he could see only one explanation.

'Esperanza is surrounded,' he said. 'The garrison is less than a hundred. The town will fall in twenty-four hours, and the advancing armies of Maduro will meet our reinforcements at Las Floras. It will be a miracle if we can hold the invaders from Santa Miranda for five days.'

'You should have kept some troops here,' said Shannet. 'You have sent every soldier in Santa Miranda. Once that army is defeated there will be nothing for the invaders to overcome.'

'To-morrow I will recruit the *peónes*,' said Don Manuel. 'There must be conscription. Pasala requires the services of every able-bodied citizen. I will draft a proclamation to-night for the President to sign.'

It was then nearly five o'clock, but none of them had had a siesta that afternoon. They were holding another of many unprofitable conferences in a room in the palace, and it was significant that Shannet's right to be present was undisputed. The President himself was also there, biting his nails and stabbing the carpet nervously with the rowels of his spurs, but the other two took no notice of him. The President and de Villega were both still wearing the magnificent uniforms which they had donned for the review of the troops that morning.

Shannet paced the room, the inevitable limp unlighted cigarette drooping from his loose lower lip. His once-white ducks were as soiled and sloppy as ever. (Since they never became filthy, it is apparent that he must have treated himself to a clean suit occasionally, but nobody was ever allowed to notice this fact.) His unbrushed hair, as always, flopped over his right eye.

Since the day before, Shannet had had much to think about. Campard's amazing cable, attributing the war to a criminal gang, had arrived, and Shannet had replied with the required information. He had passed on the suggestion of his employer to the Minister for the Interior, pointing to the undoubtedly lawless behaviour of Sheridan and the unknown; but that two common outlaws could organise a war was a theory which de Villega refused to swallow.

'It is absurd,' he said. 'They are ordinary criminals. Two men cannot be a gang. In due time they will be caught, the man Sheridan will be imprisoned, and the man Mussolini will be hanged.'

Shannet, asked for the name of the man who had assaulted him, had replied indignantly: 'He told me his name was

Benito Mussolini!' Since then, he had been impelled to make several protests against the conviction of the officials that this statement was to be believed; but the idea had taken too firm a root, and Shannet had to give up the attempt.

But now he had an inspiration.

'There can be no harm in finding out,' he urged. 'Send for the *peón* that all the trouble is about, and let us question him.'

'I have a better idea than that,' exclaimed de Villega, jumping up. 'I will send the *peón* to the garotte to-morrow, for an encouragement to the people. They will enjoy the spectacle, and it will make them more ready to accept the proclamation of conscription. I will make a holiday—'

But Shannet's brain had suddenly taken to itself an amazing brilliance. In a flash it had soared above the crude and elementary idea of sending for the *peón* and forcing him to speak. He had no interest in de Villega's sadistic elaboration of the same idea. He had seen a much better solution than that.

9

Rapidly Shannet explained his inspiration to the others. It was as simple as all great inspirations. He was now firmly convinced in his mind that Sheridan and the Unknown were at the bottom of all the trouble, and this belief was strengthened by the fact that no trace of them had been found since their escape, although both police and military had searched for them. Some of the things that the Unknown had said – before and after the interlude in which words were dispensed with – came back to Shannet with a dazzling clarity. It all fitted in.

And ready to his hand lay the key to the trap in which he was in. He saw that what the Unknown had started the Unknown could stop. It was Campard's own idea, but Shannet was more conveniently placed to apply it than his master had been. Also, he had the necessary lever within a few minutes' reach.

Lilla McAndrew.

She was the master card. Sheridan, he knew, was infatuated. And Sheridan was an important accomplice of the Unknown. With Lilla McAndrew for a hostage Shannet could dictate his own terms.

'I know I have reason!' Shannet said vehemently, while he inwardly cursed the limitations of his Spanish, which prevented him driving his ideas home into the thick skulls of his audience more forcibly. 'I know well the *Señor* Campard, for whom I have worked for years. Perhaps it sounds fantastic to you, but I know that he is not an easy man to frighten. If I had suggested this to him myself, that these two men could have plotted a war, he would have laughed me to scorn. But he has said it of his own accord, therefore I know that he must have some information.'

'I think everyone has gone mad,' said de Villega helplessly. 'But you may proceed with your plan. At least it can do no harm. But I warn you that it is on your own responsibility. The *Señorita* McAndrew is a British subject, and questions may be asked. Then I shall say that I know nothing of it; and, if the authorities demand it, you will have to be handed over to them.'

It was significant of the way in which Shannet's prestige had declined since the commencement of the war for which de Villega was inclined to blame him; but Shannet did not care. 'I will take the risk,' he said, and was gone.

In the Palace courtyard his horse was still being held by a patient soldier – one of the half-dozen left behind to guard the palace. Shannet clambered into the saddle and galloped out as the gates were opened for him by a sentry.

His first course took him to an unsavoury café at the end of the town, where he knew he would find the men he needed. He enrolled two. They were pleased to call themselves 'guides,' but actually they were half-caste cut-throats available for anything from murder upwards. Shannet knew them, for he had used their services before.

He explained what he wanted and produced money. There was no haggling. In ten minutes the three were riding out of the town.

Kelly, too late, had thought of that very possibility, as he had hinted to Sheridan in the jungle clearing that morning. But Kelly and Sheridan were still twenty miles away.

And the Saint, in the President's palatial bathroom, was leisurely completing the process of dressing himself in the clean clothes which he had found. They fitted him excellently.

Meanwhile, the men whom Shannet had left in conference were receiving an unpleasant surprise.

'God!' thundered de Villega. 'How did this *peón* escape?'

'Excellency,' said the abashed governor of the prison, 'it was during the siesta. The man fell down moaning and writhing as if he would die. The warder went to attend him, and the man grasped him by the throat so that he could not cry out, throttled him into unconsciousness, and bound and gagged him. He also surprised the gatekeeper, and hit him in the English fashion—'

De Villega let out an exclamation.

'What meanest thou, pig – "in the English fashion"?'

The governor demonstrated the blow which the gatekeeper had described. It was, in fact, the simple left uppercut of the boxer, and no Latin-American who has not been infected with our methods ever hits naturally like that.

'What manner of man was this *peón*?' demanded Don Manuel, with understanding dawning sickeningly into his brain.

'Excellency, he was tall for a *peón*, and a man of the strength of a lion. If he had washed he would have been handsome, with an aristocratic nose that such a man could hardly have come by legitimately. And he had very white teeth and blue eyes—'

'Blue eyes!' muttered de Villega dazedly for, of course, to the Latin, all Englishmen have blue eyes.

He turned to the governor with sudden ferocity.

'*Carajo*!' he screamed. 'Imbecile, dost thou not know whom thou hast let slip through thy beastly fingers? Dost thou not even know whom thou hast had in thy charge these three days?'

He thumped upon the table with his fist, and the governor trembled.

'Couldst thou not recognise him, cross-eyed carrion?' he screeched. 'Couldst thou not see that he was no true *peón*? Maggot, hast thou not heard of the outlaw Benito Mussolini, for whom the *rurales* have searched in vain while he sheltered safely in the prison under thy gangrenous eyes?'

'I am a worm, and blind, Excellency,' said the cringing man tactfully, for he knew that any excuse he attempted to make would only infuriate the Minister further.

De Villega strode raging up and down the room. Now he believed Shannet, wild and far-fetched as the latter's theory had seemed when he had first heard it propounded. The news of the prisoner's escape, and the – to Don Manuel – sufficient revelation of his real identity, provided incontrovertible proof that the fantastic thing was true.

'He must be recaptured at once!' snapped de Villega. 'Every *guardia* in Santa Miranda must seek him without rest day or night. The *peónes* must be pressed into the hunt. The State will pay a reward of five thousand pesos to the man who brings him to me, alive or dead. As for thee, offal,' he added, turning with renewed malevolence upon the prison governor, if Sancho Quijote, or Benito Mussolini – whatever he calls himself – is not delivered to me in twelve hours I will cast thee into thine own prison to rot there until he is found.'

'I will give the orders myself, Excellency,' said the governor, glad of an excuse to make his escape, and bowed his way to the door.

He went out backwards, and, as he closed the door, the Saint pinioned his arms from behind, and allowed the point of his little knife to prick his throat.

'Make no sound,' said the Saint, and lifted the man bodily off his feet.

He carried the governor down the passage, the knife still at his throat, and took him into a room that he had already marked down in his explorations. It was a bedroom. The

Saint deposited the man on the floor, sat on his head, and tore a sheet into strips, with which he bound and gagged him securely.

'I will release you as soon as the revolution is over,' the Saint promised, with a mocking bow.

Then he walked back to the other room and entered softly, closing the door behind him. De Villega was penning the announcement of the reward, and it was the President who first noticed the intruder and uttered a strangled yap of startlement.

Don Manuel looked up, and loosed an oath. He sprang to his feet, upsetting the ink-pot and his chair, as if an electric current had suddenly been applied to him.

'Who are you?' he demanded in a cracked voice, though he had guessed the answer.

'You know me best as Benito Mussolini, or Sancho Quijote,' said the Saint. 'My friends – and enemies – sometimes call me El Santo. And I am the father of the revolution.'

He lounged lazily against the door, head back, hands rested carelessly on his hips. The Saint was himself again, clean and fresh from razor and bath, his hair combed smoothly back. The clothes he had appropriated suited him to perfection. The Saint had the priceless gift of being able to throw on any old thing and look well in it, but few things could have matched his mood and personality better than the buccaneering touch there was about the attire that had been more or less thrust upon him.

The loose, full-sleeved shirt, the flaring trousers, the scarlet sash – the Saint wore these romantic trappings with a marvellous swashbuckling air, lounging there with a reckless and piratical elegance, a smile on his lips . . .

Seconds passed before the Minister came out of his trance. 'Revolution?'

De Villega echoed the word involuntarily, and the Saint bowed.

'I am the revolution,' he said, 'and I have just started. For my purpose I arranged that the Army should leave Santa Miranda, so that I should have nothing to deal with but a few officials, yourselves, and a handful of *guardias*. Wonderful as I am, I could not fight an army.'

'Fool!' croaked Don Manuel, in a voice that he hardly knew as his own. 'The Army will return, and then you will be shot.'

'Permit me to disagree,' said the Saint. 'The Army will return, certainly. It will be to find a new Government in power. The Army is the servant of the State, not of one man, nor even of one Government. Of course, on their return, the soldiers would be free to begin a second revolution to overthrow the new Government if they disliked it. But I do not think they will do that, particularly as the new Government is going to increase their pay. Observe the subtle difference. To have attempted to bribe the Army to support a revolution would have been treason, and rightly resented by all patriotic citizens; but to signalise the advent of the new Constitution by a bonus in cash to the Army is an act of grace and generosity, and will be rightly appreciated.'

'And the people?' said Don Manuel, as in a dream.

'Will they weep to see you go? I think not. You have crushed them with taxes – we shall liberate them. They could have liberated themselves, but they had not the initiative to begin. Now I give them a lead, and they will follow.'

The Saint straightened up off the door. His blue eyes, with a sparkle of mischief in them, glanced from the Minister for the Interior to the President, and back to the Minister for the Interior again. His right hand came off his hip in a commanding gesture.

'*Señores*,' he said, 'I come for your resignations.'

The President came to his feet, bowed, and stood to attention.

'I will write mine at once, *Señor*,' he said hurriedly. 'It is plain that Pasala no longer needs me.'

It was the speech of his life, and the Saint swept him a low bow of approval.

'I thank your Excellency!' he said mockingly.

'Half-wit!' snarled de Villega over his shoulder. 'Let me handle this!'

He thrust the President back and came round the table.

A sword hung at his side, and on the belt of his ceremonial uniform was a revolver holster. He stood before the Saint, one hand on the pommel of his sword, the other fiddling with the little strap which secured the flap of the holster. His dark eyes met Simon Templar's bantering gaze.

'Already the revolution is accomplished?' he asked.

'I have accomplished it,' said Templar.

De Villega raised his left hand to stroke his moustache.

'*Señor*,' he said, 'all this afternoon we have sat in this room, which overlooks the front courtyard of the palace. Beyond, as you know, is the Calle del Palacio. Yet we have heard no commotion. Is a people that has been newly liberated too full of joy to speak?'

'When the people hear of their liberation,' said the Saint, 'you will hear their rejoicing.'

De Villega's eyes glittered under his black brows.

'And your friends, *Señor*?' he pursued. 'The other liberators? They have, perhaps, surrounded the palace and overcome the guards without an alarm being raised or a shot fired?'

The Saint laughed.

'Don Manuel,' he said, 'you do me an injustice. I said I was the father of the revolution. Can a child have two fathers? Alone, Don Manuel, I accomplished it – yet you persist in speaking of my private enterprise as if it were the work of a hundred. Will you not give me the full credit for what I have done?'

De Villega stepped back a pace.

'So,' he challenged, 'the people do not know. The palace guards do not know. The Army does not know. Will you tell me who does know?'

'Our three selves,' said the Saint blandly. 'Also two friends of mine who organised the war for me. And the governor of the prison, whom I captured on his way to mobilise the guardias against me. It is very simple. I intend this to be a bloodless revolution, for I am against unnecessary killing. You will merely resign, appointing a new Government in your places, and leave Pasala at once, never to return again on pain of death.'

The holster was now undone, and de Villega's fingers were sliding under the flap.

'And you – alone – demand that?'

'I do,' said the Saint, and leapt at de Villega as the revolver flashed from its place.

With one arm he grasped Don Manuel around the waist, pinning his left arm to his side; with his left hand he gripped Don Manuel's right wrist, forcing it back, and twisting.

The President sprang forward, but it was all over in a couple of seconds. The revolver exploded twice, harmlessly, into the floor, and then fell with a clatter as the Saint's grip became too agonising to be borne.

The Saint hurled de Villega from him, into the President's very arms, and as de Villega staggered back his sword grated out of its sheath and remained in the Saint's right hand. The President's revolver was half-way out of its holster when the Saint let him feel the sword at his breast.

'Drop it!' ordered Simon.

The President obeyed.

Templar forced the two men back to the wall at the sword's point. Then he turned quickly, using the sword to fish up the two revolvers from the floor by their trigger-guards, and turned again to halt their immediate rally with the guns impaled on his blade.

From below, through the open windows, came the shouting of the sentries, and the sound of running feet thundered in the passage outside the room.

Like lightning the Saint detached the revolvers from his sword, and held them one in each hand. They covered their owners with an equal steadiness of aim.

The two shots that de Villega had fired, though they had hit no one, had done damage enough. They hadn't entered into the Saint's plan of campaign. He had betted on being quick enough to catch de Villega before he could get his hand to his gun in its cumbersome holster – and the Saint, for once, had been a fraction of a second slow on his timing. But the error might yet be repaired.

'You, Excellency, to the windows!' rapped the Saint in a low voice. 'You, de Villega, to the door! Reassure the guards. Tell them that the President was unloading his revolver when it accidentally exploded. The President will repeat the same thing from the window to the sentries below.'

He dodged out of sight behind the door as it burst open, but there was no mistaking the menace of the revolvers which he still focused on the two men.

The President was already addressing the sentries below. De Villega, with one savagely impotent glance at the unfriendly muzzle that was trained upon him, followed suit, giving the Saint's suggested explanation to the guards who crowded into the doorway.

'You may go,' he concluded. 'No harm has been done. But remain within call – I may need you shortly.'

It required some nerve to add that last remark, in the

circumstances, but de Villega thought that the Saint would not betray his presence with a shot if he could possibly help it. He was right. The President came back from the window. The guards withdrew, with apologies for their excited irruption, and the door closed. The Saint slid the bolt into its socket.

'A wise precaution, Don Manuel, to warn the guards that you might need them,' he said. 'But I do not think it will help you.'

He stuck the revolvers into his sash and picked up the sword again. It was a better weapon for controlling two men than his little knife, and much quieter than the revolvers.

'Your resignations or your lives, *señores*?' said the Saint briskly. 'I will take whichever you prefer to give, but I must have one or the other at once.'

De Villega sat down at the table, but did not write. He unbuttoned his coat, fished out a packet of cigarettes, and lighted one, blowing out a great cloud of smoke. Through it he looked at the Saint, and his lips had twisted into a sneering grin.

'I have another thing to offer, *Señor*,' he remarked viciously, 'which you might prefer to either of the things you have mentioned.'

'*Es decir*?' prompted Simon, with a frowning lift of his eyebrows.

De Villega inhaled again with relish, and let the smoke trickle down from his nostrils in two long feathers. There was a glow of taunting triumph in his malignant stare.

'There is the *Señorita* McAndrew,' he said, and the Saint's face suddenly went very meek.

'What of her?'

'It was the *Señor* Shannet,' said de Villega, enjoying his moment, 'who first suggested that you were the man behind the war. We did not believe him, but now I see that he is a wise man. He left us over half an hour ago to take her as hostage. You gave me no chance to explain that when the guards entered the room just now. But I told them to remain within call for that reason – so that I could summon them as soon as you surrendered. Now it is my turn to make an offer. Stop this war, and deliver yourself and your accomplices to justice, and I will save the *Señorita* McAndrew. Otherwise—'

Don Manuel shrugged. 'Am I answerable for the affections of the *Señor* Shannet?'

A throaty chuckle of devilish merriment shook him, and he bowed to the motionless Saint with a leering mock humility.

'I, in my turn, await your decision, *Señor*,' he said.

10

The Saint leaned on his sword.

He was cursing himself for the fool he was. Never before in his career had he been guilty of such an appalling lapse. Never would he have believed that he could have been capable of overlooking the probability of such an obvious counter-attack. Now his brain was whirling like the flywheel of a great dynamo, and he was considering, calculating, readjusting, summarising everything in the light of this new twist that de Villega had given to the affair. Yet his face showed nothing of the storm behind it.

'And how do I know that you will keep your bargain?' he asked.

'You do not know,' replied de Villega brazenly. 'You only know that, if you do not agree to my terms, the *Señor* Shannet will certainly take reprisals. I offer you a hope.'

So that was the strength of it. And, taken by and large, it didn't strike the Saint as a proposition to jump at. It offered him. exactly nothing – except the opportunity to go nap on Don Manuel's honour and Shannet's generosity, two bets which no one could have called irresistibly attractive. Also, it involved Kelly and Sheridan, who hadn't been consulted. And it meant, in the end, that all three of them would most certainly be executed, whatever de Villega decided to do about Lilla McAndrew, whom Shannet would probably claim, and be allowed, as a reward for his share in suppressing the revolution. No . . .

Where were Kelly and Sheridan? The Saint was reckoning it out rapidly, taking into consideration the age of Kelly's Ford and the reported abominable state of the roads between Esperanza and Santa Miranda. And, checking his calculation over, the Saint could only get one answer, which was that Kelly and Sheridan were due to arrive at any minute. They would learn of the abduction . . .

'The *Señora* Kelly?' asked the Saint. 'What about her?'

De Villega shrugged.

'She is of no importance.'

Yes, Mrs. Kelly would be left behind – if she had not been shot. She was middle-aged and stout and past her attractiveness, and no one would have any interest in abducting her. So that Kelly and Sheridan, arriving at the bungalow, would hear the tale from her.

And then – there was no doubt about it – they would come storming down to the palace, *guardias* and sentries notwithstanding, with cold murder in their hearts.

The Saint came erect, and de Villega looked up expectantly. But there was no sign of surrender in the Saint's poise, and nothing relenting about the way in which he stepped up to the Minister and set the point of the sword at his breast.

'I said I came for your resignations,' remarked the Saint with a deadly quietness. 'That was no idle talk. Write now, de Villega, or, by the vixen that bore thee, thou diest!'

'Fool! Fool!' Don Manuel raved. 'It cannot help you!'

'I take the risk,' said the Saint icily. 'And do not speak so loud – I might think you were trying to attract the attention of the guards. Write!'

He thrust the sword forward the half of an inch, and de Villega started back with a cry.

'You would murder me?'

'With pleasure,' said the Saint. 'Write!'

Then there was sudden silence, and everyone was quite still, listening. For from the courtyard below the windows came the rattle of urgent hoofs.

The Saint leapt to the windows. There were three horses held by the sentries. He saw Shannet and two other men dismounting – and saw, being lifted down from Shannet's saddlebow, Lilla McAndrew with her hands tied.

He could have shouted for joy at the justification of his bold defiance. And yet, if he had thought a little longer, he might have foreseen that the girl would be brought to the palace. She was not the victim of Shannet's privateering, but an official hostage. But even if the Saint hadn't foreseen it, there it was, and he could have prayed for nothing better. He saw all the trump cards coming into his hands . . .

Then he whipped round, in time to frustrate de Villega's stealthy attack, and the Minister's raised arm dropped to his side.

The Saint speared the sword into the floor and slipped the revolvers out of his sash. For the second time he dodged behind the opening door. He saw the girl thrust roughly into the room, and Shannet followed, closing the door again behind him.

'Fancy meeting you again, honeybunch!' drawled the Saint, and Shannet spun round with an oath.

The Saint leaned against the wall, the Presidential and Ministerial revolvers in his hands. On his lips was a smile so broad as to be almost a laugh, and there was a laugh in his voice.

'Take that hand away from your hip, Shannet, my pet!' went on the Saint, in that laughing voice of sheer delight. 'I've got you covered – and even if I'm not very used to these toys, I could hardly miss you at this range . . . That's better . . . Oh, Shannet, my sweet and beautiful gargoyle, you're a bad boy, frightening that child. Take the cords off her wrists, my angel . . . No, *Señor* de Villega, you needn't edge towards that sword. I may want it again myself in a minute. *Gracias*! . . . Is that more comfortable, Lilla, old dear?'

'Oh,' cried the girl, 'thank God you're here! Where's Archie?'

'On his way, old darling, on his way, as the actress said of the bishop,' answered the Saint, 'Are you all right?'

She shuddered a little.

'Yes, I'm all right,' she said. 'Except for the touch of his filthy hands. But I was very frightened . . .'

'Archie will deal with that when he arrives,' said the Saint. 'It's his business – he'd never forgive me if I interfered. Come here, my dear, keeping well out of the line of fire, while I deal with the specimens. I'm not the greatest revolver shot in the world, and I want to be sure that it won't matter who I hit.'

He steered her to safety in a corner, and turned to Don Manuel.

'When we were interrupted,' said the Saint persuasively, 'you were writing. The interruption has now been disposed of. Proceed, *Señor*!'

De Villega lurched back to the table, the fight gone out of him. He could never have envisaged such an accumulation and culmination of misfortunes. It was starting to seem to him altogether like a dream, a nightmare rather – but there was nothing ethereal about the revolver that was levelled so steadily at him. The only fantastic part of the whole catastrophe was the man who had engineered it – the Saint himself, in his extraordinary borrowed clothes, and the hell-for-leather light of laughing recklessness in his blue eyes. That was the last bitter pill which De Villega had to swallow. He might perhaps have endured defeat by a man whom he could understand – a cloaked and sinister conspirator with a personality of impressive grimness. But this lunatic who laughed . . . *Que diablos*! It was impossible . . .

And then, from outside, drifted a grinding, screaming, metallic rattle that could only be made by one instrument in the world.

'Quick!' said the Saint. 'Slither round behind Master Shannet, Lilla, darling, and slip the gat out of his hip pocket . . . That's right . . . Now d'you mind sticking up the gang for a sec. while I bail the troops? Blaze away if anybody gets funny.'

The girl handled Shannet's automatic as if she'd been born with her finger crooked round a trigger, and the Saint, with a nod of approval, crossed over to the window.

Kelly's Ford was drawn up in the courtyard, and both Kelly and Sheridan were there. Kelly was just disposing of a sentry who had ventured to question his right of way.

'Walk right in, souls!' the Saint hailed them cheerily. 'You're in time to witness the abdication of the Government.'

'Have you seen Lilla?' shouted a frantic Sheridan.

The Saint grinned.

'She's safe here, son.'

The report of an automatic brought him round with a jerk.

With the Saint's back turned, and the Saint's victory now an accomplished fact, Shannet had chanced everything on one mad gamble against the steadiness of nerve and aim of the girl who for a moment held the situation in her small hands. While Lilla McAndrew's attention was distracted by the irresistible impulse to try to hear what Archie Sheridan was saying he had sidled closer . . . made one wild leaping grab . . . missed . . .

The Saint stooped over the still figure and made a swift examination. He straightened up with a shrug, picking up his revolvers again as the first of the guards burst into the room.

'Quietly, *amigos*,' he urged; and they saw sudden death in each of his hands, and checked.

The next instant the crowd stirred again before the berserk rush of Archie Sheridan, who had heard the shot as he raced up the palace steps. A yard behind him followed Kelly, breaking through like a bull, his red head flaming above the heads of the guards.

'All clear, Archie!' called the Saint. 'It was Shannet who got it.'

But Lilla McAndrew was already in Archie Sheridan's arms.

'Here, Kelly,' rapped the Saint. 'Let's get this over. Take these guns and keep the guards in order while I dispose of the Government.'

Kelly took over the weapons, and the Saint stepped back and wrenched the sword out of the floor. He advanced towards the President and de Villega, who stood paralysed by the table.

'You have written?' he asked pleasantly.

De Villega passed over a piece of paper, and the Saint read it and handed it back.

'You have omitted to nominate your successors,' he said. 'That will be the *Señor* Kelly and those whom he appoints to help him. Write again.'

'Half a minute,' Kelly threw back over his shoulder, with his eyes on the shuffling guards. 'I don't fancy being President myself – it's too risky. I'll be Minister for the Interior, and the President can stay on, if he behaves himself.'

The President bowed.

'I am honoured, *Señor*,' he assented with alacrity.

'Write accordingly,' ordered the Saint, and it was done.

The Saint took the document and addressed the guards.

'By this,' he said, 'you know that the President dismisses *Señor* Manuel Concepcion de Villega, the Minister for the Interior, and his Government, and appoints the *Señor* Kelly in his place. To celebrate his appointment, the *Señor* Kelly will in a few days announce the removal of a number of taxes which have hitherto oppressed you. Now take this paper and cause it to be embodied in a proclamation to the free people of Pasala. Let to-morrow be a public holiday and a day of rejoicing for this reason, and also because it is now proved that there is no war with Maduro. That was a rumour spread by certain malicious persons for their own ends. See that a radiogram is sent to Estados Unidos, explaining that, and saying that they may recall the warship they were sending. You may go, *amigos*.'

There was a silence of a few seconds; and then, as the full meaning of the Saint's speech was grasped, the room rang and echoed again to a great crash of *Vivas*!

When Kelly had driven the cheering guards out into the passage and closed the door in their faces, Simon Templar thought of something and had the door opened again to send for the governor of the prison. The man was brought quickly.

'*Señor*,' said the Saint. 'I apologise for the way I treated you just now. It happened to be necessary. But the revolution is now completed, and you are a free man. I bear you no malice – although I am going to insist that you disinfect your prison.'

He explained the circumstances, and the prison governor bowed almost to the floor.

'It is nothing, *ilustrisimo Señor*' he said. 'But if I had known I would have seen to it that your honour was given better accommodation. Another time, perhaps . . .'

'God forbid,' said the Saint piously.

Then he turned and pointed to the now terrified de Villega.

'Take this man with you,' he directed. 'He is to leave Pasala by the next boat and meantime he is to be closely guarded. He will probably attempt either to fight or to bribe his escape. My answer to that is that if he is not delivered to me when I send for him, your life and the lives of all your warders will answer for it.'

'It is understood, *señor*.'

Kelly watched the departure of the governor and his prisoner open-mouthed; and when they were gone he turned to the Saint with a blank expression.

'Look here,' he said, as if the thought had just struck him – 'where's all this fightin' I've been told so much about?'

The Saint smiled.

'There is no fighting,' he said. 'This has been what I hoped it would be – a bloodless revolution. It was undertaken in the name of a justice which the law could not administer, to ruin a man more than six thousand miles away, back in London, England. He had ruined thousands, but the law could not touch him. This was my method. Your first duty as Minister for the Interior will be to revoke the original oil concession and to make out a fresh one, assigning the rights, in perpetuity, to Miss McAndrew and her heirs.' He laid a hand on Kelly's shoulder. 'I'm sorry to give you such a disappointment, son; and if you must have a fight, I'll have a round or two with you myself before dinner. But I had to do it this way. Any other kind of revolution would have meant the sacrifice of many lives, and I didn't really want that.'

For a moment Kelly was silent and perplexed before the Saint's sudden seriousness; then he shrugged, and laughed, and took Simon Templar's hand in a huge grip.

'I don't confess to know what yez are talkin' about,' he said. 'And I don't care. I suppose it's been worth it – if only to see the look on de Villega's ugly face whin yez sent him to prison. And, anyway, a laughin' devil who can run a show like yez have run this one deserves to be allowed to work things his own way.'

'Good scout!' smiled the Saint. 'Was Mrs. Kelly all right?'

'A bit scared, but no harm done. It was Lilla she was afraid for. They just tied the missus up in a chair and left her. An' that reminds me – there was a cable waitin' for me up at the bungalow, and I can't make head or tail of it. Maybe it's something to do with you.'

Kelly fumbled in his pocket and produced the form. The Saint took it over, and one glance told him that it was meant for him.

'It's from an agent of mine in London,' he explained. 'He wouldn't have addressed it to Archie or me in case anything had gone wrong and it was intercepted,'

He knew the code almost perfectly, and he was able to write the translation in between the lines at once.

P.O.P.s down trumped twelve thousand. –

The Saint wrote :

P.O.P.s fell heavily. Cleared twelve thousand pounds. Campard committed suicide this morning.

It was signed with the name of Roger Conway.

'Archie!' called the Saint, thoughtfully; and again: 'Archie!'

'They sneaked out minutes ago,' said Kelly. 'She's a sweet girl, that Lilla McAndrew . . .'

And it was so, until evening.

And at even the Saint went forth and made a tour of a number of disreputable cafés, in each of which he bought much liquor for the clientele. They did not recognise him until he started to sing – a strange and barbarous song that no one could understand. But they recognised it, having heard it sung before, with many others like it, by a certain *peón*:

> 'The bells of Hell go ting-a-ling-a-ling.
> For you but not for me;
> For me the angels sing-a-ling-a-ling,
> They've got the goods for me—'

To this day you will hear that song sung by the peasants of Santa Miranda. And if you should ask one of them why he sings it, he will answer, with a courteous surprise at your ignorance, 'That, *Señor*, is one of the songs of freedom . . .'

The Man Who Could Not Die

INTRODUCTION FROM
PAGING THE SAINT, 1945:

If (as has unfortunately been observed in certain circles) I have failed to become the supreme maestro of the whodunit in my generation, I can at least truthfully plead that this is because I never seriously tried.

I have written some whodunits, but not very many, and not all of them very good. But most of the time I have tried to exploit a mutation which you might call the 'whatisit'.

I think it was G. K. Chesterton who first claimed in a loud voice that the short story was the only satisfactory length for a whodunit, because beyond that length it was exasperating to have to contend with an entire cast of characters with masks on, clad in deceptive raiment, speaking with disguised voices in studied ambiguities, and generally attempting to give false impressions, whatever their true characters might be, entirely for the selfish purposes of the author.

It was this cogent argument which turned my interest to the whatisit, the story in which we have no serious doubt, if any doubt at all, as to the identity of the prime villain. Our problem is to discover the facts and form of his villainy, or to find means to punish him, or to circumvent his menace to the happiness of our preferred characters.

Maxwell Smith, I believe, was one of the early proponents of this style of literary architecture in the popular detective magazines – the business of frankly presenting Desperate Desmond at the outset and centering reader interest on the task of bringing him to book through the untiring efforts of Handsome Harry. And a nice job he did of it. Of course, the classic example of this design is Hugo's *Les Miserables*, in which the indefatigable Monsieur Javért dogged the footsteps of Jean Valjean to the end of the chapter.

This yarn is one of my own first experiments with this pattern, and for that reason it may be of some interest to you tireless antiquarians.

I

Patricia Holm raised her fair, pretty head from *The Times*.

'What,' she asked, 'is an obiter dictum?'

'A form of foot-and-mouth disease,' said the Saint, glibly. 'Obiter – one who obits; dictum – a shirt-front. Latin. Very difficult.'

'Fool,' said his lady.

The Saint grinned, and pushed back his chair. Breakfast was over; a blaze of summer sunshine was pouring through the open windows into the comfortable room; the first and best cigarette of the day was canted up between the Saint's smiling lips; all was right with the world.

'What's the absorbing news, anyway?' he inquired lazily.

She passed him the paper; and, as is the way of these things, the matter which had given rise to her question was of the most ephemeral interest – and yet it interested the Saint. Simon Templar had always been the despair of all those of his friends who expected him to produce intelligent comments upon the affairs of the day; to read a newspaper not only bored him to extinction, but often gave him an actual physical pain. Therefore it followed, quite naturally, that when the mood seized him to glance at a newspaper, he usually managed to extract more meat from that one glance than the earnest, regular student of the Press extracts from years of daily labour.

It so happened that morning. Coincidence, of course, but how much adventure is free from all taint of coincidence?

Coincidences are always coinciding, it is one of their peculiar attributes; but the adventure is born of what the man makes of his coincidences. Most people say : 'How odd!'

Simon Templar said: 'Well, well, well!'

But *The Times* really hadn't anything exciting to say that morning; and certainly the column that Patricia had been reading was one of the most sober of all the columns of that very respectable newspaper, for it was one of the columns in which such hardy annuals as Paterfamilias, Lieut.-Colonel (retired), Pro Bono Publico, Mother of Ten, unto the third and fourth generation, Abraham and his seed for ever, let loose their weary bleats upon the world. The gentleman ('Diehard') who had incorporated an obiter dictum in his effort was giving tongue on the subject of motorists. It was, as has been explained, pure coincidence that he should have written with special reference to a recent prosecution for dangerous driving in which the defendant had been a man in whom the Saint had the dim beginnings of an interest.

'Aha!' said the Saint, thoughtful like.

'Haven't you met that man – Miles Hallin?' Patricia said. 'I've heard you mention his name.'

'And that's all I've met up to date,' answered the Saint. 'But I have met a bird who talks about nothing else but Miles. Although I suppose, in the circumstances, that isn't as eccentric as it sounds.'

He had, as a matter of fact, met Nigel Perry only a fortnight before, by a slightly roundabout route. Simon Templar, being in a club in Piccadilly which for some unknown reason allowed him to continue his membership, had discovered that he was without a handkerchief. His need being vital, he had strolled over to a convenient shop – without troubling to put on a hat. The rest of the story, he insisted, was Moyna Stanford's fault. Simon had bought his handkerchief, and the shop assistant had departed towards the cashier with the

Saint's simoleons, when Moyna Stanford walked in, walked straight up to the Saint, and asked if he could show her some ties. Now, Moyna Stanford was very good to look upon, and there were quantities of ties prominently displayed about the shop, and the Saint could never resist anything like that. He had shown her several ties. The rightful tie-exhibitor had returned. There had been some commotion. Finally, they had lunched together. Not including the tie-exhibitor.

The rest of the story, as the Saint retailed it to Patricia Holm, was perfectly true. He had met Nigel Perry, and had liked him immediately – a tall, dark, cheery youngster, with a million-dollar smile and a two-figure bank balance. The second of those last two items Simon had not discovered until later. On the other hand, it was not very much later, for Nigel Perry had nothing approaching an inferiority complex. He talked with an engaging frankness about himself, his job, his prospects, and his idols. The idols were, at that moment, two – Moyna Stanford and Miles Hallin. It is likely that Simon Templar was shortly added to the list; perhaps in the end he headed the list – on the male side. But at the time of meeting Miles Hallin reigned supreme.

The Saint was familiar with the name of Hallin, and he was interested in the story that Nigel Perry had to tell, for all such stories were interesting to the Saint.

At that breakfast-table, under the shadow of an irrelevant obiter dictum, Simon explained.

'Hallin's a much older man, of course. Nigel had a brother who was about Hallin's age. Years ago Hallin and the elder Perry were prospecting some godless bit of desert in Australia. What's more, they found real gold. And at the same time they found that one of their water-barrels had sprung a leak, and there was only enough water to get one of them back to civilisation. They tossed for it – and for once in his life Hallin lost. They shook hands, and Perry pushed off. After Perry had been gone some time, Hallin decided that if he sat down on the gold mine waiting to die he'd go mad first. So he made up his mind to die on the move. It didn't occur to him to shoot himself – he just wouldn't go out that way. And he upped his pack and shifted along in a different direction from the one that Perry had taken. Of course he found a water-hole, and then he found another water-hole, and he got out of the desert at last. But Perry never got out. That's just a sample of Hallin's luck.'

'And what happened to the gold?'

'Hallin registered the claim. When he got back to England he looked up young Nigel and insisted on giving him a half share. But it never came to much – about a couple of thousand, I believe. The lode petered out, and the mine closed down. Still, Hallin did the white thing. Taking that along with the rest, you can't blame Nigel for worshipping him.'

And yet the Saint frowned as he spoke. He had a professional vanity that was all his own, and something in that vanity reacted unfavourably towards Miles Hallin, whom a sensational journalist had once christened 'The Man Who Cannot Die.'

'Are you jealous?' teased Patricia; and the Saint scowled.

'I don't know,' he said.

But he knew perfectly well. Miles Hallin had cropped up, and Miles Hallin had spoilt a beautiful morning.

'It annoys me,' said the Saint, with what Patricia couldn't help thinking was an absurd pettishness. 'No man has a right to Hallin's reputation.'

'I've heard nothing against him.'

'Have you heard anything against me?'

'Lots of things.'

Simon grinned abstractedly.

'Yes, I know. But has anyone ever called me "The Man Who Cannot Die"?'

'Not when I've been listening.'

'It's not a matter of listening,' said the Saint 'That man Hallin is a sort of public institution. Everyone knows about his luck. Now, I should think I've had as much luck as anyone, and I've always been much bigger news than Hallin will ever be, but nobody's ever made a song and dance about that side of my claim to immortality.'

'They've had other things to say about you.'

The Saint sighed. He was still frowning.

'I know,' he said. 'But I have hunches, old darling. Let me say here and now that I have absolutely nothing against Hallin. I've never heard a word against him, I haven't one reasonable suspicion about him, I haven't one single solitary fact on which I could base a suspicion. But I'll give you one very subtle joke to laugh about. Why should a man boast that he can't die?'

'He didn't make the boast.'

'Well – I wonder? . . . But he certainly earned the name, and he's never given it a chance to be forgotten. He's capitalised it and played it up for all it's worth. So I can give you an even more subtle joke. It goes like this: "For whosoever will save his life shall lose it . . ."'

Patricia looked at him curiously. If she had not known the Saint so well, she would have looked at him impatiently; but she knew him very well.

She said: 'Let's hear what you mean, lad. I can't follow all your riddles.'

'And I can't always give the answers,' said the Saint.

His chair tilted back as he lounged in it. He inhaled intently from his cigarette, and gazed at the ceiling through a cloud of smoke.

'A hunch,' said the Saint, 'isn't a thing that goes easily to words. Words are so brutally logical, and a hunch is the reverse of logic. And a hunch, in a way, is a riddle; but it has no answer. When you get an answer, it isn't the answer to a riddle, or the answer to a hunch: it's the end of a story. I don't know if that's quite clear—'

'It isn't,' said Patricia.

The Saint blew three smoke-rings as if he had a personal grudge against them.

'My great tragedy, sweetheart,' he remarked modestly, 'is that I'm completely and devastatingly sane. And the world we live in is not sane. All the insanities of the world used to worry me crazy, without exception – once upon a time. But now, in my old age, I'm more discriminating. Half the things in that newspaper, which I'm pleased to say I've never read from end to end, are probably offences against sanity. And if you come to a rag like the *Daily Record*, about ninety-eight per cent of its printed area is devoted to offences against sanity. And the fact has ceased to bother me. I swear to you, Pat, that I could read a *Daily Record* right through without groaning aloud more than twice. That's my discrimination. When I read that an obscure biologist in Minneapolis has said that men would easily live to be three hundred if they nourished themselves on an exclusive diet of green bananas and vaseline, I'm merely bored. The thing is a simple offence against sanity. But when I'm always hearing about a Man Who Cannot Die, it annoys me. The thing is more than a simple offence against sanity. It sticks up and makes me stare at it. It's like finding one straight black line in a delirious patchwork of colours. It's more. It's like going to a menagerie and finding a man exhibited in one of the cages. Just because a Man Who Cannot Die isn't a simple insult to insanity. He's an insult to a much bigger thing. He's an insult to humanity.'

'And where does this hunch lead to?' asked Patricia, practically.

Simon shrugged.

'I wish I were sure,' he said.

Then, suddenly, he sat upright.

'Do you know,' he said, in a kind of incomprehensible anger, 'I've a damned good mind to see if I can't break that man's record! He infuriates me. And isn't he asking for it? Isn't he just asking someone to take up the challenge and see what can be done about it?'

The girl regarded him in bewilderment.

'Do you mean you want to try to kill him?' she asked blankly.

'I don't,' said the Saint. 'I mean I want to try to make him live.'

For a long time Patricia gazed at him in silence. And then, with a little shake of her head, half laughing, half perplexed, she stood up.

'You've been reading too much G. K. Chesterton,' she said. 'And you can't do anything about Hallin to-day, anyway. We're late enough as it is.'

The Saint smiled slowly, and rose to his feet.

'You're dead right, as usual, old dear,' he murmured amiably. 'I'll go and get out the car.'

And he went; but he did not forget Miles Hallin. And he never forgot his hunch about the man who could not die. For the Saint's hunches were nearly always unintelligible to anyone but himself, and always very real and intelligible to him; and all at once he had realised that in Miles Hallin he was going to find a strange story – he did not then know how strange.

Miles Hallin, as the Saint had complained, really was something very like a national institution. He was never called wealthy, but he always seemed to be able to indulge his not inexpensive hobbies without stint. It was these hobbies which had confirmed him in the reputation that Simon Templar so much disliked.

Miles Hallin was so well known that the newspapers never even troubled to mention the fact. Lesser lights in the news, Simon had discovered, were invariably accounted for. They were 'the famous cricketer' or 'the well-known novelist' or perhaps, with a more delicate conceit, 'the actor'. Simon Templar always had an uneasy feeling that these explanations were put in as a kind of covering each-way bet – in case the person referred to should become well known without anyone knowing why. But Miles Hallin was just – Miles Hallin.

Simon Templar, even in his superlatively casual acquaintance with the newspapers, had had every opportunity to become familiar with the face of Miles Hallin, though he had never seen the man in the flesh. That square-jawed, pugnacious profile, with the white teeth and crinkled eyes and flashing smile, had figured in more photographs than the Saint cared to remember. Mr Miles Hallin standing beside the wreckage of his Furillac at Le Mans – Mr Miles Hallin being taken aboard a lug after his speedboat *Red Lady* had capsized in the Solent – Mr Miles Hallin after his miraculous escape during the King's Cup Air Race, when his Elton 'Dragon' caught fire at five thousand feet – Mr Miles Hallin filming a charging buffalo in Tanganyika – Simon Templar knew them all. Miles Hallin did everything that a well-to-do sportsman could possibly include in the most versatile repertory, and all his efforts seemed to have the single aim of a spectacular suicide; but always he had escaped death by the essential hair's-breadth that had given him his name. No one could say that it was Miles Hallin's fault.

Miles Hallin had survived being mauled by a tiger, and had killed an infuriated gorilla with a sheath-knife. Miles Hallin had performed in bull-fights before the King of Spain. Miles Hallin had gone into a tank and wrestled with a crocodile to oblige a Hollywood movie director. Miles Hallin had done everything dangerous that the most fertile imagination could conceive – and then some. So far as was known, Miles Hallin couldn't walk a tight-rope; but the general impression was that if Miles Hallin could have walked a tight-rope he would have walked a tight-rope stretched across the crater of Vesuvius as a kind of appetiser before breakfast.

Miles Hallin bothered the Saint through the whole of that week-end.

Simon Templar, as he was always explaining, and usually explaining in such a way that his audience felt very sorry for him, had a sensitivity to anything the least bit out of the ordinary that was as tender as a gouty toe. The lightest touch, a touch that no one else would have felt, made him jump a yard. And when he boasted of his subtle discriminations, though he boasted flippantly, he spoke no less than the truth. That gift and nothing else had led him to fully half his adventures – that uncanny power of drawing a faultless line between the things that were merely eccentric and the things that were definitely wrong. And Miles Hallin struck him, in a way that he could not explain by any ordinary argument, as a thing that was definitely wrong.

Yet it so chanced, this time, that the Saint came to his story by a pure fluke – another and a wilder fluke than the one that had merely introduced him to a man whose brother had been a friend of Hallin's. But for that fluke, the Saint might to this day have been scowling at the name of Miles Hallin in the same hopeless puzzlement. And yet the Saint felt no surprise about the fluke. He had come to accept these accidents as a natural part of his life, in the same way as any other man accepts the accident of finding a newspaper on his breakfast-table, with a sense (if he meditated it at all) that he was only seeing the inevitable outcome of a complicated organisation of whose workings he knew nothing, but whose naturally continued existence he had never thought to question. These things were ordained.

In fact, there was an unexpected guest at a house-party at which the Saint spent his week-end.

Simon Templar had met Teddy Everest in Kuala Lumpur, and again, years later, at Corfu. Teddy Everest was the unexpected guest at the house-party; but it must be admitted that he was unexpected only by the Saint.

'This is my lucky day,' murmured Simon, as he viewed the apparition. 'I've been looking for you all over the world. You owe me ten cents. If you remember, when you had to be carried home after that farewell festival in K.L., I was left to pay for your rickshaw. You hadn't a bean, I know that, because I looked in all your pockets. Ten cents plus five per cent compound interest for six years—'

'Comes to a lot less than you borrowed off me in Corfu,' said Everest cheerfully. 'How the hell are you?'

'My halo,' said the Saint, 'is clearly visible if you get a strong light behind me ... Well, damn your eyes!' The Saint was smiling as he crushed the other's hand in a long grip. 'This is a great event, Teddy. Let's get drunk.'

The party went with a swing from that moment.

Teddy Everest was a mining engineer, and the Saint could also tell a good story; between them, they kept the ball rolling as they pleased. And on Tuesday, since Everest had to go to London on business, he naturally travelled in the Saint's car.

They lunched at Basingstoke; but it was before lunch that the incident happened which turned Teddy Everest's inexhaustible fund of reminiscence into a channel that was to make all the difference in the world to the Saint – and others.

Patricia and Simon had settled themselves in the lounge of the hotel where they pulled up, and Everest had proceeded alone into the bar to supervise the production of cocktails – Teddy Everest was something of a connoisseur in these matters. And in the bar he met a man.

'It's extraordinary how people crop up,' he remarked, when he returned. 'I've just seen a bloke who reminded me of a real O. Henry yarn.'

And later, over the table, he told the yarn.

'I don't think I bored you with the details of my last job,' he said. 'As a matter of fact, this is the only interesting thing about it. There's a gold mine somewhere in South Africa that was keeping me pretty busy last year – it was going down steadily, and I was sent out to try and find a spark more life in it. Now, it happened that I'd come across that very mine the year before, and heard all about it, and I was rather bored with the job. Everyone on the spot knew that the mine was a dud, and it seemed to me that I was just going to waste my time. Still, the pay was good, and I couldn't afford to turn my nose up at it. I'd got into jolly low water over my last holiday, to tell you the truth, and I wasn't sorry to have something to do – even if it was boring. It was on the train to Marseilles, where I caught my boat, that I met this guy – he on his way to a luxurious week at Antibes, rot him! We got talking, and it turned out that he knew a bit about the game. I remember telling him about my dud mine, and asking him if he held any shares, because I said a rag-and-bone man might give him a price for them. He hadn't any shares, which rather spoils the story.'

'Because the mine wasn't a dud,' murmured Simon; and Everest nodded.

'It was anything but. Certainly the old borings were worked out, but I struck a new vein all on my own, and those shares are going up to the sky when my report's been passed. I gave Hallin the tip just now – I felt he deserved it.'

The Saint sat still.

It was Patricia Holm who put the question.

'Did you say "Hallin"?' she asked.

'That's right.' Everest was scraping at his pipe with a penknife. 'Miles Hallin – the racing chappie.'

Patricia looked across at the Saint, but the overflow she was expecting did not take place.

'Dear me!' said the Saint, quite mildly.

They were sitting over coffee in the lounge when Hallin passed through. Simon recognised him at once – before he waved to Everest.

'One of the world's lucky men, I believe,' Everest said, as the clamour of Hallin's car died away outside.

'So I hear,' said the Saint.

And once again Patricia looked at him, remembering his discourse of a few days before. It was a characteristic of the Saint that no idea ever slipped out of his mind, once it had arrived there: any riddle that occurred to him tormented him until he had solved it. Anything that was as wrong as Miles Hallin, to his peculiar mind, was a perpetual irritation to him, much as a note out of tune on a piano would be a perpetual irritation to a musician: he had to look round it and into it and scratch it and finger it and jigger about with it until he'd got it into line with the rest of the scheme of things, and it gave him no peace until it was settled.

Yet he said nothing more about Miles Hallin that day.

Still he knew nothing. Afterwards –

But those are the bare facts of the beginning of the story.

They are told as the Saint himself would tell them, simply put forward for what they are worth. Afterwards, in the light of the knowledge to which he came he could have fitted them together much more coherently, much more comprehensively; but that would not have been his way. He would have told the story as it happened.

'And the longer I live,' he would have said, 'the more I'm convinced that there's no end to anything in my life. Or in anyone else's, probably. If you trace the most ordinary things back to their source, you find they have the queerest beginnings. It's just one huge fantastic game of consequences. You decide to walk home instead of taking a taxi, one night, and ten years later a man commits suicide. And if you had taken the taxi, perhaps ten years later the same man might have been a millionaire. Your father stayed at one hotel instead of another, in the same town, and at the age of fifty you become Prime Minister. If he had stayed at the other hotel you would probably have ended your life in prison ... Take this very story. If we hadn't lunched at Basingstoke that day, or if we'd never gone to that house-party, or if I hadn't once gone out without a handkerchief, or even if I'd never gone to Kuala Lumpur – Leave out the same flukes in the lives of the other people involved. Well, I've given up trying to decide exactly in what year, way back in the dim and distant past, it was decided that two men would have to die to make this story.'

This is exactly the point at which Simon Templar would have paused to make his philosophical reflection.

And then he would have told how, on the following Saturday evening, the posters of the *Evening Record* caught his eye, and something made him buy a copy of the paper; and he went home to tell Patricia that Miles Hallin had crashed again at Brooklands, and Miles Hallin had escaped again with hardly a scratch, but his passenger, Teddy Everest, had been burnt to death before the whole crowd.

3

'You see,' Nigel Perry explained simply, 'Moyna's people are frightfully poor.'

'Yeah,' said the Saint.

'And Miles is such a damned good chap.'

'Yeah,' said the Saint.

'It makes it awfully difficult.'

'Yeah,' said the Saint.

They lay stretched out in arm-chairs, masked by clouds of cigarette smoke, in the bed-sitting-room which was Nigel Perry's only home. And Perry, bronzed and clear-eyed from ten days' tramping in Spain, was unburdening himself of his problem.

'You haven't seen Moyna yet, have you?' said the Saint.

'Well, hang it, I've only been back a few hours! But she'll be in later – she's got to have dinner with an aunt, or something, and she'll get away as soon as she can.'

'What d'you think of your chances?'

Perry ran brown fingers through his hair.

'I'm blowed if I know, Templar,' he said ruefully. 'I – I've tried to keep clear of the subject lately. There's such a lot to think about. If only I'd got some real money—'

'D'you think a girl like Moyna cares a hoot about that?'

'Oh, I know! But that's all very fine. Any sensible girl is going to care about money sooner or later. She's got every right to. And if she's nice enough to think money doesn't matter – well, a chap can't take advantage of that . . . You know, that's where Miles has been so white. That money he paid over to me as my brother's share in the mine – he's really done his best to help me to make it grow. "If it's a matter of £. s. d.," he said, "I'd like you to start all square."'

'Did he?' said the Saint.

Perry nodded.

'I believe he worked like a Trojan. Pestered all his friends to try and find me a cast-iron investment paying about two hundred per cent. And he found one, too – at least, we thought so. Funnily enough, it was another gold mine – only this time it was in South Africa—'

'Hell!' said the Saint.

'What d'you mean?'

'Hell,' said the Saint. 'When was this – last week?'

The youngster looked at him puzzledly.

'Oh, no. That was over a year ago . . . But the shares didn't jump as they were supposed to. They've just gone slowly down. Not very much, but they've gone down. I held on, though. Miles was absolutely certain his information couldn't be wrong. And now he's just heard that it was wrong – there was a letter waiting for me—'

'He's offered to buy the shares off you, and make up your loss.'

Perry stared.

'How did you know?'

'I know everything,' said the Saint.

He sprang to his feet suddenly. There was an ecstatic expression on his face that made Perry wonder if perhaps the beer . . .

Perry rose slowly; and the Saint's hand fell on his shoulder.

'Moyna's coming to-night, isn't she?'

'I told you—'

'I'll tell you more. You're going to propose, my lad.'

'What?'

'Propose,' drawled the Saint, 'If you've never done it before, I'll give you a rapid lesson now. You take her little hand in yours, and you say, huskily, you say: "Moyna, d'you think we could do it?" "Do what?" she says. "Get fixed," says you. "Fixed?" she says. "How?" "Keep the party clean," says you. "Moyna," you say, crrrushing her to your booosom – that's a shade north of your cummerbund – "Moyna, I laaaaaaave you!" . . . That will be two guineas. You can post me a cheque in the morning – as the actress used to say. She was a perfect lady . . . So long!'

And the Saint snatched up his hat. He was half-way to the door when Perry caught him.

'What's the idea, Templar?'

Simon turned, smiling.

'Well, you don't want me on the scene while you shoot your speech, do you?'

'You don't have to go yet.'

'Oh, yes, I do.'

'Where?'

'I'm going to find Miles!'

'But you've never met him.'

'I haven't. But I'm going to!'

Perry blocked the doorway.

'Look here, Templar,' he said, 'you can't get away with this. There's a lot of things I want to know first. Hang it – if I didn't know you pretty well, I'd say you'd gone clean off your rocker.'

'Would you?' said the Saint gently.

He had been looking at Perry all the time, and he had been smiling all the time, but all at once the younger man saw something leap into the Saint's gaze that had not been there before – something like a flash of naked steel.

'Then,' said the Saint very gently, 'what would you say if I told you I was going to kill Miles Hallin?'

Perry fell back a pace.

'You're crazy!' he whispered.

'Sure,' said the Saint. 'But not so crazy as Miles Hallin must have been when he killed a friend of mine the other day.'

'Miles killed a friend of yours? What in God's name d'you mean?'

'Oh, for the love of Pete!'

With a shrug, the Saint turned back into the room. He sat on the edge of a table; but his poise was as restless as his perch. The last thing that anyone could have imagined was that he meant to stay sitting there.

'Listen, and I'll tell you a joke,' he said. 'I'm full of jokes these days . . . Once upon a time there was a man who could not die. Joke.'

'I wish to Heaven you'd say what you mean!'

'If I did, you wouldn't believe me.'

'Not if it was about Miles.'

'Quite! And it is about Miles. So we'd have a first-class row – and what good would that do? As it is, we're getting damned near it. So why not let it go?'

'You've made suggestions—'

'Of course I have,' agreed the Saint wearily. 'And now I'm going to make some more. Lose your temper if you must, Nigel, old dear; but promise me two things first: promise you'll hang on to those shares, and propose to Moyna to-night. She'll accept – I guarantee it. With lots of love and kisses, yours faithfully.'

The youngster's jaw tightened.

'I think you're raving,' he said. 'But we're going to have this out. What have you got to say about Miles?'

The Saint's sigh was as full of patience and long-suffering as the Saint could make it. He really was trying to be patient; but he knew that he hadn't a hope of convincing Nigel Perry.

And to the Saint it was all so plain. He wasn't a bit surprised at the sudden blossoming of the story : it had happened in the way these things always happened, in the way he subconsciously expected them to happen. He had taken the blossoming in his stride; it was all infinitely past and over to him – so infinitely past and over that he had ceased to think about coincidences. And he sighed.

'I've got nothing to say about Miles.'

'You were saying—'

'Forget it, old dear. Now, will you do what I asked you to do about Moyna?'

'That's my business. Why should you want to dictate to me about it?'

'And as for those shares,' continued the Saint calmly, 'will you—'

'For the last time,' said Perry grimly, 'will you explain yourself?'

Simon looked at him over a cigarette and a lighted match, and then through a trailing streamer of smoke; and Simon shrugged.

'Right!' he said. 'I will. But don't forget that we agreed it was a waste of time. You won't believe me. You're the sort that wouldn't. I respect you for it, but it makes you a damned fool all the same.'

'Go ahead.'

'Do you remember that fellow who was killed at Brooklands yesterday, driving with Miles Hallin?'

'I've read about it.'

'He was a friend of mine. Over a year ago he told Miles Hallin about some dud shares. You bought them. Under a week ago he met Hallin again and told him the shares weren't so dud. Now Hallin's going to take the shares back off you. He killed poor old Teddy because Teddy knew the story – and Teddy was great on telling his stories. If Hallin had known that the man he saw with Teddy knew you, I should probably have had my funeral first. Miles is such a damned good chap. "If it's a matter of £ s. d," he'd have said, "I'd like me to start all square."'

'By God, Templar—'

'Hush! . . . Deducing back from that joke to the joke about another gold mine—'

Perry stepped forward, with a flaming face.

'It's a lie!'

'Sure it is. We agreed about that before I started, if you recall the dialogue . . . Where was I? Oh, yes. Deducing back from that joke—'

'I'd like Miles to hear some of this,' Perry said through his teeth.

'So would I,' murmured the Saint. 'I told you I wanted to find him. If you see him first, you may tell him all about it. Give him my address.' The Saint yawned. 'Now may I go, sweetheart?'

He stood up, his cigarette tilted up in the corner of his mouth and his hands in his pockets; and Perry stood aside.

'You're welcome to go,' Perry said. 'And if you ever try to come back I'll have you thrown out.'

Simon nodded.

'I'll remember that when I feel in need of some exercise,' he remarked. And then he smiled. For a moment he gripped the boy's arm.

'Don't forget about Moyna,' he said.

Then he crossed the landing and went down the stairs; and Nigel Perry, silent in the doorway, watched him go.

The Saint went down slowly. He was really sorry about it all, though he had known it was inevitable. At least, he had made it inevitable. He was aware that he asked for most of the trouble that came to him – in many ways. But that couldn't be helped. In the end –

He was on the last flight when a man who was running up from the hall nearly cannoned into him.

'Sorry,' said the man.

'Not at all,' said the Saint politely.

And then he recognised the man, and stopped him with a hand on his sleeve.

'How's the trade in death?' murmured the Saint.

Miles Hallin turned, staring; and then he suddenly knew where he had seen the Saint before. For an instant the recognition flared in his eyes; then his face became a mask of indignation.

'What the devil do you mean?' he demanded.

Simon sighed. He always seemed to have something to sigh about in those days.

'I'm getting so tired of that question,' he sighed. 'Why don't you try it on Nigel? Perhaps he doesn't have so much of it as I do.'

He turned, and continued on his way. As he opened the front door he heard Hallin resuming his ascent at a less boisterous speed, and smiled gently to himself.

It was late, and the street outside was dark and practically deserted. But in front of the house stood an immense shining two-seater that could only have belonged to Miles Hallin.

For a space of seconds the Saint regarded it, fingering his chin, at first thoughtfully, and then with a secret devil of merriment puckering the corners of his eyes.

Then he went down the steps.

He found the tool-box in a moment. And then, with loving care, he proceeded to remove the nuts that secured the offside front wheel . . .

Two minutes later, with the wheel-brace stowed away again as he had found it, and the nuts in his pocket, he was sauntering leisurely homewards, humming to the stars.

4

The Saint was in his bath when Inspector Teal arrived in Upper Berkeley Mews the next morning; but he presented himself in a few moments arrayed in a superb pair of crepe-de-Chine pyjamas and a dressing-gown that would have made the rainbow look like something left over from a sale of second-hand mourning.

Mr Teal eyed him with awe.

'Where did you hire that outfit?' he inquired.

Simon took a cigarette.

'Have you come here to exchange genial back-chat,' he murmured, 'or is it business? I have an awful suspicion that it's business.'

'It is business,' said Mr Teal.

'Sorry,' said the Saint, 'my office hours are twelve noon to midday.'

Teal shifted his gum across to the east side of his mouth.

'What's your grouse against Hallin?' he asked.

'Hallin? Who's Hallin? Two aitches.'

'Miles Hallin's car was wrecked last night,' said Teal deliberately.

The Saint raised his eyebrows.

'Really? Was he drunk, or did he lend the divisional surgeon a fiver?'

'The offside front wheel of his car came off when he was driving down Park Lane,' said Teal patiently. 'He was driving pretty fast, and he swerved into a taxi. He ought to have been killed.'

'Wasn't he?' said the Saint,

'He wasn't. What have you got to say about it?'

'Well, I think it's a great pity.'

'A great pity he wasn't killed?'

'Yes. Probably he wanted to die. He's been trying to long enough, hasn't he? . . . And yet it mightn't have been his fault. That's the worst of these cheap cars. They fall apart if you sneeze in them. Of course, he might have had a cold. Do you think he had a cold?' asked the Saint earnestly.

The detective closed his eyes.

'When Hallin looked at the car,' Teal explained, 'he found that someone had removed the nuts that ought to have been keeping the wheel on.'

The Saint smoothed his hair.

'Well, really, dear old broccolo,' he drawled, with a pained expression, 'is that all you've come to see me about? Are you going to make a habit of coming to me to air your woes about everything that happens in London? You know, I'm awfully afraid you're getting into the way of thinking I'm some sort of criminal. Teal, you must not think that of me!'

'I know all about last night,' Teal replied, without altering his weary tone. 'I've already seen Perry.'

'And what did Perry tell you?'

'He told me you said you were going to kill Hallin.'

'Beer, beer I – I mean, dear, dear!' said the Saint. 'Of course he was a bit squiffy—'

Teal's eyes opened with a suddenness that was almost startling.

'See here, Templar,' he said, 'it's time you and me had a straight talk.'

'I beg your pardon?' said the Saint.

'You and I,' said Teal testily. 'I know we've had a lot of scraps in the past, and I know a lot of funny things have happened since then. I don't grudge you your success. In your way, you've helped me a lot; but at the same time you've caused disturbances. I know you've had a pardon, and we don't want to bother you if we can help it, but you've got to do your share. That show of yours down at Tenterden, for instance – that wasn't quite fair, was it?'

'It wasn't,' said the Saint generously. 'But I'm afraid it appealed to my perverted sense of humour.'

Mr Teal rose ponderously.

'Then do I take it you're going on as before?'

'I'm afraid you do,' said the Saint. 'For the present, anyway. You see, I've got rather a down on Miles Hallin. He killed a friend of mine the other day.'

'He what?'

'At Brooklands. Since you're making so many inquiries about funny things that happen to cars, why don't you investigate that crash? I don't know if there was enough left of Teddy Everest to make an investigation profitable; but if it could be done, I expect you'd find that he was thoroughly doped when he got into that car. I expect you'd find, if you were a very clever investigator – or a very clever clairvoyant, like I am – that the dope took effect while they were driving. Teddy just went to sleep. Then it would be quite an easy matter for an expert driver like Hallin to crash the car without hurting himself. And, of course, it could always catch fire.'

Teal looked at him curiously.

'Is that the truth?' he asked.

'No,' said the Saint. 'I'm just making it up to amuse you. Good morning.'

He felt annoyed with Chief Inspector Teal that day. He felt annoyed with a lot of things – the story in general, and Miles Hallin in particular. There were many things that were capable of annoying the Saint in just that way; and when Mr Teal had departed, the Saint sat down and smoked three cigarettes with entirely unnecessary violence.

Patricia Holm, coming in just after the third of these cigarettes had been hurled through the open window, read his mood at once.

'What is it this time?' she asked.

Simon broke a match into small pieces as if it had done him a grievous injury.

'Teal, Nigel Perry, Miles Hallin,' he answered, comprehensively. 'Also, an old joke about Death.'

It was some time before she secured a coherent explanation. The incidents of the night before she had already heard; but he had stated them without adornment, and his manner had encouraged the postponement of questions. Now he told her, in the same blunt manner, about Teal's visit; but she had to wait until after lunch, when the coffee-cups were in front of them and the Saint was gently circulating a minute quantity of Napoleon brandy around the bowl of an enormous glass, before she could get him to expound his grievance.

'When I first spoke about Miles Hallin – you remember? – you thought I was raving. I don't want to lay on any of the "I told you so" stuff; but now you know what you do know, I want you to try and appreciate my point. I know you'll say what anyone else would say – that the whole thing simply boils down to the most unholy fluke. I'm saying it doesn't. The point is that I'm going back far beyond that share business – even beyond poor old Teddy. I'm going back to Nigel's brother, and that little story of the great open spaces that I've heard so much about. I tell you, this just confirms what I thought about that.'

'You didn't say you thought anything about it,' Patricia remarked.

'I wasn't asking to be called a fool,' said the Saint. 'I knew that as things stood I had rather less chance of convincing any sane person than I'd have of climbing the Matterhorn with my hands tied behind me and an elephant in each pocket. But you ought to see the joke now. What would you say was the most eccentric thing about a man who could not die?'

Patricia smiled at him patiently.

'I shouldn't know what to say,' she answered truthfully.

'Why,' said the Saint, with a kind of vast impatience, 'what else should be the most eccentric thing about him but the fact that he can die, and always could? Don't you understand that whatever jokes people make about death, they never make that kind of joke? There are impossibilities that are freakish and funny, and impossibilities that are freakish and unfunny; pigs with wings belong to the first kind, but men who cannot die belong to the second kind. Now, what could induce a man to pursue that second kind of joke with such a terrible eagerness?'

The girl shrugged.

'It's beyond me, Simon.'

'The answer,' said the Saint, 'is that he knew it wasn't true. Because he'd once looked death in the face – slow and deliberate death, not the kind that comes with a rush. And he found he was afraid of it.'

'Then that story about Nigel's brother—'

'Perhaps we shall never know the truth of it. But I'm as certain as I've ever been about anything that the story we're told isn't the truth. I'm certain that that was the time when Miles Hallin discovered, not that he could not die, but that he couldn't bear to die. And he saved his life at the expense of his partner.'

'But he's risked his life so often since—'

'I wonder how much of that is the unvarnished truth – how much he engineered, and how much he adorned his stories so as to give the impression he wanted to give? . . .

Because I think Miles Hallin is a man in terror. Once, he yielded to his fear; and after that his fear became the keynote of his life, which a fear will become if you yield to it. And he found another fear – the fear of being found out. He was afraid of his own legend. He had to bolster it up, he had to pile miracle upon miracle – only to make one miracle seem possible. He had to risk losing his life in order to save it.'

'But why should he have killed Teddy?'

The Saint took another cigarette. He gazed across the restaurant with eyes that saw other things.

'One fear breeds another,' he said. 'All things in a man's mind are linked up. If one cog slips, the whole machine is altered. If you will cheat at cards, you will cheat at Snakes-and-Ladders. Hallin cheated for life; it was quite natural that he should cheat for love. Because Nigel was Moyna's favourite, Hallin had to try and take away the one little thing that gave Nigel a chance. Because Teddy could have discovered the swindle, he killed Teddy. His fear drove him on, as it will keep on driving him on: it's the most ruthless master a man can have. Now, because he saw me with Teddy at Basingstoke, and then saw me last night leaving Nigel's, he will try to kill me. If he thought Nigel believed me, he would try to kill Nigel – that's why I had to tell the story in such a way that I knew Nigel wouldn't believe it. Even now, Hallin is wondering . . .'

'But if Nigel had given up the shares without suspecting anything, and then they'd soared up as Teddy said they would—'

'What would that have mattered?'

'Nigel would have known.'

'Known what? Hallin would have said he sold the shares for the best price he could get, and Nigel would never have thought that it might be a lie . . . But now – do you remember how I said I wanted to make Hallin live?'

'Yes.'

'That was the test – before I knew any of this. I wanted to see what would happen to him if he put aside his joke. I wanted to know what he would be like if he became an ordinary mortal man – a man to whom death might not be a terror, but to whom death was still no joke. And now I know.'

With her chin on her hands, Patricia regarded him. Not as she had regarded him when he had spoken of Miles Hallin before; but with a seriousness that wore a smile.

'I shall never get to the end of your mind, lad,' she said; and the Saint grinned.

'At the moment,' he murmured, 'I'm enjoying my brandy.'

And he actually did forget Miles Hallin for the rest of that afternoon and evening; for Simon Templar had the gift of taking life as it came – when once he knew from what quarter it might be coming.

His impatience disappeared. It seemed as if that talk over the coffee and brandy had cleared the air for him. He knew that trouble was coming; but that was nothing unusual. He could meet all the trouble in the world with a real enjoyment, now that he had purged his mind of the kind of puzzle that for him was gloom and groping and unalloyed Gehenna. Even the reflection that Miles Hallin had still failed to die did not depress him. He had not loosened that wheel in high hopes of a swift and catastrophic denouement, for he had known how slight was the chance that the wheel would elect to part company with the car at the very moment when Hallin was treading the accelerator flat down to the flooring; the thing had been done on the spur of the moment, more in mischief than anything else, just to pep up the party's future. And it would certainly do that.

As for Teal, and Teal's horrific warnings of what would happen if the Saint should again attract the attention of the law – those were the merest details. They simply made the practical problem more amusing . . .

So the Saint, over his brandy, swung over to a contentment as genuine and as illogical as his earlier impatience had been, and was happy for the rest of that day, and nearly died that night.

He had danced with Patricia at the May Fair, and he had thought that Patricia looked particularly beautiful; and so presently they strolled home arm in arm through the cool lamplit streets, talking intently and abstractedly about certain things that are nobody's business. And the Saint was saying something or other, or it may have been Patricia who was saying something or other, as they crossed Berkeley Square; but whoever it was never finished the speech.

Some instinct made the Saint look round, and he saw the lights of a car just behind them swerve suddenly. An ordinary sight enough, perhaps, on the face of it; but he knew by the same instinct that it was not ordinary. It may have been that he had not forgotten Miles Hallin so completely, after all.

He stopped in his stride, and stooped; and Patricia felt herself swept up in his arms. There was a lamp-post close behind them, and the Saint leapt for it. He heard the screech of brakes and tyres before he dared to look round; even then he was in time to see the pillar that sheltered him bend like a reed before the impact of the car; and he moved again, this time to one side, like lightning, as the iron column snapped at the base and came crashing down to the pavement.

Then there was a shout somewhere, and a sound of running feet; and the mutter of the car stopped.

Quietly the Saint set Patricia down again.

'How very unfortunate,' he remarked. 'Dearie, dearie me! ... Mr Miles Hallin, giving evidence, stated that his nerves had been badly shaken by his smash at Brooklands. His licence was suspended for six months.'

A constable and half a dozen ordinary citizens were rapidly congregating around the wreckage; and an unholy glitter came into the Saint's eyes.

'Pardon me one moment, old darling,' he murmured; and Patricia found herself standing alone.

But she reached the crowd in time to hear most of his contribution to the entertainment.

'Scandalous, I call it,' the Saint was saying, in a voice that trembled – possibly with righteous indignation. Or possibly not. 'I shall write to *The Times*. A positive outrage . . . Yes, of course you can have my name and address. I shall be delighted to give evidence . . . The streets aren't safe . . . murderous fools who ought to be in an asylum . . . Probably only just learnt to drive . . . Disgraceful . . . disgusting . . . ought to be shot . . . mannerless hogs . . .'

It was some time before the policeman was able to soothe him; and he faded out of the picture still fuming vitriolically, to the accompaniment of a gobble of applause from the assembled populace.

And a few minutes later he was leaning helplessly against the door of his flat, his ribs aching and the tears streaming down his cheeks, while Patricia implored him wildly to open the door and take his hilarity into decent seclusion.

'Oh, but it was too beautiful, sweetheart!' he sobbed weakly, as at last he staggered into the sitting-room. 'If I'd missed that chance I could never have looked myself in the face again. Did you see Miles?'

'I did.'

'He couldn't say a word. He didn't dare let on that he knew me. He just had to take it all. Pat, I ask you, can life hold any more?'

Half an hour later, when he was sprawled elegantly over an arm-chair, with a tankard of beer in one hand and the last cigarette of the evening in the other, she ventured to ask the obvious question.

'He was waiting for us, of course,' she said; and the Saint nodded.

'My prophetic report of the police-court proceedings would still have been correct,' he drawled. 'Miles Hallin has come to life.'

He did not add that he could have prophesied with equal assurance that Chief Inspector Teal would not again be invited to participate in the argument – not by Miles Hallin, anyway. But he knew quite well that either Miles Hallin or Simon Templar would have to die before the argument was settled; and it would have to be settled soon.

5

Nevertheless, Teal did participate again; and it may be said that his next intrusion was entirely his own idea.

He arrived in Upper Berkeley Mews the very next evening; and the Saint, who had seen him pass the window, opened the door before Teal's finger had reached the bell.

'This is an unexpected pleasure,' Simon murmured cordially, as he propelled the detective into the sitting-room. 'Still, you needn't bother to tell me why you've come. A tram was stolen from Tooting last night, and you want to know if I did it. Six piebald therms are missing from the Gas Light and Coke Company's stable, and you want to know if I've got them. A seventeen horse-power saveloy entered for the St. Leger has been stricken with glanders, and you want to know—'

'I didn't say so,' observed Mr Teal – heatedly, for him.

'Never mind,' said the Saint peaceably. 'We won't press the point. But you must admit that we're seeing a lot of you these days.' He inspected the detective's water-line with a reflective eye. 'I believe you've become a secret Glaxo drinker,' he said reproachfully.

Teal gravitated towards a chair.

'I heard about your show last night,' he said,

Simon smiled vaguely.

'You hear of everything, old dear,' he remarked; and Teal nodded seriously.

'It's my business,' he said.

He put a finger in his mouth and hitched his chewing-gum into a quiet backwater; and then he leaned forward, his pudgy hands resting on his knees, and his baby blue eyes unusually wide awake.

'Will you try not to stall, Templar – just for a few minutes?'

The Saint looked at him thoughtfully. Then took a cigarette and sat down in the chair opposite.

'Sure,' he said.

'I wonder if you'd even do something more than that?'

'Namely?'

'I wonder if you'd give me a straight line about Miles Hallin – and no fooling.'

'I offered you one yesterday,' said the Saint, 'and you wouldn't listen.'

Teal nodded, shifting his feet.

'I know. But the situation wasn't quite the same. Since then I've heard about that accident last night. And that mayn't mean anything to anyone but you and me – but you've got to include me.'

'Have I?'

'I'm remembering things,' said the detective. 'You may be a respectable member of society now, but you haven't always been one. I can remember the time when I'd have given ten years' salary for the pleasure of putting you away. Sometimes I get relapses of that feeling, even now.'

'So you do,' murmured the Saint.

'But this isn't one of those times,' said Teal. 'Just now I only want to remember another part of your record. And I know as well as anyone else that you never go after a man just because he's got a wart on his nose. Usually, your reason's fairly plain. This time it isn't. And I'm curious.'

'Naturally.'

'Hallin's right off your usual mark. He doesn't belong to any shady bunch. If he did, I'd know it. He isn't even a borderline case, like I knew Lemuel was.'

'He isn't.'

'And yet he tried to bump you off last night.'

The Saint inhaled deeply, and exhaled again through a Saintly smile.

'If you want to know why he did that,' he said, 'I'll tell you. It was because he's always been terribly afraid of death.'

'Do you mean he thought you were going to kill him?'

'That's not what I said. I certainly did say I was going to kill him; but whether he believed me or not is more than I can tell you at present.'

'Then what do you mean?'

Simon raised his eyebrows mournfully, but he checked the protest that was almost becoming a habit. After all, Teal was only a detective. One had to make allowances.

'Miles Hallin thought no one in the world knew the truth about him,' said the Saint. 'And then he found that I knew. So he wanted me to die.'

Teal compressed his lips.

Then he said: 'And what was this truth?'

'Simply that Miles Hallin is a coward.'

'Would he try to kill you for that?'

The Saint gazed at the ceiling.

'Did you take my tip about that Brooklands affair?' he asked.

'I made some inquiries,' Teal shrugged. 'I'm afraid it wasn't much use. I'm told no one could prove anything.'

'And yet you've come back to see me.'

'After that business last night. On the level, Templar, I'd be glad of a tip. You know something that I don't know, and just this once I want you to help me. If it had looked like one of your ordinary shows, I wouldn't have done it.'

'Where is the peculiar difference between this show and what you call my "ordinary shows"?'

'You know as well as I do—'

'I don't!'

The Saint uncurled from his chair like a steel spring released, and his eyes were of the same steel. The detective realised that those eyes had been levelled unwinkingly at him for a long while; but he had not realised it before. Now he saw his mistake.

'I don't know anything of the kind,' snapped the Saint, with those eyes of chilled steel; and the laziness had vanished altogether from his voice. 'But I do know that I can't swallow the joke of your coming to see me just because you want to take one of my feathers and put it in your own cap. I've got a darned good swallowing apparatus, Teal, I promise you, but it simply won't sink that one!'

Teal blinked.

'I only wanted to ask you—'

'Shucks!' said the Saint tersely. 'You've told me what you wanted to ask me. My yell is that you haven't told me the real reason. And that's what I'm going to know before we take the palaver any further. You asked me not to stall: now I'm telling you not to stall. Shoot!'

For a space of seconds they eyed one another in silence; and then the detective nodded fractionally, though his round, red face had not changed its expression.

'All right,' he said slowly. 'I'll come clean – if you'll do the same.'

The Saint stood tensely. But he hesitated only for a moment. He thought: 'Something's happened. Teal knows what it is. I've got to find out. It may or may not be important, but—'

The Saint said curtly, 'That's O.K. by me.'

'Then you start,' answered Teal.

Simon drew breath.

'Mine's easy. I suspect that the story of Hallin's luck in Australia is a lie. I know that Hallin's crazy about the same girl that Nigel Perry's in love with. I know that Hallin tried to push Perry out of the running by persuading him to put the little money he'd got into a mine that Hallin thought was a dud. I know that Teddy Everest told Hallin the mine was a dud, and later told him it wasn't a dud after all. I know Hallin faked that crash because Teddy might be dangerous. I know Hallin had planned some story to get those shares back from Perry; and I know Hallin tried to kill me because I told Perry the truth – even if Perry didn't believe me. That's all there is to it. Your turn.'

Teal's chair creaked as he moved; but his eyes were closed. He appeared to have fallen asleep. And then he spoke with a voice that was not at all sleepy.

'Moyna Stanford was kidnapped this afternoon,' he said; and the Saint swore softly.

'The hell! . . .'

'That's all I know.'

'Tell me about it.'

'There's very little to tell. She'd been down to lunch with some friends at Windsor – she walked alone to the station – and she hasn't been seen since.'

'But, burn it! – a grown girl can disappear for two or three hours without being kidnapped, can't she?'

'Ordinarily, she can,' said Teal. 'I'm just telling you what's happened. She was due to have tea with some friends of her mother's. They rang up her mother to ask why she hadn't come. Her mother rang up Windsor to ask the same question. And as soon as her mother grasped the facts she went flying to the police. Of course, Mrs. Stanford didn't get much satisfaction – we haven't got time to attend to hysterical parents who get the wind up as quickly as that – but I heard about it, and it seemed to link up. Anyway—'

'She might have run away with Perry,' said the Saint, with a kind of frantic hope that he knew instinctively to be the hope of a fool.

And the detective's reply came so pat that even Simon Templar was startled.

'She might have,' said Teal grimly, 'because Perry's also disappeared.'

The Saint stood like a statue.

Then when he spoke again his voice was strangely quiet.

'Tell me about Perry,' he said.

'Perry just went out to lunch in the ordinary way, but he never went back to the office.'

The Saint removed his cigarette from his mouth. It had gone out. He gazed at it as if its extinction was the only thing in the world that mattered.

Then he said: 'At the police-court this morning, Hallin was remanded for a medical examination. Was that the Beak's idea – or yours?'

'Largely mine,' said Teal.

'Would Hallin know?'

'He might have guessed.'

'And what happened after that?'

'Probably, he lunched with Perry. The identification isn't certain, but—'

'Has Hallin been seen anywhere since?'

'I've had men making inquiries. If you'll let me use your telephone—'

'Carry on.'

The detective moved ponderously over to the instrument; and Simon, lighting another cigarette, began to stride up and down the room.

He was still pacing the carpet when Teal hung up the receiver and turned to him again.

'Hallin hasn't been seen since lunch.'

The Saint nodded without speaking, and set off on a fresh route, his hands deep in his pockets. Teal watched him with exasperation.

'Haven't you got anything to say?' he demanded.

Simon raised his eyes from the floor.

'I've made a big mistake,' he said, as though nothing else concerned him; and Teal seethed audibly.

'For Heaven's sake!'

'Er – not exactly.'

The Saint stopped abruptly on those words, and faced about; and Teal was suddenly amazed that he could ever have associated that dark, rakish profile with trivialities.

'My mistake,' said the Saint, 'was in underrating Hallin's intelligence. I don't know why I did it. He'd naturally be quick on the uptake. And he'd realise that when those shares went up he'd be damned. Perry would have to believe me. And the rest follows.'

'What follows?'

'He got Perry away with some yarn – probably about Moyna. Then he rushed down to Windsor, caught Moyna at the station, and offered to drive her to London. But I know where they went – Perry may be there too—'

'Where?'

'Wales.'

'How d'you know that?'

'Hallin's got a place there. Damn it, Teal, d'you think you're the only durned General Information Bureau in this gosh-blinded burg?'

Teal brushed his hat on his sleeve.

'I can get a police car round here in five minutes,' he stated.

'Do it,' said the Saint; and Teal went again to the telephone – very quickly.

When he had given his instructions, he put his hat down on the table, and came and stood in front of the Saint. And suddenly his hands shot out, and moved swiftly and firmly over the Saint's pockets. And the Saint smiled.

'Did you think I was carrying the missing couple around with me?' he murmured, in the mildest of expostulation; but Teal was not amused.

'I'm remembering Lemuel,' he said briefly. 'You may be coming with me, but you're not carrying a gun.'

The Saint smiled even more gently.

'Miles Hallin is terribly afraid,' he said, addressing the ceiling. 'Once upon a time, he was just afraid of dying; but now he has an even bigger fear. He's afraid of dying before he's finished with life . . . I think someone had better carry a gun.'

Teal understood perfectly.

6

'So there you are!' Nigel Perry flung open the door of the cottage as Hallin's car pulled up outside. 'I was wondering what on earth to do. Moyna isn't here—'

'She isn't far away,' Hallin said.

He climbed stiffly out of his seat. Perry could not see his face clearly in the gloom, but something in Hallin's tone puzzled him. And then Hallin took him by the arm with a laugh.

'Come inside,' he said, 'and I'll tell you all about it.'

Inside, in the lighted room, Hallin's heavy features seemed drawn and strained; but of course he had just driven nearly a hundred and sixty miles at his usual breakneck pace.

'Heavens, I'm tired!'

He sat down, and passed a hand across his forehead. His eyes strayed towards the decanter on a side-table, and the younger man hurried towards it.

'Thanks,' Hallin said.

'I've been bothered to death, Miles!' said Perry boyishly, splashing soda-water into the glass. 'I didn't dare leave the place, in case Moyna arrived and found nobody here, and I didn't know how to get in touch with you—'

'And now I expect you're wondering why I'm here at all.'

'I am.'

Hallin took the tumbler and half-emptied it at a gulp.

'That's better! . . . Well, everything's gone wrong that could go wrong.'

'Don't you know any more than you knew at lunch-time?'

'I don't know any more, but – well, I've told you it all. Moyna rang me up – she said she was in frightful trouble – your office number was engaged, and she couldn't wait. She'd got to get out of London at once. I asked her where she was going, and she didn't seem to have any idea, I said I'd leave the key of my place in Wales with my valet—'

'But you gave it to me!'

'I've got more than one key, you idiot! Anyway, she jumped at the chance; and I promised to send you on by the first train. It was much later when I started to think that I might be able to help you, whatever your trouble was – and I got out the car and came straight down.'

'But I can't understand it!' Perry couldn't sit down; his nerves were jangled to bits with worry. 'Why should Moyna have to run away out of London? She couldn't be mixed up with any crime—'

Hallin took another pull at his drink.

'I wish I could be as sure of that as you are.'

'Miles!'

'Oh, don't be silly, Nigel. D'you think I'd believe she was in on the wrong side? There are other ways of being mixed up in crime.'

'What did you mean when you said everything had gone wrong?'

Hallin lighted a cigarette.

'I discovered something else on my way here,' he said.

'You said Moyna wasn't far away—'

'I don't think she is. I'll tell you why. As I came up the hill, I had to stop for a moment to switch over to the reserve petrol tank. While I was out of the car I heard someone speaking beside the road. He said: "Hallin's just come by." Then he said: "I'll leave him to you. I'll be waiting for Templar—" '

'Templar?'

'That's what he said.'

'But he must have known you were there.'

'He must have thought I couldn't hear. It was a pure fluke that I could. I moved a couple of steps, and I couldn't hear a sound. Some trick of echoes, I expect. However, I followed the sound, keeping in the line it seemed to move in, and I almost fell over the man. He fired at me once, and missed; and then I got hold of him. He – went over the cliff. You remember – it's very steep there—'

'You killed him?'

'Of course I did,' said Hallin shortly, 'unless he can fall two hundred feet without hurting himself. It was him or me – and he was armed. I got back into the car and drove on. Farther up the road a man stepped out and tried to stop me, but I drove right at him. He fired after me twice, but he didn't do any damage. And that's all.'

Perry's fists clenched.

'By God, if that man really was waiting for Templar—'

'Why shouldn't he have been? Remember all that's happened. We don't know what Templar's game is, but we know his record—'

'But he was pardoned a long time ago.'

'That doesn't make him straight. A man like that—'

Perry swung round. He caught at Hallin's arm.

'For God's sake, Miles – we've got to do something—'

Hallin stood up.

'That's why I came to fetch you,' he said.

'But what can we do?'

'Get back to that telephone – find where the line leads.'

'Could you find the place again?'

'I marked it down.'

'But those men who fired at you—'

'We can go another way. I know all the roads around here backwards. Are you game?' Perry set his teeth.

'You bet I am. But – if you'd got a gun or something—'

Hallin looked at him for a moment. Then he went to the desk, unlocked a drawer, and took out two automatics. One he gave to Perry, the other he slipped into his own pocket.

'That's a good idea,' he said. 'Now are you ready?'

'Yes – come on!'

It was Perry who led the way out of the cottage, and he had already started the car when Hallin climbed in behind the wheel.

They moved off with a roar, and Perry leaned over and yelled in Hallin's ear.

'They'll hear us coming!'

Hallin nodded, and kicked the cut-out over. The roar was silenced.

'You're right,' he said.

They tore down the hill for a quarter of a mile, and skidded deliriously round a right-angle turn; then they went bucketing down a steep and narrow lane, with the big car brushing the hedge on either side.

'This is the only way to get round them,' Hallin said.

The huge headlights made the lane as light as it would have been at noon; even so, it was a nightmare path to follow at that pace. But Hallin was a perfect driver. Presently the lane seemed to come to a dead end; Hallin braked, and put the wheel over; and they broadsided into a clear road.

'It's close here,' Hallin said.

The car slackened speed; after a few moments they almost crawled, while Hallin searched the side of the road. And then he jammed on the brakes, switching off the engine and the lights as he did so.

'This is the place.'

He met Perry in the road, and led off at once. For a few yards they went over grass; then they threaded a way between rocks and low stunted bushes. On his right, Perry heard a distant murmur of water. Then Hallin stopped him.

'It was just here.'

Perry heard the scrape of a match; and then he saw.

They stood beside a slight bump of ground; and there was a shallow cavity in the side of it, which seemed to have been worn away under a flat ledge of stone. And in the cavity was a telephone.

The light went out.

'I've got an idea,' Hallin said.

'What is it?'

'Suppose you took that man's place at the telephone – spoke to the men at the other end – told them some story? I'll follow the wire. I don't think the other end is far away. Give me ten minutes, and then start. You could distract their attention – it'd give me a chance to take them by surprise.'

'But I want to get near the swine myself!'

'You shall. But to start with – Look here, you know you aren't used to stalking. I could get up to them twice as quietly as you could.'

Perry hesitated; and then Hallin heard him groping down into the hollow.

'All right.' The youngster's voice came up from the darkness. 'Hurry along, Miles, and shout as soon as you can.'

'I will. Just ten minutes, Nigel.'

'Right-ho!'

Hallin moved away.

He did not follow any wire. He knew just where he was going.

In ten minutes he was squatting beside a heavily insulated switch. Beside him a trellised metal tower reached up towards the stars. It was one of many that had not long since sprung up all over England, carrying long electric cables across the country and bringing light and power to every corner of the land.

That Miles Hallin had left London late was only one of his inventions. He had, as a matter of fact, been in that spot for several hours. He was an expert electrician – though the job he had had to do was fairly simple. It had been the digging that had taken the time . . .

He had an ingenious mind. The Saint would have been sheerly delighted to hear the story that Nigel Perry had heard. 'If you must have melodrama, lay it on with a spade,' was one of the Saint's own maxims; and certainly Miles Hallin had not tyrannised his imagination.

There was also a thoroughness about Hallin which it gave the Saint great pleasure to recall in after years. Even in murder he was as thorough as he had been in fostering the legend of his charmed life. A lesser man would simply have pushed Perry over the very convenient precipice.

'But even at that time,' the Saint would say, 'Hallin clung to the idea that after all he might get away with something. If he'd simply shoved Nigel off the cliff he'd have had trouble with the body. So he dug a neat grave, and put Nigel in it to die; so all our sweet Miles had to do afterwards was to come back and remove the telephone and fill up the hole. You can't say that wasn't thorough.'

Hallin pulled on a thick rubber glove; and then he struck a match and cupped it in his other hand. He looked once at his watch. And his face was perfectly composed as he jerked over the lever of his switch.

7

'We'd better walk from here,' said the Saint.

Teal nodded.

He leaned forward and spoke a word to the driver, and the police car pulled into the side of the road, and stopped there.

The detective levered himself out with a grunt, and inspected the track in front of them with a jaundiced eye.

'We might have gone on to the top of the hill,' he said; and the Saint laughed without mirth.

'We might not,' said the Saint. 'Hallin's place is right by the top of the hill, and we aren't here to advertise ourselves.'

'I suppose not,' said Teal wistfully.

The driver came round the car and joined them, bringing the electric flashlights that were part of their outfit) and Teal took one and tested it. The Saint did the same. They looked at each other in the light.

'You seem to know a lot about this place,' Teal said.

The Saint smiled.

'I came down from London last week specially to have a look at it,' he answered, and Teal's eyes narrowed.

'Did you bring any bombs with you?' he asked.

Simon turned his flashlight up the road.

'I'm afraid I forgot to,' he murmured. 'And now, shall we proceed with the weight-reducing, Fatty?'

They set off in a simmering silence, Teal and the Saint walking side by side, and the chauffeur bringing up the rear. As they went, the Saint began to sing, under his breath, some ancient ballad about 'Oh, How a Fat Girl Can Love'; and Teal's breathing seemed to become even more laboured than was warranted by the steepness of the hill. The driver, astern, also sounded as if he was having difficulty with his respiratory effects.

They plodded upwards without speaking for some time, preoccupied with their respective interests; and at last it was Teal who stopped and broke the silence.

'Isn't that a car up there?' he said.

He pointed along the beam of his torch, and the Saint looked.

'It surely is something like a car,' admitted the Saint thoughtfully. 'That's queer!'

He quickened his pace and went into the lead. Then the other two caught him up again; he was standing still, a few yards from the car, with his flashlight focused on the number-plate.

'One of Hallin's cars,' said the Saint.

He moved quickly round it, turning his light on the tyres : they were all perfectly sound. The petrol gauge showed plenty of fuel. He put his hand on the radiator: it was hot.

'Well, well, well!' said the Saint.

Teal, standing beside him, began to flash his torch around the side of the road.

'What's that tin doing there?' he said.

'I do not know, my chubby cherub,' said the Saint.

But he reached the tin first, and lifted it up. It was an empty petrol can. He turned it upside down over his palm, and shook it.

'Did he fill up here?' said Teal, and the Saint shook his head.

'The can's as dry as a successful bootlegger's politics. It's an old one. And I should say – Teal, I should say it was put here to mark a place. Look at the mark in the grass!'

He left Teal to it, and moved along the road, searching the turf at the side. Then he came back on the other side. His low exclamation brought Teal trotting.

'Someone's doing a midnight cross-country,' said the Saint. He pointed.

'I can't see anything,' said Teal.

'You wouldn't,' said the Saint disparagingly. 'Now, if they'd only thought to leave some cigarette-ash about, for you to put under a microscope, or a few exciting bloodstains—'

Teal choked.

'Look here, Templar—'

'Teal,' said the Saint, elegantly, 'you drip.'

He sprang lightly over the ditch and headed into the darkness, ignoring the other two; and, after a moment's hesitation, they followed.

The assurance with which the Saint moved over his trail was uncanny. Neither of the others could see the signs which he was able to pick up as rapidly as he could have picked up a plain path; but they were townsmen both, trained for a different kind of tracking.

Perhaps they travelled for fifty yards. And then the Saint stopped dead, and the other two came up on either side of him. His lighted torch aimed downwards, and they followed it with their own; but again neither of them could see anything remarkable.

'What is it this time?' asked Teal.

'I saw an arm,' said the Saint. 'An arm and a gun. And it went into the ground. Put your lights out!'

Without understanding, they obeyed.

And, in the darkness, the Saint leapt.

His foot turned on a loose stone, throwing him to his knees; and at the same time he heard a metallic click that meant only one thing to him; an automatic had been fired – and had failed to fire.

He spun round. Holding his torch at arm's length away from him, he switched it on again. And he gasped.

'Nigel!'

The boy was wrestling with the sliding jacket of the gun. It seemed to have jammed. And he bared his teeth into the light.

'You swine!' he said.

The Saint stared.

'Nigel! It's me – Simon Templar—'

'I know.'

The automatic reloaded with a snap, and Perry aimed it deliberately. And then Teal's hand and arm flashed down into the beam of light, caught Perry's wrist, and twisted sharply upwards. Another hand snatched the gun away.

'You devils!'

Perry got his wrist free with a savage wrench, and rolled out of the hole where he had been lying. He gathered himself, crouched, and leapt at the light. Simon put out one foot, and brought him down adroitly.

'Nigel, don't be a big boob!'

For answer the youngster squirmed to his feet again, with something like a sob, and made a second reckless rush.

The Saint began to feel bored.

He switched out his torch, and ducked. His arms fastened about Perry's waist, his shoulder nestled into Perry's chest; he tightened his grip decisively.

'If you don't stop it, Nigel,' he said, 'I'll break your back.'

Perry went limp suddenly. Perhaps he had never dreamed of being held with such a strength. The Saint's arms locked about him like steel bands.

'What's the matter with him?' inquired Teal lethargically, and Simon grunted.

'Seems to have gone loco,' he murmured.

Perry's ribs creaked as he tried to breathe.

'It's all right,' he said. 'I know all about you. You—'

'I've got him,' said Teal unemotionally; and the Saint loosened his hold and straightened up.

He had dropped his torch in the scuffle. Now he stooped to grope around for it; and it was while he was stooping that another light came. It came with a sort of hissing crackle – something like blue lightning.

'What the kippered herring was that?' ejaculated Teal.

The Saint found his torch and turned its rays into the hollow where Perry had been lying. And the blue lightning came again. They all saw it.

And then the Saint laughed softly.

'Good old Miles,' he drawled.

'Electric,' Teal said dazedly.

'Electrocution,' said the Saint, mildly.

There was a long silence. Then:

'Electrocution?'

Perry spoke huskily, staring at the hole in the ground, where the beams of three flashlights concentrated brilliantly.

'Good old Miles,' said the Saint again.

He pointed to the blackened and twisted telephone, and a dark scar on the rock. And there was another silence.

Teal broke it, sleepily.

'Some fools are born lucky,' he said. 'Perry, what yarn did Hallin tell you to get you there?'

'Miles didn't do that—'

'I suppose I did.' Teal tilted his torch over so that it illumined his own face. 'You know me, Perry – you met me yesterday. I'm a police officer. Don't talk nonsense.'

It was an incisive speech for Teal.

Perry said, in his throat: 'Then – where's Moyna?'

'That's what I want to know,' remarked the Saint 'We'll ask Miles. He'll be coming back to inspect the body. Shut your faces, and douse those glims!'

The lights went out one by one, and darkness and silence settled upon the group. Without a sound the Saint stepped to one side. He rested his torch on a high boulder, and kept his finger on the switch.

Then he heard Hallin.

At least, he heard the faint soft crunch of stones, a tiny rustle of leaves . . . He could see nothing. It was an eerie business, listening to that stealthy approach. But the Saint's nerves were like ice.

A match flared suddenly, only a few yards away. Hallin was searching the ground.

Then the Saint switched on his light. He caught Hallin in the beam, and left the light lying on the rock. The Saint himself stepped carefully away from it.

'Hullo,' said the Saint unctuously.

Hallin stood rooted to the ground. The match burned down to his fingers and he dropped it.

Then his hand jerked round to his pocket . . .

'Rotten,' said the Saint calmly; and his voice merged in the rattle of another shot.

From a little distance away two more lights sprang up from the darkness and centred upon Hallin. The man twisted round in the blaze, and fired again – three times. One of the lights went out. The other fell, and went out on the ground as the bulb broke. Hallin whipped round again. He sighted rapidly, and his bullet smashed the Saint's torch where it lay.

'Teal, did he get you?'

The Saint stepped swiftly across the blackness; and Teal's voice answered at his shoulder.

'No, but he got Mason.'

The Saint's fingers touched Teal's coat, so lightly that the detective could have felt nothing. They crept down Teal's sleeve, jumped the hand, and closed upon the torch . . .

'Thanks,' said the Saint. 'See you later.'

He jerked at the torch as he spoke, and got it away. The

detective made a grab at him; but Simon slipped away with a laugh. He could hear Hallin blundering through the darkness, and he followed the noise as best he could. Behind him was another blundering noise, and a shout from Teal; but the Saint was not waiting.

Simon went on in the dark. He had eyes like a cat, anyway; and, in the circumstances, there might be peculiar dangers about a light . . . Then it occurred to him that there might be other live wires about, and he had no urge to die that way. He stopped abruptly.

At the same time he found that he could no longer hear Hallin. On his right he heard a muffled purling of water; behind him Teal was still stumbling sulphurously through the gloom, hopelessly lost. The detective must have been striking matches, but Simon could not see them. A rise of ground must have cut them off.

Warily the Saint felt around for another boulder, and switched on his torch as he had done before. The result startled him. Hallin's face showed up instantly in the glare, pale and twisted, scarcely a yard away; then Hallin's hand with the gun; beyond Hallin, the ground simply ceased . . .

'Precious,' said the Saint, 'I have been looking forward to this.'

He hurled himself full length, in a magnificent standing tackle; his arms twined around Hallin's knees. Over his head, the automatic banged once, but the light did not go out. Then they crashed down together.

The Saint let go, and writhed up like an eel. He caught Hallin's right wrist, and smashed the hand against a stone. The gun dropped.

Simon snatched it up, scrambling to his feet as he did so; and one sweep of his arm sent the weapon spinning far out into the gulf.

The Saint laughed, standing up in the light.

'In the name of Teddy Everest,' he said, 'this is our party. Get up, Miles Hallin, you dog!'

8

Hallin got up.

He was shorter than the Saint by three or four inches, but twice as heavy in the bone, with tremendous arms and shoulders. And he came in like a charging buffalo.

Simon side-stepped the first rush with cool precision, and shot in a crisp left that caught Hallin between the eyes with a smack like a snapped stick; but Hallin simply turned, blinking, and came again.

The Saint whistled softly through his teeth.

He really wasn't used to people taking those punches quite so stoically. When he hit a man like that, it was usually the beginning of the end of the fight; but Hallin was pushing up his plate for a second helping as if he liked the diet. Well, maybe the light was bad, thought the Saint; and accurate timing made a lot of difference . . . And again he side-stepped, exactly as before, and felt the blow which he landed jolt right up his arm; but this time he collected a smashing drive to the ribs in return. It hurt him; but Hallin didn't seem to be hurt . . .

The Saint whistled even more softly.

So there was something in Hallin, after all. The man fought in a crouch that made scoring difficult. His arms covered his body, and he kept his chin well down in his chest; he wasn't easy . . .

The Saint circled round to get his back to the light, and for the third time Hallin rushed at him. Simon went in to meet him. His left swung over in a kind of vertical hook that stroked down Hallin's nose, and Hallin raised his arms involuntarily. Lashing into the opening, the Saint went for the body – right, left, right. He heard Hallin grunt to the thud of each blow, and he smiled.

They closed.

Simon knew what would come next. He was old in the game. He wrenched his body round, and took the upward kick of Hallin's knee on the muscles under his thigh. At the same moment he jerked Hallin's other leg from under him, and they went down together.

Hallin fought like a fiend. His strength was terrific. They rolled over and over, away out of the light of the torch, into the darkness, with Hallin's hands fumbling for the Saint's eyes ... The Saint knew that one also. He grabbed one of Hallin's fingers, and twisted; it broke with a sharp crack, and Hallin screamed ...

The Saint tore himself away. He was rising to one knee when his other foot seemed to slip into space. He clutched wildly, and found a hold on the roots of a bush; then Hallin caught him again. With a superhuman heave the Saint dragged himself another foot from the edge of the precipice; and then his handhold came clean out of the ground, bringing a lump of turf with it. He dashed it into Hallin's face.

They fought on the very brink of the precipice. Simon lost count of the number of blows he took, and the number he gave. In the darkness it was impossible to aim, and just as impossible to guard. One of them would get a hand free, and hit out savagely at the dark; then the other would do the same; sometimes they scored, sometimes they missed. The rocks bruised them at every movement; once they crashed through a bush, and the twigs tore the Saint's face.

Then he landed again, a pile-driving half-arm jolt that went home, and Hallin lay still.

Gasping, the Saint relaxed . . .

And at once Hallin heaved up titanically under him, and something more than a fist struck the side of the Saint's head.

If it had struck a direct blow Simon's skull would have been cracked like an eggshell; but Hallin had misjudged his mark by a fraction. The stone glanced from the Saint's temple; even so, it was like being kicked by a mule. It shook the Saint more than anything else in the whole of that mad struggle, and sent him toppling sideways with a welter of tangled lights zipping before his eyes. He felt Hallin slip from his grasp, and slithered desperately away to his left. Something went past his cheek, so close that he felt it pass, and hit the ground beyond him with a crunching thud . . .

He touched another bush, and crawled dizzily round it. On the other side he dragged himself up – first to his knees, then, shakily, to his feet. He could hear Hallin stumbling about in the blackness, searching for him; but he had to rest. Every muscle of his body ached; his head was playing a complete symphony . . .

Then he heard the bush rustle; and he had not moved.

He strained his eyes into the obscurity. The steady beam of the torch was a dozen yards away; suddenly he saw Hallin silhouetted against it. Hallin must have seen him at the same moment. The Saint ducked instantaneously, and the rock that Hallin hurled at him went over his head. Simon saw that rock also, for the fraction of a second, in the same silhouette: it was the size of a football.

Hallin came after it without a pause. Simon could see him clearly. With a gigantic effort the Saint gathered his strength and met the rush with a long straight left that packed every ounce of power he could muster. Hallin was coming in carelessly now: the blow took him squarely on the mouth and sent him flying.

The Saint stood still. As long as he could keep his position he had a precarious advantage. He saw Hallin's silhouette again, for a moment – but only for a moment. Then nothing. He realised that Hallin had also seen the point . . .

He began to edge away, with his ears alert for the slightest warning sound. And then he saw another light – the light of a match, moving through the darkness a few points from his torch. At the same time Teal's shout reached him faintly.

Without hesitation Simon plunged towards the electric torch.

Again he guessed exactly what Hallin would do – and he was right. The man had already crept round behind him – that gave the Saint a lead – but, as he ran, Simon heard the other coming up behind. A hand touched his arm; then Hallin cursed, and the Saint heard him fall.

Simon reached the light, switched it out, and swerved away. He heard Hallin running again, but the man went right past him and did not turn back.

'Where are you, Templar?'

He heard Teal's voice, closer at hand; as the Saint blundered after Hallin, his path took him towards the voice; presently he switched on his light again, and Teal himself showed up, red-faced and perspiring.

'Have you seen him?' rapped the Saint.

'No,' said the detective shortly. 'Didn't you kill him?'

Simon answered with the ghost of a laugh.

'Unfortunately I failed. But there's still time. He must have gone between us. Come on!'

He started off again, and Teal had to follow.

As they ran the Saint said: 'This'll take us towards the road, anyway. He's sure to make for that. Where's Perry?'

'I sent him back to the car,' said Teal short-windedly. 'With Mason.'

'Which car?'

'Hallin's.'

'You sap! That's where Hallin'll be making for—'

'Perry's got his gun back.'

'Oh! . . . How's Mason? Dead?'

'Don't know. Shot through the lungs. Perry carried him.'

'Learn anything from Perry?'

'Not much. I didn't wait.'

They went on quickly. Hallin could no longer be heard, but the Saint was certain about the road. And the road would take Hallin to something else . . .

They came out of the scrub on to level turf, where the going was easier. Down to his left the Saint saw a pair of headlights. He turned, hurrying on.

'Mind the ditch.'

He lighted the detective over, and followed with a leap. As his feet touched the road he heard Perry's challenge.

'Stop where you are!'

'But this is us,' said the Saint.

The car turned a little, and the headlights picked him up. In a moment the car itself swept up beside them.

'You haven't seen Miles?' demanded Simon, with one foot on the step.

'Not a sign.'

'And you haven't heard anything?'

'Only you. I thought—'

'Damnation!' said the Saint, in his gentle way. He looked up and down the road, listening intently, but he could hear nothing. Then he swung on to the running board.

'He's sure to have struck the road somewhere,' he said crisply. 'Teal, hustle yourself round the other side . . . Can you put this thing along, Nigel?'

'I'll do my best.'

'Off you go, then.'

Teal climbed on to the step at the other side, and the car started again with a jerk, and gathered speed. As Perry changed up, Teal leaned over to be pessimistic.

'He'll see us coming a mile away if he is on the road,' he said.

'I know,' said the Saint savagely. 'Perhaps you'd rather run.'

He did not care to admit how pessimistic he himself felt. He was certain that Hallin must make for the road sooner or later; but he also knew that Teal's remark was perfectly justified. In fact, if it had been merely a question of capturing a fugitive, the Saint would have given it up forthwith. But there was another reason for the chase, and this very reason also gave it a faint chance of success. It was Perry who made the Saint speak of it.

'He told me Moyna wasn't far away,' Perry said. 'Have you any idea what he meant?'

'What he said,' answered the Saint grimly. 'He brought Moyna with him, but he didn't take her to the cottage. I don't know where he took her; but I'll bet he told you the truth. She won't be far away.'

Perry said, in a strained voice: 'Oughtn't we to be looking for her, instead of chasing him?'

'We're doing both at the same time,' said the Saint quietly. 'Wherever she is, that's where he's gone. Miles Hallin is going to have his life.'

'I – I can hardly believe it, even now,' said the youngster huskily.

Simon's hand rested on his shoulder.

'I hope you won't see it proved,' he said. 'But I know that Hallin has gone to find Moyna.'

Teal cleared his throat.

'He can't have got as far as this, anyway,' he remarked.

'Right as usual, Claud Eustace.' The Saint's voice was preternaturally calm. 'He must have gone down the hill. Turn the car round, Nigel, and we'll try the other line.'

Teal understood, and held his peace. Of course Hallin might easily have gone up the hill. He would have stepped off the road, and they might have passed him . . . But Perry could be spared the argument . . . And yet Teal did not know how sincerely the Saint was clinging to his hope. Simon himself did not know why he should have clung to the hope as he did, against all reason; but the faith that spurred him on was above reason. The Saint simply could not believe that the story would end – the way Teal thought it must end . . .

'This is where we started from.' The Saint spoke to the lad at the wheel in tones of easy confidence. 'We could stop the engine and coast down, couldn't we? Then we'd hardly make any noise . . .'

They went on with no sound but the soft rustle of the tyres. Simon did not have to mention the headlights. Those would give their approach away even more surely than the drone of the engine; but Simon would have invented any fatuous remark to save Perry's nerves.

They reached the bottom of the hill, and Teal was the first to see the police car standing by the road where they had left it. He pointed it out as Perry applied the brakes.

'He can't have come this way, either,' Teal said. 'If he had, he'd have taken that car.'

'I wonder if he saw it,' said the Saint.

He dropped off into the road, and his flashlight spilled a circle of luminance over the macadam. The circle moved about restlessly, and Teal stepped from the car and followed it.

'Looking for footprints?' inquired the detective sardonically, as he came up behind the Saint; and at that moment the light in the Saint's hand went out.

'Blood,' said the Saint, very quietly.

'That's a nasty word,' murmured Teal.

'You everlasting mutt!' Simon gripped his arm fiercely. 'I wasn't swearing. I was telling you something!' He turned. 'Nigel, turn those headlights out!'

The detective was fumbling with a matchbox; but the Saint stopped him.

'It's all right, old dear,' he drawled. 'This gadget of yours is still working. I just thought we'd better go carefully. Hallin's been past here. He didn't take the car, so he can't have had much farther to go.'

'But what's this about blood? Did you use a knife?'

'No,' said the Saint, smiling in the darkness. 'I hit him on the nose.'

9

Moyna Stanford had been awake for a long time.

She had roused sickly from a deeper sleep than any she had ever known; and it had been more than half an hour before she could recall anything coherently, or even find the strength to move.

And when her memory returned – or, rather, when she had forced it to return – she was not much wiser. She remembered meeting Miles Hallin at Windsor station. He had insisted on driving her back to London, and she had been glad to accept the invitation. In Slough he had complained of an intolerable thirst; they had stopped at a hotel, and she had been persuaded to join him in an early cup of tea. Then they had returned to the car ...

She did not know how long she had slept.

When she awoke, she was in darkness. She lay on something soft, and, when she could move, she gathered that it was a bed. She had already discovered that her wrists and ankles were securely bound ...

Presently she had learned one or two other things. That it was night, for instance, she learned when she rolled over and saw a square of starlight in one wall; but her hands were tied behind her back, and she could not see her wrist-watch to find out what hour of the night it might be. Then she lay still, listening, but not the faintest sound broke the silence. The house was like a tomb.

She had no idea how long she lay there. She did not cry out – there would be no one to hear. And she could see no help in screaming. Later, the sound of a car passing close by told her that she was not far from a road – a country road, or there would have been more cars. There was never such a silence in London. Later still – it was impossible to keep track of time – she scrambled off the bed, and hobbled slowly and laboriously to the window. It was very dark outside; she could see nothing but a black expanse of country, in which no particular features were distinguishable, except that the horizon was ragged against the dimness of the sky, as if it were formed by a line of hills. She might have been anywhere in England. The window was open, and she stood beside it for a long while, wondering if another car would pass, and if the road would be near enough for anyone in the car to hear if she called; but no other car came. After a time she struggled back to the bed and lay down again; it was difficult and wearying for her to stand with her feet tightly lashed together, and her head was swimming all the while.

Then the drug she had been given must have put forth one final kick before it was finished with her; for she awoke again with a start, though she had no recollection of falling asleep. The sky through the window looked exactly the same: she was sure that she had only dozed.

She was shivering – she did not know why. Strangely enough, when she had first awoken she had been aware of no fear; that part of her brain seemed to have stayed sunken in sleep. But now she found herself trembling. There was a tightness about her chest; and she waited, tense with a nameless terror, hardly breathing, certain that some distinct sound had roused her.

Then the sound was repeated; and she would have cried out then, but her throat seemed paralysed.

Someone was coming up the stairs.

A faint light entered the room. It came from under the door, and traced a slow arc around half the floor. The creak of another board outside sent an icy qualm prickling up her spine; her mouth was dry, and her heart pounded thunderously . . . The next thing would be the opening of the door. She waited for that, too, in the same awful tenseness: it was like watching a card-castle after a sudden draught has caught it; she knew what must come, it was inevitable, but the suspense was more hideous than the active peril . . . The rattle of a key in the lock made her jump, as if she had been held motionless by a slender thread and the thread had been snapped by the sound . . .

Involuntarily she closed her eyes. When she opened them again Miles Hallin was re-locking the door on the inside, and the bare room was bright with the lamp that he carried.

Then he turned, putting the lamp down on a rough wooden chair, and she saw him properly. She was amazed and aghast at his appearance. His clothes were torn and shapeless and filthy; his collar had burst open, and his tie was half-way down his chest; his hair was dishevelled; his face was smeared and stained with blood.

'Are you awake?' he said.

She could not answer. He advanced slowly to the bed, peering at her.

'You are awake. I've come back. You ought to be glad to see me. I've nearly been killed.'

He sat down, and put his head in his hands for a moment. Then he looked at her again.

'Killed!' His voice was rough and shaky. 'One of your friends tried to kill me. That man Templar. I nearly killed him, though. I'd have done it if I'd been alone. We were on the precipice. There's a two hundred foot drop. Can you imagine it? You'd go down – and down – and down – down to the bottom – and break like a rotten apple – Ugh!' He shuddered uncontrollably. 'It was terrible. Have you ever thought about death, Moyna? I think it must be dreadful to die. I don't want to die!'

His hand plucked at her sleeve, and she stared at him, fascinated. His quivering terror was more horrible than anything she had ever imagined.

'I can't die!' he babbled. 'Don't you know that? It's in all the newspapers. Miles Hallin – The Man Who Cannot Die! I'm big, strong – Templar couldn't kill me, and he's strong – I can't – go down – and lie still and – get cold – and never move any more. And you rot. All your flesh – rots . . . In the desert, I thought about it. D'you hear about Nigel's brother? We tossed for who was to die, and he won. And he didn't seem to mind dying. I pretended I didn't mind, either. And I walked with him a long way. And then – I hit him when he wasn't looking. I took the water – and left him. He – he died, Moyna. In the sun. And – shrivelled up. He's been dead – years. Sometimes I can see him . . .'

The girl moistened her lips. She could not move.

'Ever since then I've been dead, too. I've never been alive. You see, I couldn't tell anyone. Acting – all the time. So – I've always been alone. Never been able to tell anyone – never been with anyone who knew all about it – who – who was frightened, like I was. Until I met you. I knew you'd understand. You could share the secret. I was going – to tell you. And then Templar found out. I don't know how. Or he guessed. He sees everything – his eyes – I knew he'd try to take you away from me. So I brought you here. I'm going to – live. With you. He won't find us here. I bought this place for you – long ago. It's beautiful. I don't think anyone's ever died here. Moyna! Moyna! Moyna!'

'Yes?' Her voice was faint.

'I wish you'd speak. I was – afraid – you might be going to die. I had to drug you. You know I drugged you? I couldn't explain then – I had to bring you here, where we could be alone. Now I'll untie you.'

His fingers tugged at the ropes he had put on her. Presently her hands were free, and he was fumbling with her feet, crooning like a child. She tried to master her trembling.

'Miles, you must let me go!'

'I'm letting you go,' He held up the cords for her to see, 'And now – we're all right. Just you and me. You'll be – nice to me – won't you, Moyna?'

His arms went round her, dragging her towards him.

'Miles.' She strove to speak calmly, though she was weak with fear – 'You must be sensible! You've got to get me back to London. Mother will be wondering what's happened to me—'

'London?' He seemed to grasp the word dully. 'Why?'

'You know I can't stay here. But you can come and see me to-morrow morning—'

His blank eyes gazed at her.

'London? To-morrow? I don't understand.' Suddenly he seized her again. 'Moyna, you wouldn't run away! You're not going to – to leave me. I can't go to London. You know I can't. I shall be killed. We've got to stay here—'

She was as helpless as a babe in his hands. He heard nothing more that she said.

'Moyna, I love you. I'm going to be good to you. I'm going to look after you – tell you – everything—'

'Miles,' she sobbed, 'oh, let me go—'

'Just – you and me. And we'll stay here. And we – won't die – ever. We won't die—'

'Oh, don't—'

'You mustn't be afraid. Not of me. We won't be afraid of anything. We're going to stay here – years – hundreds of years – thousands of years, Moyna, you mustn't be frightened. It'll be quite all right—'

'Take your hands off me—'

'But you do love me, don't you? And you're not going to leave me alone. I shan't be frightened of anything if you're here. In the dark, I can see Perry – sometimes. But I shan't mind—'

She fought back at him desperately, but against his tremendous strength she felt as weak as a kitten. She screamed aloud.

Somewhere a shout answered her. She heard a splintering crash, then someone leaping up the stairs. Another shout! 'Moyna, where are you?'

She cried out again. Hallin let her go. She fell off the bed and flung herself at the door. He caught her again there. 'They're coming,' he said stupidly.

Then his eyes blazed. He dragged her away with a force that sent her flying across the room. In an instant he had reached her. She stared in horror at his face, pale and twisted under the smears of blood, only a few inches from her own.

'They're going to kill me,' he gasped. 'I'm going to die! Moyna, I'm going to die – die! . . . And I haven't lived yet. Loved you—'

She half rose, but he threw her down again. The strength that she had found went from her. She felt that she would faint at any moment. Her dress tore in his hands, but the sound seemed to come from an infinite distance. There was a mighty pounding on the door. 'Open it. Hallin!' someone was shouting. 'You can't get away!' Hallin's whole body was shaking.

'They can't kill me!' he croaked. 'Moyna, you know that, don't you? I can't be killed. No one can ever kill me—'

'You fool!' came a voice outside. 'You won't break the door down that way. Why don't you shoot the lock out?'

Hallin raised himself slowly from the bed. His eyes were like a babe's.

'Shoot out the lock,' he said dreamily. 'Yes – shoot out the lock—'

With her hand to her mouth Moyna Stanford watched him reel across the room.

He spoke again.

'It's dreadful to die,' he said.

On the landing outside, the Saint was focusing his flashlight on the door, and Teal's automatic was crowded against the keyhole.

The lock shattered inwards with a splintering crash, and Simon hurled himself forward.

Inside the room he heard a heavy fall, and the door jammed half-open. Then Teal and Nigel Perry added their weight to the attack, and they went in.

'Nigel!'

The girl struggled up and stumbled, and Perry caught her in his arms,

But Teal and the Saint were looking at the man who lay on the floor, very still, with a strange serenity on his upturned face.

'He wasn't so lucky after all,' said the detective stolidly.

Simon shook his head.

'We never killed him,' he said.

He fell on his knees beside the body; and when he stood up again his right hand was red and wet, and something lay in his palm. Teal blinked at it. It was a key.

'How did that get there?' he demanded.

'It was in the lock,' said the Saint.

IO

In the full panoply of silk hat, stock, black coat, flowered waistcoat, gold-mounted umbrella, white gloves, striped cashmere trousers with a razor-edged crease, white spats, and patent-leather shoes (reading from north to south), Simon Templar was a vision to dazzle the eyes; and Chief Inspector Claud Eustace Teal, meeting the Saint in Piccadilly in this array, was visibly startled.

'Where are you going?' he asked.

'I have already been,' said the Saint. 'They do these things at the most ungodly hours. If you want to know, an infant has this day been received into the Holy Catholic Church. I personally sponsored the reception.'

The detective was suitably impressed.

'Moreover,' said the Saint, 'it was christened Simon. Now I call that real handsome.'

'What does Perry call it?' inquired Teal; and the Saint was shocked.

They walked a little way together in silence, and then Teal said: 'The Commissioner's been waiting for an answer to his letter.'

'I have meditated the idea,' said the Saint. 'As a matter of fact, I thought of heading down to see him this afternoon.'

'What were you going to say?'

Simon's umbrella swung elegantly in his hand.

He sighed.

'The idea is amusing,' he murmured. 'And yet I can't quite see myself running on the side of Law and Order. As you've so kindly pointed out on several occasions, dear old horse-radish, my free-lance style is rather cramped now that you all know so much about me; but I'm afraid – oh, Teal, my bonny, I'm terribly afraid that yours is not the only way. I should become so hideously respectable before you finished with me. And there is another objection.'

'What's that?'

The Saint removed his shining headpiece and dusted it lovingly with a large silk handkerchief.

'I could not wear a bowler hat,' he said.

Teal stopped, and turned.

'Are you really going to refuse?' he asked; and Simon nodded.

'I am,' he said sadly. 'It would have been a hopeless failure. I should have been fired in a week anyway. Scotland House would become a bear-garden. The most weird and wonderful stories would be told in the Old Bailey. Gentlemen would write to *The Times* – Teal, I don't want to become a wet blanket. But I might want that arm again—'

'Templar,' said the detective glumly, 'that's the worst news I've heard for a long time.'

'Is it?' drawled the Saint, appearing slightly puzzled. 'I thought everyone knew. It's the hand I drink with.'

'I mean, if you really are going on in the same old way—'

'Oh, that!'

The Saint smiled beatifically. He glanced at his watch.

'Let us go and have lunch,' he said, 'and weep over my wickedness. I'm such a picturesque villain, too.' He sighed again. 'Tell me, Teal, where can a policeman and a pirate lunch together in safety?'

'Anywhere you like,' said Teal unhappily.

Simon Templar gazed across Piccadilly Circus.

'I seem to remember a very good restaurant in the Law Courts themselves,' he remarked. 'I lunched there one day just after I'd murdered someone or other. It gave me a great sensation. And this, I think, is my cue to repeat the performance. Come, Algibald, and I will tell you the true story about the Bishop and the Actress.'

The End

Watch for the sign of the Saint!

If you have enjoyed this Saintly adventure, look out for the other Simon Templar novels by Leslie Charteris – all available in print and ebook from Mulholland Books

You've turned the last page.

But it doesn't have to end there . . .

If you're looking for more first-class, action-packed, nail-biting suspense, join us at **Facebook.com/ MulhollandUncovered** for news, competitions, and behind-the-scenes access to Mulholland Books.

For regular updates about our books and authors as well as what's going on in the world of crime and thrillers, follow us on **Twitter@MulhollandUK**.

There are many more twists to come.

MULHOLLAND:
You never know what's
coming around the curve.

HODDER